Show River

River

The Bell Chronicles
Book 1

JL Curtis

Books by JL Curtis

The Grey Man- Vignettes
The Grey Man- Payback
The Grey Man- Changes
The Grey Man- Partners
The Grey Man- Twilight
The Grey Man- Sunset

Rimworld- Into the Green
Rimworld- Milita Up
Rimworld- The Rift

Short Stories/Novellas by JL Curtis

Rimworld- Stranded
The Morning the Earth Shook
The Grey Man- Down South
The Grey Man- Generations
April Fool

(Kindle only)

Anthology Collected by JL Curtis

Calexit- The Anthology
Burnt Ends
Tales Around the Supper Table

Author's Note: This is a work of fiction. Names, characters, places, and incidents are a product of the author's imagination. Locales and public names are sometimes used for atmospheric purposes. Any resemblance to actual people, living or dead, or to businesses, companies, events, institutions, or locales is completely coincidental.

Published by JLC&A. Available from Amazon.com in Kindle format or paperback book, printed by Amazon.

Showdown on the River- The Bell Chronicles Book 1/ JL Curtis. -- 1st ed.
ISBN-13: 9798706744328

DEDICATION

To those who came before us, who tilled the ground,
built on the land, and left their legacies for us.

ACKNOWLEDGMENTS

Thanks to the usual suspects, you know who you are

Thanks to my editor, Stephanie Martin

Cover art by Tina Garceau

Table of Contents

Chapter 1

The east side of Horsehead Crossing was a roiling mass of bawling cows, dust, flies, and tired cowboys and horses. The air stank of burned hair, wood fires, and unwashed men under the cold, clear late March sky.

Rio Bell inhaled with a sense of pride. Twenty-two, a little under six foot tall, lean, with light brown hair and piercing blue eyes, this was his first time as the boss on a drive, and he was in his element. Just then a big old brindle steer decided to make a break for it. Rio touched his spurs to the buckskin, wishing he was up on Red, his roan. "C'mon boy, let's go get him!"

The buckskin took off from a standing start as Rio pulled his gloves tight. Reaching for the lasso, he shook out a loop. "Oh no you don't, you miserable hunk of beef," he mumbled as the brindle got within about twenty yards of the breaks on the Pecos. He threw the loop and caught the nose and one horn, dallied the rope on the horn of the saddle, and sat back as the buckskin planted all four hooves.

The brindle hit the end of the rope and spun. Rio thought the buckskin was going to the ground, but it recovered its legs just as the brindle turned and charged them. He mumbled a curse, "Aw, sumbitch, not now," as the buckskin fought to stay out of the way of the steer's horns. He was trying to undo the dally and stay in the saddle at the same time, while the buckskin and brindle did their dance of death.

Rio finally managed to get the dally loose, but the brindle kept coming. *Enough of this,* he thought as he fought to get the loop off the Remington on his belt. He finally worked it loose and drew the pistol just as the brindle brushed his chaps with the tip of its horn. He drew and fired as fast as he could and put one round through the brindle's eye, dropping it in its tracks.

The buckskin crow-hopped one more time, then backed away slowly. Rio let him back up six or eight steps. He stepped out of the saddle and almost fell, but caught himself on the stirrup and tied the buckskin to a mesquite bush. Pulling his gloves off, he spat to try to get some dryness out of his mouth and started coughing. Rio had just pulled his canteen off the saddle as Flynn came riding up, rifle out.

He looked down at Rio. "You look like crap, and that poor buckskin is wore slap out. What the hell were you shooting at?"

"That damn brindle steer that's been giving us trouble for two days. Sumbitch made a break for it, and I went after it. It turned on me, so I killed it. I guess Pronto will have plenty of beef for a while."

"How many times did you shoot? You were shooting real fast," Flynn said with a grin.

"Twice I think, John."

He laughed. "Better check, I think you emptied it."

"Nah, I couldn't," he drew the pistol, pulled the hammer back to half cock and went cylinder by cylinder, each one had been fired. "Damn if I didn't. Didn't realize it." He quickly pulled a spare cylinder out, tapped the wedge out and slipped the new cylinder in, then tapped the wedge back in, and eased the hammer down on an empty chamber before slipping it back in his holster.

"Get scared, things happen. How many more are we going to kill or lose?"

After he took a drink, shaking the canteen ruefully, he said, "I don't know. But all this," he swung his arm, "is money on the hoof! The tally is twenty-two hundred head, mixed stuff. We're only supposed to deliver two thousand. Well, make that twenty-one hundred ninety-nine head," he said, kicking the brindle's carcass. "These were the last road brands, need to make sure we have both the Bar B and Rafter B irons with us if we pick up any more cows along the way. We should be able to line them out in a couple of days."

"Why wait?"

"Need a day to rest up the horses, get the last provisions for the chuck wagon, and we're waiting on another thirty horses for the remuda." He patted the buckskin's neck as it stood, legs apart and head down. "We need to let the crew get a rest day too. I think we've got three more riders coming, if Pa could find them. With only fifteen riders, we're gonna be a little short before it's over."

Flynn took off his hat, revealing black hair going grey, and nodded. "Probably. Gonna be a long drive to Wyoming, but doing the gather out here saves us a week or so."

Rio shrugged. "Yep, no point in driving the cows east to turn around and drive 'em back this way. More money this way than taking them up the Chisholm trail. Pa did this trail a couple of times with Goodnight, and I did one drive last year from Fort Belknap to Fort Laramie. We're going to shade east and not go over Raton pass. Costs too much. We're not paying a dime a head to Dick Wootton.

Flynn cocked a leg around the horn and spit. "What about Indians?"

"Word is Comanches and Kiowas aren't raiding yet. Maybe we can get a head start on them. The Arapaho have moved up into Wyoming and Montana after Red Cloud's war and the treaty at Fort Laramie, and that's as far north as we're going. Old man Story is going to take delivery there and have his hands drive the cows on up to the Story Ranch in Montana."

"That'll save us, what, a month?"

"Probably. I figure we should be back in Texas no later than September." Rio groaned as he swung back into the saddle, "I'm too old for this."

Flynn laughed. "You're what, all of twenty? Hell, other than Pronto and Arthur, I'm the oldest one here, and I'm barely thirty-three. And I told your dad this is my last drive."

Rio grinned through the dust, "You know I'm twenty...two for another few months. You want to be the trail boss?"

"Oh, no. That's all on you. You're young and stupid enough to take that on," he said with a smile. "Honestly, Rio, I'm getting too broke down to do this every year. Lissy is turning five and keeps wanting daddy to come home on a regular basis. Your dad offered me a position as the ranch foreman, and he's willing to let me raise horses on my own time. I think I'm going to take it. Cattle drives are for you youngsters."

Rio nodded. "I keep hearing that, but how do you explain Pronto?"

Flynn laughed. "Well, it's simple. Pronto is crazy as hell. He *thinks* he's around seventy, and all he talks about are those damn mountains. And bears, huge elk, all his buddies, and the rendezvous, but apparently he was never sober enough to remember *all* of the rendezvous. That's what he blames for both his squaws he married. Personally, I think he wanted something to warm his tent in the winter."

"You ever tell him that?"

"What do I look like? A fool? That old man is still snake quick with that hogleg, and I've seen what he can do with that Bowie he carries."

Rio sighed as the memory of the last drive, and Pronto's slicing and dicing of the Comanche who thought he was easy prey, played out in his mind. The sheer amount of blood that was everywhere by the time Pronto finished him off had made Rio puke and a couple of the other drovers turn shades of green. Pronto? Well, Pronto didn't even turn a hair, and as far as Rio knew, he hadn't ever given it a second thought.

You hear about gunfighters, but I wonder how many people that old man has killed? He's been out here since he was fourteen or so, which makes fifty years on or beyond the frontier. And we're just now seeing law come this way.

The rattle of a wagon interrupted that chain of thought as Pronto drove the chuck wagon over. "Just had to kill a tough steer, didn't ya, boy? Couldn't find me a nice tender heifer, could ya?"

Rio glanced up at him and saw that he was smiling. "A heifer I could have handled, that steer didn't want to do anything but kill me."

"Looks to me like you won."

"Want some help skinning him out?"

Pronto spat. "Hell no, you yonkers waste too much meat. Got a couple o' fires goin'. What I can't cook 'fore it spoils, I'll turn into jerky. There's brick chili and biscuits cookin' over by the bedrolls. Go watch it, and don't let it burn, I know Boyle is gonna wander off like he allus does. I'll be a while over here."

Rio shook his head. "I'm..."

Flynn laughed. "Pronto, you do know he's supposed to be the trail boss, right?"

Pronto spat again. "Don't care. He wants to be in charge, he's in charge of the food. Now go 'way."

***

Noon the next day found Rio up on Red, his favorite horse, out checking the herd and looking for any trouble. One of the things he was specifically looking for was any lame beeves, as they wouldn't be able to keep up and would be a waste of time. He was also checking counts with the various drovers as he worked his way around the herd. He found the black cowboy named Arthur sitting quietly on his horse under a tree, just watching a couple of hundred cows grazing. "What's going on, Arthur?"

"See that piebald cow 'bout halfway to the river?" He pointed languidly to the right.

"The one with a little space around her?"

"I think she might be our bell cow. This bunch came from Cronin's place, up by Pecos. Wherever she goes, this whole bunch follows her."

He thought about it for a minute, "Joshua Cronin put what, five hundred head in?"

Arthur nodded. "Yep. Juan and I went up and got 'em last week, along with a dozen mustangs."

"Well, we don't have one, so it might be worth a try. You want to get a rope on her and bell her now?"

"Not yet. I'd give it a day or two once we get 'em movin'. But I'd like to push this bunch to the front and see what happens. She don't seem to spook, I rode within a rod of her and she just looked at me."

"You're not usually wrong, so let's go with that idea. I'm guessing you already talked to Flynn?"

Arthur's face split into a grin. "Why young Rio Bell, what makes you think I, a poor black man, would go behind my bosses back?"

Rio laughed. "Because you two do that on a regular basis? Poor? Hell, you're getting paid more than I am. So is Flynn! I think Pa is paying you two to babysit me."

"No, suh. You're a man growed. Been one since you were fourteen. John and I watched you grow up, especially after the war. You learned to ride young, and you know how to use that pistol, and your rifle. We've taught you all we can, and I know John is quitting after this drive. I may too." He glanced at his left hand, hidden in a glove, "You know I don't carry a pistol, and you know why." Patting the butt of the shotgun sticking up in front of the saddle, "Betsy and me, we do what is needful of doing."

Arthur came back to the ranch in late 1863, if I remember right. He was in grey and came from Natchez. He'd been hurt, shot in the hand... wrist? And it hadn't been treated. But he was a freeman. His pappy had come west with grandpa, worked as a farrier on the ranch before the war, but he went to war with Pa. He went missing during the war, but Pa hired him to take care of the horses, and he's done that ever since he made it back.

He nodded. "And you scare the hell out of people with that thing."

"Most people tend to stop and think when they look down Betsy's barrels. She don't back up worth a damn," Arthur glanced to the east, "And it looks like the remuda is here, along with your Pa. I hope they all got shoes. Orlando was supposed to take care of that."

Rio laughed. "You just want to do the shoeing and sit in your nice warm workshop, don't you?"

"I'm getting old too. I'm almost forty. And I'm getting' to the point I don't like to leave home. I don't like cold. And this is gonna be a long cold trip."

"Let's go see what Pa and Eli brought in the wagon and what he has to say."

"Lead on, boss."

A half hour later, the supplies had been transferred to the chuck wagon, the horses added to the remuda, and three new riders made introductions. Ed Bell, tall, spare, and going grey, tied his horse to the rear of the now empty wagon, hopped up into the bed, waved his hat, and yelled, "Gather round!"

The cowboys not already standing around rode over, and he looked at each of them, "Men, I don't have a lot to say. You're going to be the first herd up the trail, as best we can tell. You've got a herd to deliver to Nathan Story at Fort Laramie. Rio is the trail boss, he's been over the trail and knows where he's going. Some of you went up last year, and some are new. If you have questions, ask one of the old hands. As far as I know, there aren't any Indians on the warpath yet. Regular cowhands get forty a month and found, you new fellas prove out, you'll get that as well. Any questions?"

He looked around again, then said, "I want to see *all* of you back at the ranch in September." He hopped down and motioned to Rio and Eli, who got down and followed him around the wagon. "The Peterson kid, Hoyt, is young, thirteen maybe fourteen, but they need help. His ma died a couple of months ago, and his da has two more kids at home. I'm going to pay him directly so only give Hoyt five dollars a month. Pronto has seven hundred in gold in the chuck wagon and you still have the two hundred I gave you. That should allow you to pay any tolls that people throw up, or the Indians, and give you enough to buy supplies as necessary."

"What about ammo? I didn't..."

"Brought another thousand rounds of forty-four and a hundred shotgun rounds for Arthur. Five hundred rounds of fifty-two and fifty-six for the carbines should get you all the way up there. Neither the Peterson kid or Cavanaugh kid had a pistol, so I gave them a couple of those Colt Navy conversions we had at the ranch, with the old flap holsters. I brought five hundred rounds of thirty-six caliber to feed them. If I were you, I'd make Peterson the wrangler. He can ride, and he can shoot a little. Not sure how good he would be with the herd. Cavanaugh was punching cows for Gonzales but wanted to make more money. Jesus Rodriquez is a cousin of Juan's from across the river. He can ride, and he's good with a riata."

"We'll fold them in. Why are you sending Boyle? He's...not going to want to take orders from me."

"You're the trail boss. He gets out of line, fire his ass and be ready to back it up with your gun. Shawn's probably going to leave when you get to Wyoming, anyway. He's run out his string here, but he's still a top-notch hand when he puts his mind to it. When are you leaving?"

"I plan on pushing across the river tomorrow and getting them lined out the day after. First couple of days will shake out both the cows and the crew, or so you taught me."

Ed shook his head. "Smart-alecky kids. Your ma sends her love." He reached out and hugged Rio, "Take care, Son. We want you back safe."

"I'll do my best, Pa," he reached in his jacket, handing a folded piece of paper to his dad, "Oh, I wrote this for Uncle Ethan. I want to try to see him on the way back."

Eli scuffed the dirt then looked at his older brother with a grin. "Pa's gonna...going to let me go with the Suttons up to Kansas over the Chisholm trail this year. I'm...going to be handling the remuda!" He looked quickly to see his dad walking off and said softly, "I wish I was goin' with you."

Rio impulsively hugged Eli and realized they were almost the same height. "You need to start easy. You're doing the same thing I did. The trail is going to...make a man out of you. Just remember, you gotta *earn* your keep."

Eli hugged him momentarily, then pushed him away. "I'm sixteen! I'm almost as big as you are! And Pa's going to let me take a pistol with me."

Biting his lip, Rio said, "Keep it in the holster. Do your job. I'll see you in September."

Ed came around the wagon. "Let's go, Eli. We need to get back to the ranch." Turning to Rio he added, "I'll get the note to Ethan to Butterfield. It should be there in a month." He shoved it in his pocket and climbed onto the wagon seat, picked up the reins, and headed east as Rio stood watching.

Rio sighed and thought, *Well, what do I do now? I need to put a schedule together with a rotation, and scouts...gotta put somebody out front...* Rio swung back into the saddle and turned toward the chuck wagon. *Damn you, Pronto, I'm supposed to be leading, not...wait! If they see me doing this and other jobs, they can't say I'm not willing to do anything they are doing.*

Chapter 2

A month up the trail, Rio smiled as Pronto drove the chuck wagon into the camp. "'Bout time you got back! I thought we were going to have to send the crew in to search the bars for you," he said with a laugh.

"Shaddap, boy. Damn quartermaster at Fort Sumner was a real shit. He wanted to double and triple check everything. And he had to go to the colonel and get his permission to take gold in payment. I had to get some seasonings in town, and I got something to eat, too. Took my time coming back, since I got three dozen eggs back there packed in straw, and a slab of bacon. Figured you boys might like to have bacon and eggs for breakfast for a change."

"Bacon and eggs? You're forgiven! Hell, why wait for breakfast?"

"Cause my ass is draggin', and I ain't gonna cook them with the beans tonight."

Rio sighed. "Alright. I won't say anything to the others. If I did, you'd be mobbed."

Pronto spit. "I can take care of mobs," he said with a grin. "They might not like *how* I take care of it, but I could." Rio shivered, remembering that Pronto was not someone that you wanted to piss off. "You bedding them down here?"

"Yeah, today is a month on the trail, and I figured we needed a little bit of a break. Maybe let a few of the fellas go into town tonight. We're a little ahead of where I thought we would be, and there's good water and feed here."

Pronto shrugged, "You're the boss. You goin' in?"

"Nah, I went in last year, and I didn't care for it. How many of them do you think will want to go in?"

Pronto climbed down with a groan, putting his hands in the small of his back and stretching. He scratched his beard, then said, "Arthur won't. Morgan probably won't. Flynn," he rocked his hand back and forth, "Maybe. McCormick will, Jesus and Juan will. Tobin will. The kids will want to go, too. The others? No idea."

"I figured we can let half the crew go tonight, or all of them, depending on how many wants to go. Peterson can't, he's not got any money. Cavanaugh maybe, but he's been pretty quiet."

Pronto spit and nodded. "Both them kids're working out pretty well. I been working with Peterson on his gun handling. Cavanaugh's been doing some huntin', he's a pretty good rifle shot, and he's young enough to enjoy stalking the game."

Rio was surprised, "You've been working with them?"

"If they're going to be handling guns around me, I want to know I can trust them with 'em. Peterson's a little slow, but he's accurate. He's learning accuracy counts, and reloading those old conversions are a pain. I showed them some tricks, and they picked 'em up quick. I got 'em both carrying extra wedges in their pockets, too. They ain't lost any wedges yet, but they will," he said with a cackle.

Rio remembered Pronto training him and grimaced. "Slapped the pistol, did you?"

"Yep, just as he was takin' the wedge out to replace the cylinder, and it come apart just like yours did. Left him holdin' the frame and nothin' else. But he found all the parts, even the wedge. He ain't made that mistake since."

Pronto just grinned as he turned away, starting to unhitch the mules. Rio rode away chuckling under his breath and took a quick pass around the herd, letting the little grulla step out. *I gotta remember this horse. She's got some spunk.* He rode north from the herd, and topping out on a little rise, he looked north. *Now it gets interesting. We're getting into the breaks, and it's going to slow us down some. I figure we've been making ten, maybe twelve miles a day... Even with the days getting longer, I hope we can make six, maybe eight miles a day through this stuff. At least we're first, so there is plenty of grass, and thankfully it's been a wet spring, so we haven't had to do any long pushes for water.* He inhaled deeply, sighed and turned the grulla back toward the herd, letting her have her head.

***

It turned out that only half the hands wanted to go into town, and Rio let all of them go, asking Flynn to go along and ride herd on them as necessary. "John, I know you didn't particularly want to go, but they do need somebody to keep them from getting stupid." He handed him a $20 gold piece. "At least get yourself a decent meal, and a bath if you want one."

Flynn chuckled. "First time I've ever got paid to go to town." He flipped the gold piece in the air, caught it, and slipped it into his vest pocket. "A warm bath would be good thing. Maybe soak these old bones for a while, and I'll be less grumpy. I'll do my best to keep 'em out of trouble."

"Thanks, John. That's all I ask."

Pronto rang the triangle, "Supper's up! Come and get it, 'fore I throw it out!"

Flynn laughed. "Enjoy the beans, Rio. We'll be back by morning."

Rio grinned and waved as he turned toward the chuck wagon. Getting a plate of beef and beans, he sat on the log near the fire and grimaced as he took the first bite. *They're gonna get a good meal, and I'm eating beef and beans. I hope this is the end of that damn brindle's meat. He was a chewy sumbitch.* He ate the rest of the meal without comment as the crew rode off, heading for town and laughing and joking.

After he cleaned his plate, he looked around, "Arthur, you and I'll take the next night herd turn." He thought for a second, "Morgan, you and Peterson want to relieve us at midnight?"

Morgan got up slowly, heading for the chuck wagon. "Sure boss. Right, Hoyt?"

The young cowboy nodded. "I don't have a watch."

Morgan replied, "I do. I'll make sure you're up."

Tobin groaned, "Guess that means I got the last guard, right boss?"

Rio nodded, "Sorry Tobin. I'll go relieve...you get along with Gonzales better, right?"

"Sure, boss."

"Okay, I'll go relieve him now. I'll tell Miller you'll relieve him at eight, Arthur."

Arthur shrugged. "I can go now, iffn you want."

"No, Miller won't be doubling back like Gonzales."

Rio went over to the remuda, found the grulla and threw a lasso on her. He got her saddled up, coiled his lasso and hung it off the saddle horn, checked to make sure the thong was on his pistol, and mounted up. The sun was just sinking in the west as he rode slowly out to the herd, scanning for either of the cowboys riding around the herd. He finally saw a hat bobbing to the northwest and turned in that direction. A couple of minutes later, he saw Gonzales, and waved his hat.

Gonzales pulled up, and Rio rode over to him, "Raoul, I'm relieving you early. I need you to double back with Tobin at four AM."

Gonzales shook his head. "Knew I should have gone to town, Boss," he said jokingly.

Rio laughed, "You had your chance."

"Jesus is young. He deserves the chance. Me, I'm saving to marry Lupe when we get back. I don't need to spend the money."

"Lupe? Lupe that came over from Reardon's ranch? Really? Congratulations, Raoul!"

Gonzales smiled, "I knew her in old Mexico. We are from the same village. When Juan was killed by that bull last year, she didn't want to stay on that ranch. Too many memories. Juanita is her cousin and got her a job on your ranch." He shrugged. "We have been talking. Neither of us is young, but we are comfortable with each other."

Rio nodded. "Well, I hope you're comfortable with beef and beans. That's supper. I hope this is the last of that damn brindle steer."

"It is food, boss. Better than nothing. Thank you for relieving me early."

"*De nada.*" Gonzales rode off toward the chuck wagon as Rio looked around, *Dammit, I didn't ask him which way he was riding. But he's right handed, so probably counterclockwise.* Twenty minutes later, just as the sun set, he met Miller coming the other way. "Everything okay, Charles?"

Miller pulled up. "So far, boss. Where'd Raoul go?"

"I relieved him early, he's doubling back with Tobin at four."

Miller chuckled. "Better him than me. Beef and beans again?"

"Yep. Pronto should have something different tomorrow, he brought supplies back."

"Good! Your bell cow is bedded down."

Rio smiled, "Good to know. This little grulla likes to step out, so I might be moving around a little faster than normal."

Miller patted the neck of the dun he was riding, "This one's a plodder. He ain't fast, but he's steady. A good night horse. See ya when I see ya, boss."

Rio nodded and trotted toward the front of the herd, trying to keep the grulla from picking up speed, "Slow down, you. This ain't a race, and you're gonna be hauling me around for the next six hours." She twitched her ears at him but slowed as he pulled on the reins. He scanned the herd, looking for any problems and saw probably three quarters of the herd bedded down. The ones remaining up were cropping grass and lowing softly.

Five hours later, Rio's butt was hurting, and he was having trouble staying awake, he'd been humming The Little Log Cabin in the Lane, and started singing it. The grulla humped her back a couple of times and laid her ears back, and Rio said, "Okay, okay, no singing. I'll just sit up here and be quiet."

A few minutes later, he and Arthur met, "Looks like things are quiet, but we're losing the stars."

Arthur replied, "Yep, getting a few puffs of wind, too. Looks like most of the herd is down."

Rio pulled out his watch and lit a match. "Another half hour to go."

"Good. I'm tired."

"Me too. It's going to feel good to get off this horse."

Arthur chuckled, "You relieved Raoul early. It's your own fault, Rio."

"I know. But fair is fair."

"And the men appreciate it. Including the fact that you take your turn at drag. Some of them figured your bossing the drive would go to your head."

Rio shook his head, "No, Pa would have my ass if I tried that. I saw what Bolton did last year, and I vowed never to do those things if I ever got put in charge."

Arthur laughed. "That's why nobody hires him a second time. And he always has problems getting hands. Once is enough with him, even if he does bring the herds through."

Rio asked curiously, "Then why does he keep getting hired?"

"He gets the herds through. One more round?"

"Yeah. Meet me at the southwest corner of the herd. That's closest to the camp. That'll make the turnover quicker."

"Youza boss."

Rio laughed as he rode on, *Arthur is something else. We're lucky to have him, but sometimes I wonder about him.* A half hour later, Morgan and Peterson cantered out of the camp as Rio pulled up where Arthur was waiting. "Josh, Hoyt, it's quiet, but we've lost the stars. Wind's been picking up a little then laying down. Most of the herd is down and don't seem too restless."

Morgan nodded. "Got it, boss. Which way you been riding?"

"Counterclockwise."

"Okay, I'll take that. Hoyt, you take clockwise."

Peterson replied, "Okay. Slow riding, right?"

Arthur said, "Slow and easy. Take your time, ain't no rush."

"There isn't anybody out here but us, the only thing you might see or hear is our other hands coming back from town. Hopefully quietly, but I'm not betting on that."

Everyone chuckled at that, and Morgan said, "Let's go, Hoyt."

Rio and Arthur rode back to camp, each with their own thoughts. After turning the horses into the remuda, Rio said, "Pronto will have a surprise for breakfast, so you might want to get up in the morning."

Arthur laughed. "With Pronto it's always a surprise. 'Night, boss."

"Night." Rio dropped his saddle and saddle blanket next to his bedroll and sat down with a thump. Pulling his boots off, he wiggled his toes and sighed, "Oh, that feels good!" Unbuckling his gun belt, he hung it on the wagon wheel next to him and unrolled the bed roll, draping it over the saddle. He rolled onto it with a groan and fell asleep in minutes.

**

A bright flash and a loud boom startled Rio out of a deep sleep, momentarily stunning him. As he fought to figure out what was going on, he heard a rumble and mooing cattle. He froze, *Stampede... Oh...* Bolting up, he stomped his feet into his boots, frantically slinging his gun belt around his hips, and he heard Arthur yelling, "Stampede! Everybody up!"

Pronto rolled out of the back of the wagon with a grunt, hobbling toward the remuda cussing. Rio grabbed him, "No! Stay here and guard the wagon. If anybody comes in, get them on a fresh horse as soon as you can."

Grabbing his saddle, bridle, and saddle blanket, he ran toward the remuda. Dropping them, he pulled the lasso loose, shook out a loop, and dropped over the first horse he saw close enough to him that he could make it out. The horse reared, but he hung on to the rope, then pulled on it, getting the horse to come to him. Taking a chance, he stood on the lasso, quickly throwing the saddle blanket on, smoothing it out, and swinging the saddle on. Knotting the cinch strap, he pulled the bridle off his arm, quickly got the bit in the horse's mouth, fastened the bridle, and slid the lasso off its neck.

He heard the cattle stampeding away from the camp, and he quickly swung into the saddle. As he did, he heard a single shot. *Damn. That...isn't good. I hope that was an accident.* He lightly touched the spurs to the horse, and it bucked a couple of times, then started away from all the noise. He reined it around, touched the spurs to it again, and it took off at a dead run.

A bolt of lightning, followed almost immediately by another clap of thunder startled both Rio and the horse. It shied and almost put Rio in the dirt. He continued to chase the herd, slowly catching up with it, and praying the horse didn't step in any holes and break a leg.

What seemed like hours later, he could finally make out individual cows, and he realized the other hands had managed to turn the herd back on itself. The herd had finally stopped running but continued milling and lowing. As the light grew brighter, he could see them still rolling their eyes and cattle scattered across a wide section of the plain. He reined the dun to halt, and it dropped its head, sides heaving, as foam flecked its muzzle.

"Sorry horse, didn't mean to ride you that hard." Rio patted its shoulder, feeling the sweat. Then he felt his own legs start cramping. He groaned and swung down, going to his knees as his legs gave out.

The horse nuzzled his hair as he tried to get up, finally pulling himself up using the stirrup. Rio stood wavering and frantically undid his pants so he could piss. He looked around, hoping no one saw him, then buttoned back up and started walking the horse back toward the herd. He saw Flynn riding around the herd, leading a horse and waved. Flynn rode over to him, "You alright, Rio?"

"I think so, but this dun is wore out. When did you get back?"

"We rode out as soon as we heard the thunder. Couple of the fellas are a little worse for wear."

Bitterly, Rio looked around, "It's going to take us days to round up all these critters."

Flynn nodded. "Yep, but we'll get it done. At least none of them ran off a cliff that we know of. I brought a spare for you."

"Thanks, let me change my tack over, and I'll get started." Rio pulled his saddle and blanket off the dun and moved it to the pinto, then the bridle, replacing the hackamore. He put the hackamore on the dun and swung back into the saddle.

As he swung up, Flynn said, "No, you need to go back and get some coffee and food in you. We're cycling people back now. You keep going, and you're going to get hurt."

Rio bristled, "John, we need—"

"Dammit, Rio, we need you thinking. *Not* just reacting. Nothing you do right now is going to be worth a shit. You're in charge, so *take* charge."

"Alright. Fine. Start trying to get the strays back to the herd. Get somebody up here to hold the front of the herd here. I'll send the first two people I see up here to help you."

Flynn nodded. "That's more like it."

Rio picked up the hackamore and rode slowly back toward the camp, *John's right. I am in charge, and God knows how many cows we lost. Gotta get them back, somehow...*

Looking up, he saw that the sky was clear overhead, and the heavy clouds had moved off to the east. He saw Tobin first and told him to head north, find Flynn and hold the herd. A mile or so later, he saw Morgan and told him the same thing. He'd ridden almost six miles before he saw the chuck wagon in the distance, and he shivered, *It's a miracle I didn't kill myself last night. Five, six miles? Damn.* He rode up to the remuda, took the hackamore off the dun and patted it on the neck, "You done good, horse." Turning, he rode over to the chuck wagon, swung out of the saddle and tied the pinto to the tailboard.

Pronto looked at him, relief in his eyes as he handed Rio a plate of bacon and eggs, topped with a biscuit. "Glad to see you, boy."

Rio slumped down on the log, balancing the plate on his knees, "Damn glad to be here, Pronto." He ate quickly, then got up. "Have we accounted for everybody?"

Pronto glanced at him, then straightened up. "Everybody 'cept the boy. Peterson. Ain't seen him come in. You and him were the last two."

Rio froze. "What? Why didn't you tell me?"

Pronto growled at him, "What good would it have done? You needed to eat. Now drink your damn coffee. Flynn and Arthur are out checking."

Rio remembered, "I heard a shot last night...just after...the stampede started."

Pronto nodded, "I remember that. Didn't hear another one."

"No. No, I didn't either. I shouldn't have put him out there. He didn't know—" *Where could Hoyt be? No, he's gotta be alive, just not on his horse. He'll be found...*

"Stop it, dammit. He was drawing a man's pay and doing a man's job. He knew the risks. And we don't know where he is. He may be chasing cows down in the breaks."

***

Late that afternoon, Rio was riding back toward camp to change horses when he found what was left of Peterson and his horse, thanks to the circling buzzards. From the position, he must have been nearly dead center in front of the herd when they stampeded. After he threw up, he pulled his pistol and fired three rounds. Arthur was the first one there, and he took one look at Rio, looked at the mess on the ground, and took off his hat. "Lord, take this young man into your arms. He died trying to do the right thing."

Flynn rode up next, took one look and said, "Not much we can do. I'd say we bury him right here."

Rio replied, "There isn't enough left to bury, John. It's hard to separate what was Peterson and what was the horse."

Arthur said, "At least he didn't know what hit him. A thousand or more cows running over him—"

"He knew," Rio said bitterly, "He knew. He got off one shot. I wonder if that was to kill the horse."

"Might have been. Looks like he's north of the horse, so that would make sense. He tried to make a bulwark, probably never had a chance to drop a cow."

Pronto rode up on a mule, just as Cavanaugh and Gonzales came from the herd. Cavanaugh asked in horror, "Is that..." He turned away, throwing up violently.

Gonzales paled and took his hat off. "*Madre dios.*"

Pronto slid off the mule, and Rio realized he'd ridden it bareback. He pulled his skinning knife out and poked around, "Looks like his gun was out of the holster. It's either broke or buried somewhere around here." He looked up at Rio, "We need to go get rocks and pile 'em over them. Make a cairn right here. Ain't enough left to bury. I'll do a cross we can plant." He got up, wiped the knife clean on his pants and swung back up on the mule, then turned back to camp.

Four hours later, all the remaining cowboys stood around an eight foot by six foot by three foot cairn of rocks as Pronto pounded the top of a wooden cross into the ground at the end of the cairn. The cross piece simply said *Hoyt Peterson died here April 10, 1871.*

Rio took off his hat, "The only prayer I can remember is the twenty-third Psalm. It ain't the right one, but maybe he'll understand." He scrubbed his face, then recited, "The Lord is my shepherd; I shall not want. He maketh me to lie down in green pastures: he leadeth me beside the still waters. He restoreth my soul: he leadeth me in the paths of righteousness for his name's sake. Yea, though I walk through the valley of the shadow of death, I will fear no evil: for thou art with me; thy rod and thy staff they comfort me. Thou preparest a table before me in the presence of mine enemies: thou anointest my head with oil; my cup runneth over. Surely goodness and mercy shall follow me all the days of my life: and I will dwell in the house of the Lord forever. Lord, receive Hoyt into your house and give him peace. Amen."

A chorus of amens followed, and Rio looked up at the sky, tears in his eyes. He stood for a moment, then put his hat back on, "Alright, let's go to work. We got cows the gather up. I'm going to the fort to send a message to Pa that Hoyt's been killed. I'll be back as soon as I can. Flynn you're in charge."

He mounted Red, touched his heels to his flanks as he turned west toward the fort and let Red run, dreading the message he would have to send when he got there, *I killed Hoyt as sure as anything. Shouldn't have sent him out there. He didn't... Oh God. His parents... I should have taken the second shift, then he'd be alive.* Tears rolled freely down his face as the import of being in charge hit him. *I don't want this. How many more will I kill through stupidity? Or lose the herd...*

Chapter 3

After almost a week of chasing cows, Rio finally decided to move the herd on up the trail. Two hundred fifty-four cows short, even after poking in damn near every draw in the area, and grousing from the hands, including the two new hands, Dan Williams, another Texas cowboy, and Felix Estevez, up from Juarez. Pronto had made another run into the Fort for provisions and news that there was a herd about a week behind them. Flynn had pointed out that losses were going to happen, and they'd done all they could. Rio grumbled but nodded, and they lined the herd out the next morning.

Riding around the herd, he chanced on Arthur in the process of hazing a couple of mossy horns back into the herd. Arthur said, "Glad you got us moving. Guys were getting down pretty bad, seeing Peterson's cross every time they rode out."

Rio grimaced. "Yeah, but we're down cows. And Flynn says we'll lose more. Plus, we gotta eat. I know that's why we kept a few mulies in the herd, but—"

Arthur laughed harshly. "Oh, don't worry boss, we'll probably pick up three, maybe four hunnert head between now and Laramie. Ever herd loses some, and the next herd picks up some. Allus happens that way. We'uns might get a few mavericks, too, they be free for the branding."

Rio nodded. "That's right, we picked up around two hundred last year, noted their brands, and I think

Pa sent the owners the money for them. I don't remember that many mavericks, though."

"Scouts find 'em, they brand 'em right there and cut 'em if they need it. You never got to scout last year, did you?"

"Nah, Pa was more interested in my learning how to run the herd. I haven't scouted since the last trip up the Chisholm Trail in sixty-nine, and that wasn't much more than route, where to bed down, crossing conditions, and Indians, so it's been two years and a bit."

Juan came riding through the drifting dust and slid to a stop beside Rio. "Injuns ahead. Jesus said a bunch of them are on a ridge ahead and to the left of the herd. Pronto told me to find you and tell you to meet him at the chuck-wagon. Oh, and Jesus thinks there is a big chief and a medicine man with 'em."

Rio shook his head. "Dammit, that's the last thing we needed right now. Hate to ask you, but can you take over for me back here?" When Juan nodded, Rio cantered into the dust with a wave of his hand. Fifteen minutes later, he reined up at the chuck-wagon. Seeing Cavanaugh driving, he asked, "Where's Pronto, Rene?"

Cavanaugh nodded toward the back of the chuck-wagon, "He's gettin' some stuff he needs to meet with the Injuns. He wanted you to rustle up a horse for him if you got here afore he's ready."

Rio nodded. "Yeah, I want to get up on Red, so I'll go do that now. Tell Pronto I'll be back in ten or so minutes." He peeled off and headed toward the remuda where Jeb and one of the new hands, Estevez, were helping with the herd. He rode around the remuda until he spotted Red, then whistled. Red, ears pricked, saw him and pushed through the herd to him, nuzzling his hand as he climbed down from the grulla he was riding and stripped the tack from it. He quickly got the roan saddled and lassoed a piebald that was on the edge of the remuda and led it back to the chuckwagon.

It surprised him to see Pronto climb down from the chuck wagon in buckskins, but Rio said nothing as he pulled down a saddle blanket, saddle and bridle. Pronto quickly saddled the piebald, then reached back into the wagon and pulled out a small sack that he looped around the saddle horn. "Tabaccy, Injuns prize good stuff for their peace pipes. Bring money to pay the toll, too. This area, these will probably be Mescalero Apache." He flicked the reins and led off at a trot. A few minutes later, he said, "Tell the boys to cut out a few head, maybe three, four. Some of those mulies that aren't going to make it."

Rio saw Williams, another one of the new hires, and Flynn off in the distance. He rode over to Williams. "Dan, go get Flynn and tell him we need three or four mulies or whatever he can cut out quickly. Gonna do some trading with the Indians."

Williams nodded. "Will do, Boss." He turned and hightailed it toward Flynn as Rio cantered to catch back up with Pronto.

Pretty soon they could see the Indians lining the ridge top, and Pronto chuckled. "Games. They love to play games. Here's how we're going to play this. We're going to ride up to the center of their group, but not try to climb the ridge. Make them come to us. Let me do the talking. When I give you the signal, you tell me real loud, two steers. That's how many we'll give them."

Rio could only nod, as this was really the first time he'd be directly opposite Indians without backup.

They rode out at an angle, stopping about fifty yards from the ridgeline which had several trails down it. Pronto chuckled and whispered, "That is Santana. Guess old Barranquito either died or got too old to lead the tribe." He squinted. "And that's Gorgonia with him. He's the old medicine man, so I guess Santana is the new chief."

Flynn and Williams stopped a hundred yards behind them with five cows, and Pronto raised his arm and waved, the Indian waved back, and a dozen of them started down the ridge. A few minutes later, they reined up twenty or so feet from Rio and Pronto. Pronto talked to them in their language, and Rio heard Santana and Gorgonia's names, with both of them smiling. They went back and forth, and Pronto said, "They want to know why we don't go over Raton Pass."

Rio said, "Don't want to pay the toll, and there is plenty of graze out here. Also, less chance of cows getting borrowed on the way over the pass."

Pronto coughed to cover a laugh and gave what Rio guessed was a long-winded explanation. Rio thought to himself, *I really need to learn some Indian talk. Spanish just isn't enough. And it's not like Pronto didn't try to teach me...* More back and forth occurred, and Rio watched the Indians as Pronto talked. The one brave on the far end didn't like what was going on, alternately glaring and probably muttering under his breath. His horse was also restive, picking up on his rider's anger. Rio was relieved that they weren't in war paint and didn't appear to be that heavily armed. He counted eight rifles among the dozen, with Gorgonia and the others armed only with bows and knives.

Pronto said, "They want a toll. They'll take half what we would have paid for Raton."

Rio nodded. "Okay. Hold your hand out and I'll drop the five gold pieces into it in plain sight." Pronto's hand came up, and Rio reached into his vest pocket, carefully grabbing five gold pieces, then dropping them one by one into his hand.

After another extended back and forth, Pronto moved his hand back and extended two fingers, so Rio took that as his cue and looked at Santana. "Give them two steers. We would not want them to starve, and we don't want them to raid our cattle either. Especially after we paid the toll.'

Pronto nodded at him, then turned back and started another long-winded explanation. As he did, the one brave Rio had been watching pulled out a coup stick, yelled and kicked his horse into a gallop at Rio.

Without a thought, Rio drew and fired in one smooth motion. The end of the coup stick flew away, and the brave's horse suddenly started bucking. Smoke curling from the pistol, Rio looked down the entire rank of Indians. Seeing no other reaction, he holstered his pistol and said, "Give them three steers, as an apology for pulling my gun on that brave. And please tell them that the next one that tries that will get shot in the head, not the coup stick."

He turned his horse, leaving Pronto to talk to them, and rode back to Flynn. "Cut out the two mulies and that grey sumbitch and head them toward Pronto."

Flynn smiled. "Good! I'll be glad to see that damn steer gone 'fore he kills somebody." He and Williams cut the two other cows, leaving them with Rio, and headed the other three at the Indians, then rode back with Pronto to where Rio was sitting.

Rio asked, "So, what was that all about?"

Pronto glared at him. "Did you really have to shoot at that dumbass? He was just gonna count coup on you with his stick. That was a helluva chance you took trying to shoot the stick."

Rio smiled. "I wasn't shooting at the stick. I was shooting at his right ear. Tried to nick him to get his attention. That damn stick just happened to be in the way."

Pronto's eyes got big, "You what?"

"Wasn't gonna give that sumbitch a chance at me. I wasn't sure what he was going to do."

"Well, you know you made an enemy for life, don't you?"

Rio shrugged. "Not the first one I've made. Let's move the cows as far as we can before we bed them down tonight." He gigged Red to a canter and rode back to the herd in silence.

***

They pushed hard for the next week, thankful for the good weather, finally coming to the Canadian River. Pronto had swum the chuck wagon across at first light, after telling Rio he'd move a mile north and make camp just clear of the breaks. Rio nodded and swung back to the herd, finding Flynn, and between them, they placed the cowboys to keep the herd moving and managing both sides of the river.

He helped Cavanaugh and Arthur get the remuda across, then turned back again as the first of the herd came into view. Rio cussed the icy water again as he rode into the river, driving the first of the cattle across.

It was only a little over girth deep on the chestnut, but he had to keep his feet in the stirrups since the horse knee reined. The bell cow bawled but kept on going, made it to the other bank and climbed slowly out. The other cattle lowed and bawled, but followed along in a compact group. He splashed on across, turning the bell cow and the first few cows north. Everything was going fairly well until he heard a cow bawling in terror and looked back to see the ornery steer than had been a right pain in the ass mired halfway across the river, thirty yards east of the rest of the herd.

Rio cussed again, got his lasso off the saddle and shook it out, then shivered as the chestnut buck jumped down into the river and splashed him. *Glad the saddlebags are waterproof. I'm about half tempted to let that sumbitch stay here and drown.* He threw a loop and the steer dodged it, apparently sinking deeper in the muck and bawling even louder. *Ah damn... you sumbitch!* He retrieved the loop and tried again, with no success, and shook his head. Rio was not over ten feet from the steer when the chestnut took a step, sank and jumped back, dumping Rio in the water. He came up spluttering, grabbed his hat and cussed, then let the current carry him to the steer. Dropping the loop over its head, he yelled, "Back! Back!" The chestnut obediently backed up, the rope came taut and Rio pulled himself back to the horse then climbed back into the saddle.

He patted the horse's neck then said, "Okay, boy, let's drag his ass out. Back. Good boy! Back! Back!" The chestnut snorted as the steer came slowly out of the mud and scrambled to get its hooves under it. Rio turned the horse and dragged the steer all the way to the north side of the river before he shook the loop loose and smacked him on the ass, driving him toward the other cows.

Looking down at himself he ruefully mumbled, "Well, I needed a bath anyway." Rio reined up and rummaged around in the saddlebag until he found the piece of oilcloth and pulled it out. Flipping the thong off, he pulled his pistol from its holster. Rio dumped the rounds out of the cylinder, shook them and sighed with relief when they all rattled. After wiping the revolver down and drying it as well as he could, he wiped each round and slipped the rounds back in, holstered the pistol and slipped the thong back over the hammer.

By the time the last of the herd was across, over five hours later, Rio'd been dumped in the water twice more, and even Red was feeling the workout, but as far as he could tell, they had lost no steers. He rode the mile up to the chuck-wagon and slid from the saddle with a groan, prompting Pronto to look up at him with a laugh. "What's your problem, boy?" The wind shifted slightly, and he added, "Other than you stink! Get the bar soap and go wash off. There's some soaproot in the side cabinet for your hair."

Rio said, "I'll do that, but I'm going to drink a cup of coffee first. How long has it been since you had a bath?"

Pronto laughed. "I had one afore we left. I might get one today, since I need to wash my clothes. Rene needs one too!"

Cavanaugh looked up. "A bath? Where?"

Rio poured a cup of coffee to hide his grin. "In the river. Just make sure it's upriver of the crossing. And go in at least pairs. One bathes, one guards. And put on clean clothes. Otherwise you get stuff in your crotch that's not good."

Flynn trotted up with Gonzales and Estevez just as Rio finished his coffee and rinsed the cup out. He dug around in the side box and pulled out a sprig of soaproot and the bar of soap. "Get your clean clothes, Rene. Time for a bath."

"Do I gotta?" Rene asked.

"Yep, you stink too." He looked up. "Raoul. You and Estevez want to guard for us, then we'll do the same for you?"

A glance passed between them and Raoul said, "Sure, Boss. Lemme get some clean stuff out of the wagon."

Fifteen minutes later, the four of them rode back to the river and down onto a sandbank. Tying the horses to a piece of driftwood, Rio hung his pistol and belt over the saddle horn, then stripped out of his clothes and splashed into the river, cussing. A morose Rene Cavanaugh followed him in as the two Mexicans stood guard.

Estevez glanced at Rio's chest and saw three bullet scars, with another in his left bicep. He whistled softly and said, "Looks like the boy has seen some action."

Raoul laughed. "Yeah, the Rio Kid has seen a bit."

"Rio Kid? Him? I ain't never seen any of his graveyards."

Raoul said softly, "I have." He looked around then continued, "Right after the war, Rio was...seventeen, maybe eighteen. The ranch was gettin' started back up. He and his little brother were out checkin' cows when they found a bunch had been run off. Rio sent Junior back to get help, and he started following the trail. By the time we got lined out after him, he had a couple hour lead on us. We'd just topped the little ridge down at Lajitas. You know where that is?'

Estevez nodded. "Good place to cross the river."

"It was almost dark. And Rio had caught up with five Mexes that had stolen about fifty head. He rode right up amongst 'em, and one of them cut down on him. By the time we could get down there, he'd been shot twice, but all five of them were dead from headshots. He was sittin' on the ground trying to reload that old Remington with one hand and cussin'."

"Five head shots?"

Raoul nodded. "Five head shots, in near darkness, from horseback. Took two days to get back, and the last day was in the back of a wagon. Didn't think he was gonna live. Six months later, Rio, Flynn and two other hands delivered some cows to Fort Bliss down there at Magoffinsville." He looked around again, then smiled. "Apparently some vaquero with a problem decided to try to pistol whip Rio. He got one swing in and Rio took the *pistola* away from him, slapped him with it, and dropped it in the dirt as he started to walk off. Another vaquero cursed at him and pulled his *pistola*, got off one round that hit Rio on the chest, and Rio drilled that one with another head shot just as the first one charged him with a knife. He put that one down with another headshot, and that was it. Flynn said the entire thing didn't last a minute. That's when they started calling him the Rio Kid."

Estevez cocked his head, "Did you hear something?"

Raoul started to answer when his horse whinnied. "Rio," he yelled as he reached for the pistol and belt hanging on Red's saddle. Just as he did, five Mescalero Apaches came out of the breaks, breaking into ululating war cries as they raced their horses toward the river. Rio turned and slogged toward the sandbank as Raoul slung the belt toward him, then slid his rifle from the scabbard. Estevez was cursing as he fought his horse while trying to get his rifle free.

Raoul came up with the Spencer as he heard the first shots from the Apaches and involuntarily ducked as a bullet whistled by his head. He heard the bang of Rio's Remington in front of him as he brought his rifle up and knocked one Indian from his horse with his first round. By the time he levered a fresh round into the Spencer, cocked it, and lined up on a second Indian, the Indian pitched off the back of his horse.

He looked over at Estevez and saw that he had finally gotten his rifle out, even as his horse was still buck jumping, when he heard Rio yell, "Where's Rene?"

Looking frantically around, he didn't see him until he noticed a head come up twenty yards downriver. "Rene! Swim to shore! It's all over!" He saw Rene wave and looked down at Rio, "He's okay. He's down river a bit. You hit?"

Disgusted, Rio said, "No, I'm fine. But I lost the damn soap and my good shirt."

Raoul burst out laughing as Rio stomped up on the sandbar and started pulling his dry union suit on. "We just got raided by Apaches, and you're worried about soap and your shirt?"

He heard Estevez mutter, "*Un hombre muy malo. I will go get Cavanaugh and see if I can find the soap and shirt,*" just as a half dozen cowboys rode up, rifles and pistols out, yelling questions.

Rio finished pulling on a shirt and put his belt and holster on as he stomped his feet into his boots. He looked around and yelled. "Shut up! We got attacked by five Apaches. Flynn, take a few of the boys across the river and back trail 'em. Arthur, you, Williams, and Juan go git them bodies and drag them back up here...well, over on that side of the river." He took his wet pants and wrung them out as well as he could, then hung them over the saddle skirt just as Pronto rode up on a mule. "Apaches. I think one of them was the one I clipped the coup stick on."

Pronto winced and mumbled something, then said, "I don't think Santana woulda sent him. More like he and his buddies been trailing us, looking for a time to ambush us...or you."

Estevez came back with a sopping wet, naked Cavanaugh riding behind him. Cavanaugh slid off the horse and said, "Found your shirt. And I saved the bar of soap," holding out the wet shirt.

He took it. "Thanks." Pointing to Raoul and Estevez he added, "Weren't for these two, they woulda had us."

Pronto smiled and said, "What you gonna do now?"

Rio thought for a second and grinned. "I think I'll send them back tied to their horses with their weapons. That should send a message." He mounted Red and trotted back across the river, meeting Arthur and the others on the far bank. Looking down, he nodded. "Yep, that's the sumbitch. See the scratches on the right side of his face, that's splinters from when I shot the coup stick." Seeing Flynn and the others coming back with five Indian ponies, he laughed. "Soon as they get here with the horses, tie 'em on a horse and lead 'em back out of the breaks and turn 'em loose."

Chapter 4

Days turned into weeks, into almost a month as they pushed the herd further and further north. They had been amazingly lucky, weather-wise. Having seen two major storms form behind them, including one that came thundering out of the Rockies just before dawn in late June. They'd let the herd run, since they stampeded north. Rio knew from last year, there wasn't really anything to hurt them short of the Arkansas River, and they were still twenty miles south of there. By the time Pronto caught up to the herd, it was seven hours later, and he was still grumpy. When Rio asked him why, he pulled out a hailstone the size of his fist. "Damn thing almost brained me. It was nigh on to half again as big when I picked it up. Lucky I got the canvas down, otherwise it woulda been destroyed. And I got mules limping from getting hit by hailstones. Plus, I'm gettin' low on supplies. I gotta go into Pueblo afore we get to the river."

Rio nodded and sighed. "That means the...men will want to go in."

"Give 'em five dollars. But make them take a bath first. Most of 'em will eat and buy some possibles, I don't see too many drinking."

"We've been on the trail for...a little over three months. Another month to go, we're supposed to deliver the cows...end of July. We might make it yet."

"And Story's got another month of driving them to get them to his range. A month to fatten them up and the weather will turn cold on him."

"It didn't seem this long last year," Rio grumbled.

Pronto laughed. "You weren't in charge last year. Big difference. I'll also check if there are any messages or telegrams for ya."

The good news was that Williams and Green had found another fifty head of longhorns during their scout that morning. Rio smiled as he rode up to them, "Jeb, where did you and Don find them?"

Green looked down at the ground for a minute, then mumbled, "They wuz up a box canyon off to the west. Don saw some tracks, and we followed them. All of 'em have brands, so we put the Rafter B on them so folks'd know they are part of this herd. We found seven Bar B cows in that bunch."

Williams handed him a piece of paper torn from his tally book. "Here's the brands we got."

Rio nodded. "Thanks. That's good work, gents!" He turned as Flynn and Arthur rode up. "Another fifty steers, John!"

Flynn nodded, and Arthur laughed. "You happy now, Rio? That puts us back up over two thousand head, and we still got a month to go."

"Arthur, you know why I was worried. So many things can still go wrong, and we got a long way to go yet."

Arthur smiled as the two cowboys pushed the new steers into the herd. "Boss, I know'd that. Jus' like you want everthing to go perfect. Ain't gonna happen, we'll do the best we can, we allus do. You done good so far."

Rio dropped his head momentarily, then looked between the two of them. "There is so much I don't know. If it wasn't for y'all and Pronto—"

Flynn smiled as he interrupted. "Rio, you're making it work. The cowboys respect you because there isn't a job that you won't do. Most trail bosses wouldn't even think about riding drag once, much less taking a turn regularly. Just like the night herding, same thing. But...if we don't find some water soon, they're gonna run when they smell water. We ain't had any good water since we crossed the Purgatory, and they're gettin' dry. I'm guessing they'll probably run tomorrow, and we need to let 'em run. They'll stop when they hit the river, we just need to keep all of 'em pointed in the same direction. It's probably a good thing Pronto is breaking off tomorrow morning to go to Pueblo for supplies. That way we won't have to worry about him being in the way."

"We won't have much in the way of food for two days until he gets back. And the men are going to want to go into Pueblo."

Arthur took his hat off and wiped his balding skull. "Probably. And we'll probably lose a cow or two in the run to the river. We'll end up eating them 'til Pronto gets back. Allus do, remember last year?"

Rio rubbed the back of his neck and sighed. "Yeah, I remember. We lost, what, thirty head?"

Flynn added philosophically, "We'll lose what we lose."

"As long as it's not any cowboys," Rio snapped, and they both nodded. *I don't need to jump them. Hell, if it wasn't for them, I...wouldn't be here.* He added, "Sorry. Didn't mean to snap. It's just that...I don't want to lose anybody for a stupid reason." Three of the steers Green and Williams had brought back were trying to make a break back west, and Rio took off after them. Arthur rode to catch up as Flynn sat on his horse, shaking his head and smiling.

***

They had done little more than start the herd moving before there was a loud bawling from the front of the herd as the bell cow and others started trotting. Rio, riding point, yelled to Juan, "They smell water, they're gonna run! Get out!" Rio pulled the grulla around and put the spurs to her, breaking for the left side of the herd as he heard Juan whoop. He made it to the edge of the herd as more and more cows started trotting, then running flat out as he turned north, skirting the edge of the herd and pushing the ones that tried to bolt west.

Two hours later he found the remuda trailing the herd, trotting along nicely bunched, with Cavanaugh and Morgan hazing them north. "You need a horse, Mr. Bell?" Cavanaugh asked as they came within earshot.

"Yeah, this one is wore out." Rio climbed down, stripped off the saddle, saddle blanket and bridle, then slapped the little grulla on the haunch. "Go on, girl, you deserve a break." He dropped the bridle on the saddle blanket and walked in circles, trying to stretch his legs and get some feeling back in his feet.

Morgan had dabbed a loop on a chestnut and led her over, handing the lasso to Rio. "Thanks! Hopefully, the river'll stop 'em. Williams said the Arkansas is bank full, so we might get a break for a day or two." He slipped his bridle on the fresh horse, then handed the lasso back to Morgan.

As he was coiling his lasso back up, Morgan asked, "We gonna get to go into Pueblo? What with no chuck wagon..."

Rio laughed. "I knew that was coming. Yes, if the river is up as much as I think, we'll split the crew and let half go in one day and half the next. But you gotta take a bath first."

Morgan replied, "I got no problem with that. You gonna give us a draw?"

"Five dollars. That's plenty to get something to eat and some possibles. Don't get drunk, Pueblo's got a lot of miners there."

"Oh, I 'member last year. Sloan got stomped in that fight he got into. He ain't been right since and can't work no more. I gotta work. I got a wife and kid back home."

Smiling, Rio said, "So you can be a good example."

Cavanaugh rode up and said, "Good example of what, Mr. Bell?"

Tightening the cinch, Rio mounted with a groan. "Morgan's a good example of what not to do in town. Ask him about Sloan." With that, he turned and cantered back toward the herd. As he topped the little ridge and looked down on the Arkansas, he whistled. *Damn, we're not crossing for two or three days. It's not bank full, it's out of the banks, and probably gonna be some cows bogged in.* The cows spread out a half mile wide, some up to their quarters in the water, others up to their hocks, but none trying the main current. He counted riders and was relieved that everyone was present and up on horses.

As he rode down toward the river, he glimpsed Flynn on the east side of the herd, pulling out his rifle and the crack as he fired, and a cow dropped. Riding over, he looked and saw the broken fetlock. "Only one?"

Flynn shoved the rifle back in the scabbard and shrugged. "One that we know of. Who knows how many got trampled getting here. At least this one is off to the side, and this little mound will do for a campsite, since Pronto isn't here."

Rio got down and shook his legs, then turned to Juan as he rode up. "Let's gut her and skin her out. John, you want to get the crew sorted and get the night riders over here, I'll tell them what the plan is."

He nodded and rode off as Boyle rode up. "Rio, what you going to do about crossing?"

"We're not, Shawn. River's too high. You want to round up some wood while we get started butchering? Cavanaugh and Morgan should have the pans and beans with the remuda. When they get here, we'll start supper."

Boyle rode off grumbling, and Juan laughed as he wielded his Bowie knife. "He does not like getting wood, does he?"

Chuckling, Rio replied, "Shawn is Boston Irish. According to Pa, they're raised on mother's milk to object to authority of any kind."

"Ah, I wondered why he never would go to Spanish Town."

He heaved on the cow's leg, grunting, "Let's flip this sumbitch over and get the rest of the hide off. We can stack the guts, tie the hide up, and somebody can drag it downwind from the camp."

"*Sí, Señor.*"

They finally got the herd bedded down, and the cowboys ate the steaks and beans that Rio and Juan had cooked. As they ate, Rio laid out his plan for half the drovers to go to town at a time, reminding them it was a mining town and advising them to pair off. The night riders got the same word when they came in for their food, and Rio finally unrolled his bedroll and laid down as the fire guttered in the breeze. *I hope Flynn can ride herd on everybody. It's been a long time since they've been to town. I gotta let Cavanaugh go, too. He never got to go in to Fort Sumner.*

***

Rio rode slowly into Pueblo, conscious that he would have to send off another telegram to his pa. Why, Shawn, why? You stupid... He rode slowly to the undertaker's place, Flynn riding silently beside him. They reined up and got down, tied the horses to the hitching rail, and Rio stepped up on the boardwalk. Opening the door, he motioned Flynn through it and followed him in.

A door to the back of the building opened, and a tall, skinny, balding man, dressed all in black, looked out. "What can I do for you?"

Rio swallowed the lump in his throat and replied, "You have one of my men here. I...need to make arrangements for his...burial."

"The cowboy?"

Rio snapped, "He has...had a name. Shawn Boyle!"

The man came all the way through the door. "I didn't have a name. They just tole me to come get his body. He got kilt by some miners."

Flynn interrupted, "Not killed, murdered. He was down and out, and they put the boots to him."

The man shrugged. "Dead is dead. Twenty dollars for a coffin and burial on Boot Hill. Or do you want to take him with ya? Headboard is an extra five dollars. Good clothes is an extra three dollars."

Rio said through gritted teeth, "I want to see him."

The undertaker shrugged again. "He's back here. 'Taint purty." He held the door open and Rio steeled himself as he looked, then walked through the door. Boyle lay on the sawn table in the back, already bloating. Shawn...Shawn, why couldn't you leave the booze alone? Now you paid the price. I hope your soul finds some peace wherever you are now.

"I kin put his clothes back on him, iffen you want."

"Where are his boots?"

"Dunno. He didn't have any on when we went to git him."

Rio turned to Flynn. "John?"

"I don't know. I went for the sheriff as soon as I saw the body. Cavanaugh was there, but down on the floor. I think he'd been kicked or something."

"Cavanaugh said he was..." Reaching in his pocket, he pulled out a twenty dollar gold piece and counted out five silver dollars. "I want him buried today. We will watch to make sure you do it right."

"Ain't no call to—" the undertaker looked at Rio's face, gulped and said, "I'll get right on it. Gotta get a wagon to carry—"

"Just get it done. Let's go see the sheriff, John." They walked down the street to the small plaza and crossed it to the jail. Walking in, it surprised Rio to see three men sitting there. One heavyset older man with a star sat behind the desk, and two younger, fitter men sat one to each side of the desk, leaning back in their chairs. "Sheriff?"

"Cafaro. I'm the sheriff. This about your boy that got hisself killed?"

"I think the word is murdered, Sheriff."

Cafaro shook his head. "Nope. Your dandy took on four miners. He was drunk as a lord. He wouldn't stay down and they kept telling him to stay down."

Flynn said very softly, "Is that why I heard one of them say to put the boots to him? He was already down and out when I got there."

The sheriff looked up at Flynn. "You the one that pulled a gun and shot the ceiling?"

Flynn smiled. "Yeah, you want to arrest me?"

One of the deputies started to get up, "I'll arr—"

Rio hooked his chair leg, dumping him on his ass. As the deputy reached clumsily for his gun, Rio said, "Go ahead. I'll let you get it out before I kill you." Watching the deputy, he said, "Sheriff, I want the men that murdered Boyle. A beating is one thing, murder is something else again."

The deputy slumped back on the floor, his hands well clear of his gun as the sheriff said, "They're gone. Ain't seen them since that night. Dunno where they went."

Rio nodded grimly, "Well, I guess we'll handle it our way. I'm ramrodding the first herd up the trail this year. We'll put the word out with a description and a reward if we don't get 'em first. Oh, and we'll pass the word back down the trail to avoid Pueblo."

Cafaro laughed. "You?" He looked at Flynn, "You're the trail boss, right? Not this...kid."

Flynn's grin showed teeth as he replied. "No, he's in charge. And I ride for the brand. We've got two thousand head down in the flats right now. And the Rafter B takes care of its own. Boss, I think I'm gonna go prowl a bit. See if I can scare up some names for those four."

Rio smiled as he turned. "Sounds good to me. I want at least two of them myself." They walked out of the sheriff's office as if they didn't have a care in the world about being back shot, but both watched the reflections in the windows until they were well down the street. "What now?"

Flynn chewed his lip. "I think I'll go talk to the bartender and see if I can find anybody that was in the bar. You need to get a telegram off to your dad. And it wouldn't be a bad idea to get something to eat."

Behind them, Cafaro turned to the deputy and blew out a breath. "Kinda glad you didn't try anything. Them two were primed to go."

The deputy got slowly to his feet and shivered. "That...he's a stone killer. His eyes...he...was looking through me. Damned cowboys."

The sheriff licked his lips, but said nothing, just stared at the closed door.

Two hours later, Rio and Flynn watched the undertaker and two helpers lower Boyle's coffin into the grave on Boot Hill, his headboard laid at the head of the grave. They got it down and stood back waiting. Flynn nudged Rio who started, looked around, and took his hat off. "Guess we don't have a preacher. The only thing that comes to mind is Psalms twenty-three. The Lord is my shepherd; I shall not want. He maketh me to lie down in green pastures: he leadeth me beside the still waters..." He finished with "Amen," then jammed his hat back on, turning away without another word.

Mounting up, they rode back through town as Rio asked, "Did you find out anything?"

Flynn grimaced. "Got two names. Rolly and Mac McClintock. They were the ones that apparently started the fight and put the boots to Boyle. The other two," he shrugged, "Nobody seemed to know who they were, other than miners."

"And are nowhere to be found, right?"

"Skipped town yesterday morning. Apparently on the railroad with tickets to Denver. They're known troublemakers, brothers from Cornwall."

"So, Cornish hard rock miners?"

Flynn nodded. "And most seemed glad for them to go. This wasn't the first time they killed somebody. Apparently killed another miner at a mine down here in an argument over a pick. The other two, nobody seemed to know or remember their names."

"I want them. Somewhere, somehow, I want them," Rio ground out. He turned Red toward the river and added, "Let's go back to the herd. Nothing else we can do here. I want to talk to Cavanaugh again."

Flynn nodded thoughtfully and followed him down the trail.

***

Rio and Flynn rode back into the camp as Pronto was wrapping linen around Cavanaugh's chest. They swung down, and Rio asked, "What happened?"

Pronto finished tying off the bandage and glared at Rio. "Broke ribs. Two, maybe three. All I can do is strap him up. Slapped a beefsteak on his eye, maybe he'll be able to see outta it in a coupla days." He gently pushed Rene down in the back of the wagon and turned to Rio. "What'd you find out?"

Glancing at Flynn, Rio sighed. "We buried Boyle. I sent telegrams to Pa and gave a teamster heading for Fort Sumner a letter for the next herd coming up. Flynn found...two names of the four that put the boots to Shawn."

Pronto took one look at Rio's face and said cautiously, "John?"

Flynn looked around then up at the sky, finally saying, "Rolly and Mac McClintock. Hard rock miners from Cornwall. They left on the train north this morning. The other two, nobody seemed to know. Nobody knows who tripped Shawn or who kicked him. Bartender was happy to say the brothers were gone.

They've been trouble for a while. Mine owners don't seem to care."

A murmur of voices from the rest of the crew startled Rio, and he turned Red. "We're not going to find them anytime soon, but I'm not going to let it go either. And we're *not* going to trash the town. We've got a herd to deliver. After that...we'll see. I don't see them going too far if they're miners."

Surprising him, Pronto added, "Yep, plenty of time. We'll find 'em sooner or later. River's been going down today, we should be able to get across tomorrow."

"That's the plan. So nobody goes to town tonight. We're going to need everyone tomorrow. If you're not on night herd, eat and get some rest." The cowboys grumbled at that but scattered to do what needed done.

Pronto stirred the pot of beans and said, "Biscuits goin' on pretty quick. I'll fry up the steaks as soon as I can grease the pan." As the others drifted away, he continued softly, "Rio, you made the right call. Boys ain't gonna like it, but you did the right thing. Just remember that."

Rio shrugged. "I want those sumbitches. I want them bad. But...we got a job to do." Pronto nodded, and Rio reined Red around, then headed for the herd to check on the cowboys guarding it and give them the word.

Chapter 5

The next morning, as soon as it was light enough to see, Pronto took the chuck wagon across the ford and headed north. As soon as he was clear, Arthur and Rio pushed the bell cow down to the ford. She went right on in, swam about ten yards, and her whole bunch followed right along. By noon they had the herd across and lined out north. Flynn trotted up to where Rio was sitting on a little rise looking back at the drag. "Grass looks good. I'm guessing eight, maybe nine days to Denver."

Rio looked at the sky seeing it was clear from horizon to horizon with a light breeze blowing off the mountains. "Yep. I hope we don't get any more storms. I'll be happy with eight days. What do you think about pushing them a little?"

Flynn rocked his head side to side. "Eh, maybe. Days are pretty long right now, but we want them to be able to graze too. This is the best grass we've seen, and it should only get better the further north we go. We should be west of the buffalo herds, and so far the Indians are peaceable."

Rio took a swig from his canteen, shoved the cork back in and said, "So far. Now that we're north of the Mescalero's range. Pronto says they don't mess with the Utes much."

"Anybody with any sense doesn't mess with the Utes. They're probably the best horsemen of all the Indians." Flynn added, "Gonna go scout a bit. I remember we lost some cows around here last year."

Rio nodded as he left, then pointed Red's nose toward the drag. "C'mon, Red, let's get to work. At least the dust ain't blowing today." Red twitched his ears, and Rio laughed as they cantered toward the drag.

The days flew by, at least to Rio, as they pushed the herd north. While long, the days were the easiest they'd had the entire drive, with plenty of graze for the cows, enough water to keep them quiet, and no real weather issues. It was also quite a bit cooler as they moved higher in elevation the further north they got. But Rio noted that just doing basic things took more wind out of him, and the horses didn't last a whole day. They were changing horses twice a day at the minimum, and poor Cavanaugh was getting beaten up by the constant hustle to keep the cowboys supplied, in addition to his busted ribs. Juan had dropped back and helped the last two days, with Rio's tacit agreement after seeing Rene just about in tears trying to throw a loop.

Eight days after they left the Arkansas, they turned the herd onto the graze east of Denver, and Rio watched as a wagon was driven slowly through the herd to where Pronto had parked the chuck wagon. Cocking his head, he sniffed. *What the hell is this? Does Pronto know whoever is... Guess I better get my butt over there and figure out what's going on.* He trotted the grulla down toward the wagons and reined up next to Pronto. "What's going on?"

"Supplies. I ordered them when I was in Pueblo. Figgered it was easier than driving into town. 'Sides, Charlie likes getting out of the store once in a while." Pronto walked around to the back of the wagon, Rio trailing along curiously. "Charlie! Glad you made it. You got everthing I wanted?"

The stout, gray haired man hopped down from the wagon, moving a lot better than Rio thought someone that big should be able to move. "Pronto, haf I ever not had vat you vanted?" He glanced at Rio. "Dis your helper?"

Pronto laughed. "Charlie, meet my boss, Rio Bell. Rio, this is Claus von Striken, he runs the biggest general store in Denver."

Von Striken shook his head and smiled at Rio. "My apologies, sir. Vith Pronto, I never know vhat is true and vhat is not." He extended his hand as he bowed slightly from the waist.

Rio shook hands with him. "Don't feel bad, Claus. Neither do we. How did Pronto talk you into this?"

"Charlie, please. Pronto thinks ahead. He telegrammed me an order, and I haf had riders checking the graze for the last three days. Ven they say a herd was coming, I knew it vas your herd, so here ve are."

"How much do we owe you?"

Von Striken took out an order sheet, then put on a pair of spectacles. "Barrel of flour, three gallons molasses, fifty pounds lard, two pounds butter, twenty pounds sugar," the recitation continued through the dried fruit and dry goods, and he finally said, "Fifty-nine dollar, fifteen cents."

"Fifty-nine?" Rio turned. "Pronto, what the hell—"

"Blankets. I got ten. At three apiece, good price."

Rio threw up his hands and mumbled, "Think I'm made outta money." He walked around and climbed in the chuck wagon, reached into the hidden chamber and pulled out the tin box. Pulling out three twenty dollar gold pieces, he slid the box back into its hiding place and climbed stiffly out. He proffered the three gold coins to the merchant, "Thank you, I know seventy-five cents isn't much, but maybe it'll help with the cost of bringing it out here."

Von Striken nodded, "Danke. Now ve transfer supplies."

Pronto whistled and yelled, "Need to move supplies if you want to get fed!"

Grumbling, Henderson, Juan, Flynn, and two others came over, and they quickly moved the goods from one wagon to the other. Henderson looked contemplatively at the bundle of blankets and asked, "Can I buy one? I ain't got one, and it's gonna get cold."

Pronto flashed a grin at Rio as he said, "For a price, Henderson, for a price."

***

They got the herd more or less bedded down on the graze, and Rio had let the hands that didn't get to go to town in Pueblo go in with five dollars in their pockets after cautioning them about getting drunk or getting into fights. As the cowboys galloped off toward Denver, Arthur chuckled. "Ain't sure you're doin' the right thing, Boss. Them boys ain't gonna be in any shape to push cows come tomorrow."

Rio grinned. "Let 'em learn the hard way. I did. 'Sides, I owed it to them, and they'll keep their horns pulled in after what happened to Boyle. And by letting them go in early, most of them will be back by dark. Five dollars don't go far in Denver."

Pronto grumbled, "And we're gettin' low on funds. We got twenty or so days left on the trail, and the only places to get supplies are Boulder or Fort Collins, and both are supporting miners, so everything is pricey."

Rio told Henderson and Estevez to scout north to see what the grass and water situation was, then caught the grulla and saddled up. Riding out, he caught up to Cavanaugh, who was riding slowly clockwise around the cows. "Rene, how are you doing?"

"Still hurts a little, but Mr. Flynn wanted me to start working some with the cows to learn what they do. The remuda is fairly easy, horses being herd animals."

Rio nodded. "Cows are dumb. The slightest thing will spook them, and if one goes, they usually all go. Just remember, if anything happens and you're out front when they stampede, get clear, then worry about trying to turn them."

Cavanaugh looked down at his saddle. "Peterson. Believe me, I remember that lesson."

"Good. Lesson time is over. I'll get you relieved at noon."

"Thanks."

Rio continued around the herd and found Ted Green sitting staring at a brindle steer. "What's going on, Ted?"

"That sumbitch is thinkin' 'bout runnin'. Ever time I ride off, he eases away from the herd."

"Well, we could push him deeper in the herd. And I'll check with Pronto to see if we need another beef." Pulling his lasso off his saddle horn, he nodded. "Let's push him for now." Twenty minutes later, they'd pushed the steer deep into the herd, and Rio said, "Good enough."

Cavanaugh had caught up to them and watched as they rode carefully back out of the herd. "What y'all doing?"

Green answered, "Pushing a troublemaker deep into the herd. Makes it harder for him to cause trouble." Pointing at the brindle, "Did you see the brindle we were working?"

"The one with the piebald face marking?"

"Yep, that one. Keep an eye on him if he starts working out toward the edge as you come around."

Rio added, "It'll take him a while to work back out, y'all get back to circling the herd. I'll go talk to Pronto." The two cowboys nodded and rode off in opposite directions as he turned and rode back to the chuck wagon.

After talking to Pronto, he stripped the saddle off the grulla and crawled under the wagon to get a little sleep. He woke a little before four, got up, stretched and buckled on his pistol, stomped his feet into his boots and put his hat on before he walked around the wagon. Pronto grumbled, "Sleeping beauty is awake. I was about to send Rene over to kiss you."

Rio shook his head. "Gonna take night guard, so I wanted to get a little rest."

"Supper be ready in...'bout an hour. Rene, hop up in the wagon and get that packet of spices out o' the tin under the seat."

Cavanaugh hopped up in the wagon, then crawled over the seat, mumbling as he started digging for the tin. Arthur came around the back of the wagon and stopped suddenly. "Riders comin', Boss."

Rio looked up as Pronto jerked around and said urgently, "Rene, stay in the wagon. Stay outta sight." Pronto got up and stirred the fire, then sat on a log on the opposite side, and casually slid his holster into his lap.

Rio looked around as he bit his lip. "Don't know what they want. Everybody stay calm. Looks like six of them riding down the edge of the herd. Wonder what they're looking for?"

Arthur slid back behind the wagon and out of sight. "Prolly, lookin' for range cows that got mixed in."

Rio nodded. "Possible." The six riders broke off from the herd and cantered to the chuck wagon. They pulled up in a cloud of dust, and he said politely, "Light and sit. We've got coffee."

The big, slovenly rider on the black, wearing a black vest with a tin star on it, said brusquely, "Ain't got time. We're...I'm the brand inspector. You scraped up some range cows, we're gonna cut the herd and do a brand check on them."

Rio looked up as the rider pushed his horse forward, forcing Rio to step back. The cowboy to the right of the leader was subtly gigging his horse, making it dance, and Rio realized he was staring at Rio, hand hovering over his pistol. The one on the leader's left was sitting placidly on his horse, but his hand was resting on his thigh, just below his holster. *They're going to try to buffalo us, and if that doesn't work they're going to shoot. Gotta take the young guy first, then the older guy. Hopefully somebody can take out the three hanging back...* Rio dropped his hands to his side, then stepped into the horse as he said, "Whoa! Get control of your horse!" He reached up and grabbed at the bridle as he slipped the thong off his pistol. "You're not cutting our herd. There aren't any range cows—"

"Shut up kid. I seen local brands, we're gonna cut your herd. Ain't much you can do about it, is there?" he asked with a smirk.

Rio started to answer, but Cavanaugh yelled, "Look out!" A rifle banged, and suddenly horses were dancing, kicking up dust. Rio shot the young guy twice under the nose of the horse he held as it reared, knocking him backward even as he frantically swung his gun toward the older guy, getting off one round. The horse reared again, and he fired up at the leader without thinking as he saw him chopping down with his pistol. He pitched backward off the horse as Rio was hit by the horse's hoof. Falling back from the impact, he frantically rolled to the left, gun up, looking for the other three riders. All he saw were horses with empty saddles bolting away from the noise and bodies on the ground.

He got to his feet with a groan, then fell when he took a step. "Bastard shot my heel off." He went to push off with his left hand and moaned when his shoulder gave out. He got up on the second try, hobbling as he looked around while the gun smoke and dust drifted away. He saw Pronto with smoke curling from the barrel of his pistol and saw Arthur snapping Ol' Betsy closed. He went to take his hat off and realized it wasn't on his head. Looking around he found it a couple of feet behind him. He went to pick it up and saw Dan Williams lying on the ground, a bullet hole through his forehead, a blanket still covering his torso. He limped over and carefully pulled the blanket up over his head. "I'm sorry, Dan. You deserved better than to be shot for nothing." He vaguely heard Pronto yelling something as he reloaded and checked each of the bodies on the ground. He snapped up when he saw movement, his pistol coming up until he realized it was Cavanaugh climbing out of the wagon.

Cavanaugh was crying, tears running down his face as he hit the ground and collapsed into Pronto's arms. Rio heard him say, "I kilt a man. I done kilt a man. I didn't want to do that."

Pronto held him and said loudly, "You saved us, Rene. Iff'n it hadn't been for your warning, we might all be dead."

Rio stood back with Arthur as Cavanaugh added, "I saw," pointing to the body closest to the wagon, "I saw him thumb the hammer back on his rifle. I...yelled and...I shot him."

Arthur walked over to the slovenly man lying on the ground, leaned down and grunted. "Rio, you need to see this." Rio walked over and looked down as Arthur sighed. "That badge is fake. It's just a piece of tin somebody stamped out with Inspector on it."

Henderson and Estevez came charging up, rifles out as Rio held up his hand. "It's all over. Corey, I need you to ride to town and get the sheriff or one of his deputies out here as soon as you can. Tell them to bring a wagon to haul the bodies off."

Henderson touched the brim of his hat as he said, "I'm gone, Boss." He turned his horse and cantered down the trail toward Denver as Estevez started to dismount.

"Felix, can you round up their mounts?"

"*Sí, Señor.*"

"Don't touch any of the bodies, leave 'em where they are 'til the sheriff gets here."

Arthur looked at him then said gently, "Rio, you need to sit down. You're bleeding."

"What?" He looked down and saw blood running down the front of his shirt and suddenly got lightheaded. Arthur and Pronto eased him down on the stump Pronto had been using.

Pronto gently pulled the shirt away from his shoulder and looked under the collar. "Don't look like a bullet hole. Looks like a hoof caught you. Ain't bad, but I need to treat it. Rene, get me that bottle under the seat."

Rio shook his head. "No! Gotta wait for the sheriff. Can't be smellin' like booze when he gets here. Don't want him to think I was drunk and shot for nothing."

Pronto rocked back. "Well, I guess you're just gonna hurt for a while then."

He started to shrug and winced as he moved the shoulder. "Guess so. We might as well eat, gonna be a while before they can get here." Pronto shook his head and started banging pans, grumbling to himself as he went back to cooking.

***

Two hours later, the sheriff, Len Walters, early fifties, burly with graying beard and hair rode up with a deputy. He sat on his horse for a minute, carefully looking at the bodies on the ground before he dismounted. "Looks like you boys had yourselves a fight here."

Rio got up with a groan. "I'm Rio Bell, I'm the trail boss. We...they wanted to cut the herd, claimed we'd swept up local cattle. I know we didn't have any range cattle, cause we pushed them all off before the herd got here."

"Len Walters. For my sins, I'm the sheriff of this here county," he said waving his hand.

"Sheriff, you need to see this," the deputy said, standing over the younger man on the ground.

"What is it, Cameron?" the sheriff asked testily without turning.

"It's Bobby Evans!" Cameron pointed to the slovenly man in black, "And Ben Smith."

"What? Evans *and* Smith?" He walked quickly over and looked closely at them. "Damned if it isn't. Both shot in the face, too." He toed the body on the other side of Smith over and chuckled. "And TJ Roberts."

He walked over where the other three lay, and the deputy said, "Michaels, Wyden, and I don't know who this one is, his face is...gone."

Walters came back and looked at Rio closely. "You good with a gun, Son?" Arthur snorted and the sheriff glanced at him, saw the shotgun, and asked, "You take out two of them?"

"Yessir, one with each barrel. Didn't even get a chance to reload. Happened so quick. Bossman, he be good enough with a pistol."

Rio tried to deflect the conversation saying, "They shot Dan Williams, one of our cowboys as he slept." Hobbling over, he pulled the blanket back. "He didn't even have a gun. He was asleep."

A half hour of explanations of where everyone was, who shot who, and Pronto doctoring the cut on his shoulder that was already turning blue led Rio to ask, "So, who did we shoot, Sheriff?"

Walters smiled. "Well, you took care of a half dozen troublemakers that we could never catch in the act. Smith was the brains behind them and ran the stables on the east side of town. Bobby Evans was a hired gun that worked with him and has killed at least three men in gunfights in the last year."

The sound of many horse's hooves interrupted the sheriff as the rest of the cowboys, with Flynn in the lead, came pounding into camp, sliding to a stop. A number of rifles were in cowboy's hands, but not pointed at anyone as Flynn bailed off his horse. "You alright, Rio?"

He waved a hand as he sat on the stump and Pronto worked over his shoulder. "Got kicked by a horse and got a boot heel shot off. Other than that, I'm fine. The sheriff seems to be all right with everything, too."

Walters nodded. "Don't see a problem. Smith was a grifter and con man. Y'all took out him and his crew in a fair fight. You don't mind, I need you to come to town and give me a signed statement that I can file. Wagon should be here shortly to pick up the bodies. What do you want to do with your cowboy?"

Flynn replied, "We passed a wagon headed this way, he's a mile or so over the hill. Who got killed?"

"Dan Williams."

Flynn glanced at Rio then turned to the sheriff. "Is there a cemetery in town we could bury him in? Not Boot Hill?"

Walters thought a minute. "Yeah, he could be buried in City Cemetery. You know if he was religious?"

Rio spoke up, "He said he was raised Catholic."

Walters nodded. "They have a section. I think the cost is around twenty-five dollars, more if you want a preacher to preach over him."

Rio shook his head. "No, we'll say words for him. Tomorrow?"

"Probably tomorrow after noon. The undertaker will have to knock a coffin together for him."

"Fine. A few of us will be in, in the morning I guess." Ruefully holding up his leg, he added, "I need a pair of boots or a cobbler."

The deputy, Cameron said, "Probably Heiser's. I think they might do them. I know they do saddles. There might be others, but I don't know where they are."

"Thanks."

Walters said, "I need to get back, I'll leave Cameron here to escort the wagon back. Can I expect you in the morning?"

Rio nodded. "I'd like to get my boot fixed, I'll be by your office as soon as I get that done, if that is alright."

"That's fine. I know y'all aren't going to run off, not with this herd to take care of."

"Thank you, Sheriff. I appreciate your understanding."

"Well, I appreciate your taking care of bidness," Walters said with a grin.

Pronto said, "Peel outta that shirt, and lemme see how bad you're hurt. Rene, get that bottle o' whisky out from under the seat."

Rio sat down and started unbuttoning his shirt as Pronto poured some of the whisky over his hands.

Chapter 6

Rio woke to Pronto's cussing and pans banging, along with the smell of burning buffalo chips. It was chilly, and barely twilight, but he only saw stars when he turned and looked out from under the wagon. He went to get up and groaned as he tried to put weight on his shoulder, prompting Pronto to ask softly, "Need a hand, Rio?"

He grunted as he slid out. "I can do it, just gotta get..." He levered up using the wagon and continued, "Sore. Damn sore."

"Well, that horse got you good. I don't *think* anything is broke, but since we're going to town, you might want to get a sawbones to look at it."

"Depends. I don't know how much time we'll have, and I want to get my boot fixed."

Pronto mumbled something, spit in the fire and said, "Biscuits be ready in a few minutes. Got eggs and bacon. Lemme whip up breakfast an' we can go."

"We?" He grunted as he stomped his feet into his boots and teetered until he got his balance, "Damn that sumbitch for shooting off my heel."

"Better your heel than you. Sheriff wants signed statements. That's you, me, Rene, and Arthur."

Rio nodded. "Might as well. Otherwise, might be questions asked." *I wonder if I can find another hand, or do we need one? We're...two men down, but we've only got another...twenty days, probably need to find somebody.*

As the cowboys woke up, dressed, and ate, Rio thought about what needed to be done and finally called Flynn over. When he walked up Rio said, "I'm going to leave you in charge. Me, Pronto, Rene, and Arthur have to go give statements to the sheriff. I'm going to see if I can find another hand or maybe two for the last push." He almost fell when he went to take a step and added, "Gonna get my damn boot fixed too!"

Flynn snickered. "Makes sense. You might pick up a couple of hands heading back north. When do you want to roll out?"

"Tomorrow morning. We've got twenty days, give or take, to get to Fort Laramie from here. I'd rather get on up there than not."

"I agree. I'll get the boys lined out to be ready to move. Nobody to town, right?"

"Nope. Just us, and we'll be back as soon as we can."

"I'll get Red saddled for you."

"I can—"

"No, you can't. Not with that bum shoulder. Matter of fact, you need to see a doc while you're in town."

Rio huffed a breath, "Fine. I'll see a damn doc if I can find one."

***

Mounting Red was interesting without a boot heel. He finally went around and mounted from the right side. *Glad I trained Red to be mounted from either side, if I hadn't this would have been...a mess. Can't lift my damn arm, no heel to stop my foot sliding through the stirrup...* Pronto came around the back of the wagon riding one of the big Missouri mules that pulled the chuck wagon. "Let's go. I got things to do."

Arthur and Cavanaugh came up, and Rio swung Red. "John, we'll be back as soon as we can."

Flynn nodded. "We'll be right here." Rio shook his head and smiled as he gigged Red up to a canter, leading off toward Denver.

An hour and a bit later, they rode into Denver, and Cavanaugh's mouth dropped open as he looked around. "Ain't never seen this many people or houses, or businesses neither. How do they live all crowded up like this?"

Arthur pointed up the street. 'Boss, that looks like a cobbler up there. See the boot?"

"Let's see if it's open. Not having a heel on this boot is...I can't really ride too well right now." They drew up in front of the shop, and Rio dismounted, handing the reins to Arthur. "Hold Red, would you, please?" He hobbled up to the front and knocked, then knocked again.

Moments later, a little old man with a fringe of grey hair surrounding his bald dome opened the door. "Can I help you?"

"If you're a cobbler, can you fix a boot? Put a heel on it?"

"Sì, come in." He held the door open, and Rio limped in. "I am Luigi. Sit and take boot off, please."

Rio slumped on a bench and tried to get his boot off, but with the bad shoulder, he couldn't. "I'm sorry, I...my shoulder. I can't get it off."

Luigi pulled up another bench and sat down. "Give me your foot." Rio lifted his leg, and Luigi pulled the boot off, tsking as he did so. "What did you do to this boot?"

"I got the heel shot off."

"Ah," he examined the boot, turning it and looking from various angles. "I can fix." He looked down at Rio's toe sticking out of his sock and added, "You need socks. Good socks." He took the boot and disappeared into the back of the shop, and Rio heard banging and cursing in some funny language. *Luigi? I wonder...Italian? It kinda sounds like Mex a little bit, but...* His attention was diverted by a pair of boots sitting on the counter. *Oh, those boots. They sure are nice.* He limped over and looked at each one, seeing the detail and quality. He looked down at his ruefully. *Beat the hell outta mine. But I'm afraid to ask what they cost. I wonder if he sells socks?* Wiggling his toe back into the sock he tapped his foot and limped back to sit down. A couple of minutes later, Luigi came out of the back, boot repaired and holding a pair of socks.

He handed the socks to Rio and said, "This is what you need. Boots are rough inside. This double toe and heel sock. Protect foot better."

"How much do I owe you?" he asked as he laboriously pulled the boot back on.

"Fifty cents. You want socks, a dollar."

Rio's head jerked up. "*Fifty* cents for a pair of socks? That's..." he shook his head. "I can't afford that. I usually get five pairs for that." He pulled out a silver dollar as he got up and stomped his foot down into the boot. "Ah, much better."

Luigi took the dollar and gave him a fifty cent piece in change. "Good socks better, last longer. Buy cheap, get cheap."

Rio glanced at the counter. "How much for the boots?"

"Ten dollar."

Rio sighed. "Can't afford that either. Thank you for fixing my boot." He turned and left as Luigi stood there shaking his head and mumbling in Italian. *Maybe on the way back, if I've got any money left. Maybe...*

An hour later, they walked out of the sheriff's office, with Sheriff Walters pointing across the street catty cornered from his office. "Doc Martin is up the steps on this side of the building. He's old and grumpy, but he's good. Been around here since...I think eighteen-sixty. 'Preciate y'all coming in." He snapped his fingers. "Oh yeah, you need to go by Wells Fargo. Wyden and Van Horn had rewards on their heads."

"Rewards?"

"Yeah, it's a new thing. Wells Fargo is offering rewards for robbers. And Wyden and Van Horn, he was the other one we couldn't identify, robbed a train six months ago."

Rio nodded. "Thanks, Len. We'll go by as soon as I get Doc to take a look at my shoulder." He looked at the others and said, "If y'all want to go look around a bit, I don't know how long the doc will take to look at my shoulder. Be back here in a half hour?"

Pronto grinned. "I kin do that. C'mon boys."

Rio shook his head as he stepped off the boardwalk and walked toward the stairs. Climbing slowly, he knocked on the door and heard a grumpy voice growl, "Come in. It's open!" He opened the door and stepped in to see a lanky old man, white haired, dressed in a rumpled black suit getting up from a desk. "Light and sit, boy. What's your problem?"

"Uh, Doc Martin, I got...kicked by a horse yesterday." He pointed to his left shoulder, adding, "Pretty sore. And I got some scrapes."

"Take your shirt off and lemme see." He reached in his vest pocket and pulled out a pair of wire rimmed spectacles and fussily put them on, adjusting the earpieces over his ears. He blinked owlishly at Rio as he tried to get the shirt off. "Here, lemme help." Reaching up, he lifted the collar away from his neck and surprisingly gently peeled the shirt off Rio's shoulder. "Got an impressive bruise there, Son. Who bandaged you up?"

"Our cook, Pronto. He...washed the scrapes out with a bottle of whisky."

"Better'n nothing," Martin mumbled. "Dusty, bring me a pan of water and the carbolic, will ya?"

They heard a soprano voice from the back, "On the way, Doc." A small blonde lady came through the back door, balancing a pan of water and a bottle of something with a pad of linen.

"Thanks, Dusty."

"Be right back, I'll get you the white soap." She ducked back into the door and was back moments later with a bar of white soap as Martin rolled up his sleeves.

Washing his hands, he gently peeled the rude bandage off Rio's shoulder, mumbled to himself and dipped a piece of the linen in the carbolic mixture. Gently dabbing it on the scrapes, he mumbled, "Might burn a bit. Gotta clean you up." Twenty minutes later, a freshly bandaged Rio walked gingerly back down the stairs, a dollar poorer, but with another bandage in a paper sack to be changed in two days.

He'd no sooner gotten the sack stuffed in a saddlebag when the others rode up. Pronto asked, "You ready, Rio? I need to get back afore they eat all the food."

"Need to go by Wells Fargo first."

"I know where it is," Pronto said as he turned his mule.

A short ride later, the four of them stopped in front of the Wells Fargo office, and Rio said, "Lemme go see what we need to do." Reaching in his pocket, he pulled out the two posters Sheriff Walters had handed him with his signature on them. Rene grabbed Red's reins as Rio stepped up on the boardwalk. Opening the door, he walked in and stood at the counter as an older skinny, balding man talked with a miner at a desk in the corner. A minute or so later, the two shook hands and the miner stumped out with a smile on his face, folding a piece of paper.

The old man asked, "Can I help you?"

Rio laid the two wanted posters on the counter. "Sheriff Walters said I needed to come collect the rewards on these two."

The old man took the papers, looked at them and said, "Hmmm, be right back. I know Len was in this morning." He disappeared into a back room, and Rio heard a low voiced conversation, but couldn't make out any words. The old man came back with a small sack and said, "Two hundred dollars," he spilled the gold pieces out on the counter and counted them, then put them back in the sack. "Here ya go. Sheriff said you did a good job."

"Thanks. We got off lucky." Rio walked out, shoved the sack in his saddlebag and mounted. Turning to Pronto, he asked, "How are we sitting for socks?"

"Socks? Whatta you mean, socks?"

Rio asked patiently, "Do we have any socks in the spares box?"

Pronto shrugged. "Prolly not. Ain't sumthin' I worry about."

"Let's go back by the cobbler on the way out." Rio led them back down the streets until they found the cobbler's shop, and he tied Red to the hitching post.

"Be right back." He went up and found the door unlocked, went in and said, "Luigi, you here?" The cobbler came out of the back, and Rio asked, "You got twenty pair of those good socks?"

"Sì, twenty pairs I have. I make you deal. Eight dollars, twenty pair."

"Done!" Luigi disappeared into the back, and Rio pulled a twenty dollar gold piece out of his belt. Luigi came back with the socks, counted out the pairs, then wrapped them in butcher paper and tied them with twine.

He made change and asked curiously as he handed the twelve dollars back, "All for you?"

"No, I've got a herd of cows out on the flats and a bunch of cowboys. We're going up to Fort Laramie."

"Sì, you will need warm socks up there."

Rio nodded. "Probably. And I do appreciate it." He walked out and flipped the package to Pronto. "New socks for everybody, plus some spare pairs."

Rene said, "I ain't never had socks."

Rio didn't know what to say, so he swung up and said, "Anything else?"

Arthur chuckled. "No, Boss. Let's go before something else happens."

***

The sun was just peeking over the horizon when they started lining the cows out to the north with the old bell cow still leading the way. Flynn trotted up and asked, "Didn't get any more riders?"

Rio rolled his eyes. "Dammit, I *knew* there was something else I was going to do after we saw the sheriff yesterday. Pronto...no, it's my fault, John. I just flat forgot."

Flynn shrugged. "Well, we'll get through. Just hope we don't lose anybody else. Biggest problem is going to be keeping them moving with all the good grass up this way."

"I'm sorry. I'll...fill in wherever I can."

"Good! I was hoping you'd say that," Flynn said with a grin.

"Least I can do."

The cattle made an easy dozen miles before Juan and Arthur finally turned the bell cow and the herd leaders late in the afternoon as they reached a large meadow in a shallow bowl with a creek running through it. Pronto had already set up the chuck wagon off to the side by the creek and apparently caught a few fish while he was waiting on the drive to catch up to him. Cavanaugh had just hazed the last of the remuda down into the bowl and was sitting tiredly on the little rise watching the horses when Flynn rode up. "You okay, Rene?"

"Yessir. Kin I ast you a question?"

Flynn looked curiously at him and said, "Ask away."

"How come you talk so good?"

Smiling sadly, Flynn answered, "Rene, I've been educated at one of the finest universities in these United States. The University of Virginia in Charlottesville." He shook his head. "I even read for the law. But that was all before the war." He looked up at the stars appearing as the sun set behind the Rockies and shook his head again.

"But, if'n you're edu...educated. Why are you out here?"

Flynn looked him in the eye and asked, "You have any brothers or sisters?"

"Nosir."

"Be glad. I...my older brother and I didn't get along. We...our family bred some of the finest horses in Virginia. I...left home in fifty-seven with two horses, Samson and Delilah. They were my inheritance, if you will." He stopped and looked out over the camp as darkness fell then continued softly. "I ended up with a little place outside Austin before the war." He sighed. "Went back after the war, there wasn't anything left. Family was dead, house was burned, horses were gone. I'd served with Edward, Rio's dad during the war. Asked him if I could come work for him and breed horses. That's what I've been doing."

Cavanaugh was quiet for a minute, then said softly, "I'm sorry, Mr. Flynn. Didn't mean to bring up—"

Flynn laughed. "No, just reality, Rene. You ought to get Pronto talking sometime."

"Nuh uh. He scares me. He mumbles Bible stuff all the time, and he's meaner than a snake!"

"Nah, Pronto is an ol' softy. He knows the Bible because he was snowed in one winter and that was all he had to read. Said he read it four or five times. He's hard, but he's fair. He raised those mules from colts he bought off a traveler." He glanced at Cavanaugh again. "You like the horses, don't you?"

"Yessir. Better'n cows. But Paw says I need to know everthing I can when I'm growed up."

"Practical experience is good, but so is education. Don't neglect it, you hear me?"

"Yessir."

"I'm going to check the night riders; you go get something to eat before Pronto throws it out."

"Yessir. I be going."

Flynn sat for a couple of minutes watching as Cavanaugh rode carefully down to the camp, then swung east to catch up with Juan, who had the first night shift, along with Jeb Green. Jeb was another of those young cowboys that Edward seemed to be hiring as Flynn and others became more managers and less riders as the range expanded, and the older guys either bought their own ranches or took easier work. Shaking his head, he decided this was his last drive. Time to let the young cowboys have their turns.

Chapter 7

The days ran together as they pushed the herd north, finding another fifty head along the way, but the Texas cowboys got nervous with the Rockies rising to the west of them, cutting off their view of the sky and the land. The smell of pines drifted down on the winds that sometimes roared down the canyons and dumped out on the plains, scaring both the cowboys and the cattle.

Rains came in bands, sometimes for days on end as the cattle tore up the wet ground, causing Rio to wince at the damage they were doing, but Flynn reminded him this was normal for August in this part of the country. It had gotten colder, too, some mornings there was even a light frost on the grass. Rio rode out to take his turn on the drag and relieve Igor Rogov, one of the cowboys that had caught on with the herd as they moved north. "I'll take it, Igor. Anything I need to know?"

Rogov shook his head. "No, sir. All is quiet. As quiet as cows will be. I tink another veek ve be there. Rain, mebbe snow before long." He pointed to the tops of the mountains. "Snow already marches down!"

Rio shook his head. "You really like the cold, don't you?"

Rogov laughed loudly. "Am Cossack. All Cossacks love cold and snow! I go help Pronto now." He turned his horse and trotted toward the side of the herd where Pronto would be setting up camp for the night.

"Crazy Russians," Rio said sotto voce. *But he can ride like few I have ever seen! I wonder how he came to be here?*

He met Jeb Green as he crossed behind the herd chasing an older steer. "Head him off, will ya, Jeb?" he yelled. Green cut in front of the steer, causing him to turn back toward the herd, and Jeb laughed as Rio rode up.

"You're slowing down, Boss, you don't normally let them get away from you."

Disgusted, Rio grumbled, "I think this damn pinto is shying from the cows. She just ain't willing to close on them. Gotta tell Rene and Arthur. Maybe she's trying to throw a shoe, but...she ain't getting the job done."

That evening, Rio, Pronto, and Flynn sat around the campfire discussing the approach to Fort Laramie. Pronto said, "Need to swing a little east. Them little ridge lines are a pain. And we need to cross both the Laramie and North Platte to get to the holding grounds."

Flynn nodded. "Yeah, I'd rather cross south of the Fort. Otherwise it's another four, maybe five days up to Bennett's Crossing. I'm pretty sure Nelson Story is going to push straight up the Bozeman Trail, since he's got probably another fifty days on the trail to get to Paradise Valley."

"Think Mr. Story himself will come down here?" Rio asked.

"Probably. I know I would if I was spending fifty thousand dollars!" They all laughed at that, and Flynn continued, "Story knows cows. He did this the first time in sixty-six. He knows what he wants, and they have to be able to survive the winter. He may not take them all, but I know the fort needs them to feed the Indians, so we'll get a sale either way."

Rio nodded. "Shit. I just thought of something." He turned to Pronto. "What are we going to do with the chuck wagon?"

Pronto shook his head. "Boy, you need to use your head for somethin' beside a hat rack. Little late to worry 'bout that ain't it?" Flynn just smiled as Pronto added, "Gonna sell it to Story. They ain't bringin' one all that way. I'm keepin' the mules though."

Rio sighed. "Sorry. I just..." Flynn and Pronto laughed at him, and Rio just shook his head.

***

A week later, Rio and Flynn sat in the Colonel's office as they completed the sale. Story said, "I'm taking two thousand head for fifty thousand dollars." He pushed a bank draft from the First National Bank of Denver across the table to Rio.

Colonel Grover, the fort commander, nodded. "And I'm taking two hundred forty-nine cows for six thousand two hundred and twenty-five dollars." He turned to the post supply officer. "Lieutenant, please go get the money from the safe." The lieutenant nodded and left the room as Grover turned back to Rio and Flynn. "Do you need a place to pay off your cowboys?"

Rio glanced at Flynn and said, "Yes, sir, if you don't mind."

The colonel nodded. "Feel free to use the porch of my adjutant's office to pay them. I'll have the adjutant provide you a table and chairs. How long will you remain in the area?"

"Not long, sir. I think most of the cowboys want to head back home to Texas."

Story laughed. "And you boys don't like being cold, do ya? I figure we'll move out tomorrow, as soon as we finish stocking the chuck wagon."

Flynn grinned ruefully, "Not just the boys, us old guys don't like it either." That prompted a round of laughter, and he added, "Besides, there isn't much to do here, compared to Fort Collins or Denver, and the boys haven't seen a lot of whisky or women on this trip, so they want to blow off some steam."

The lieutenant came back with a bag that clanked when he dropped it on the table. He started laboriously counting the twenty dollar gold pieces and putting them in stacks of twenty-five. Twelve stacks and ten extras, plus five silver dollars sat on the table when he was done. The colonel said, "Thank you, Lieutenant, you may leave the bag." He turned to Rio. "This is the amount we agree upon, correct?"

Rio nodded. "Yes, sir. Thank you, sir."

Colonel Grover smiled. "Then I think we're done, and your cowboys are probably waiting to get paid, are they not? Mr. Story, as always, a pleasure to see you, sir."

Nelson Story stood and said, "Thank you for sharing your office, Colonel. I'm heading back to the herd, and I'll keep my cowboys out of the fort tonight."

Rio dug sixty dollars out of the stack of money and stood up, "Mr. Story, could you please give thirty dollars apiece to Igor Rogov and Will Samuels? They said they work for you and came up with us from Denver. I figure I owe them for the help."

"Thank you. I'll make sure they get it and know that you remembered to pay them," he said with a smile. "And tell your dad I said hello, and thanks for the timely delivery of the herd. You're a credit to your family, Rio."

Rio blushed at the words, and Flynn laughed as Story walked to the door. Rio said, "Well, guess we better go pay our folks. John, you want to round them up while I get with the adjutant?"

Flynn smiled. "I don't think there will be much rounding up required. I think they're all over at the sutler's store now." He went out as Rio was shoving the money into the bag, then pulled his shirt up and slipped the bank draft into the money belt he had around his waist.

***

An hour later, all of the cowboys had been paid, with some taking all of their pay, some only half their pay. Gonzales, Miller, Tobin, and a couple of others were riding out immediately, wanting to get back to Texas as soon as they could. Rio added enough money for them to take the railroad and steamships all the way to Galveston, knowing at least some of them would get off and ride back down the Chisolm Trail back home. Rio called Arthur and Cavanaugh off to the side as the other cowboys, laughing and horsing around, headed for the small bar in the sutler's store. "Arthur, Rene, you each have an additional one hundred dollars coming. These are the rewards for the guys each of you shot during the attempt to cut the herd. Rene, I know dad was giving your folks most of your paycheck, but if I were you, I'd be careful about telling them about this money. I'm not sure your momma would appreciate how you earned it."

Cavanaugh gulped and turned pale, remembering what he'd done, but he put out his hand. Rio dropped five gold pieces in it and turned to Arthur, who grinned and said, "I ain't proud, I'll take it. Better him in the ground than me."

Rio smiled. "If it hadn't been for y'all, none of us might be here today. So I owe y'all a debt of thanks personally, too!"

Rene asked, "What am I supposed to do with all this money?"

"Whatever you want. But I'd suggest you hide most of it," Arthur said. "I can show you how to do that."

Rio nodded. "Never let 'em know how much money you really have. Somebody will try to rob you, or swindle you out of it, or borrow it and never pay it back." Arthur led Cavanaugh away from the rest of the cowboys, talking quietly to him as Flynn stepped out of the adjutant's office.

"What are you going to do with the draft and the gold, Rio?"

Chuckling, Rio said, "Well, I was hoping to talk you into taking the draft and a good bit of the gold with you, since I know you're headed south tomorrow. I'm planning to go see my Uncle Ethan down by Fort Collins, and I was going to meet up with Pronto in Denver in three weeks, then take the train and steamboat back to Galveston."

Flynn rolled his eyes. "You're gonna dump that on me?" Then he smiled. "Your dad said you wanted to go see Ethan, and I wanted to come straight back, so Edward gave me a money belt to put the draft and any gold in. He told me to make sure you had enough money to bail out any of our cowboys and pay for the train and riverboat fares for anybody wanting to go back that way. I figure you probably need around two thousand dollars to do that."

Rio bit his lip. "Yeah, I didn't want to think about that, but it...makes sense. We made it, now we...gotta get the cowboys back home, but I do want to see Uncle Ethan. I haven't seen him in two years."

"Yeah, tell him I said hello. He and I...well, he changed after the...what happened when he got back from the war."

Rio shrugged. "I know the story. He came back and found that his wife and son had been killed in an Indian raid and nobody let him know."

"Right or wrong, what could he have done? He left in sixty-nine, went up the trail with Goodnight, and fell in love with the mountains. I don't blame him for wanting to get away, and Edward treated him right. He swore he'd never set foot back in Texas, basically cut off dealings with the family, other than you and Edward."

"I know. I think...anyway, if you could take the money back, I'd appreciate it." Rio grimaced and walked back into the adjutant's office. Flynn followed. Rio slipped the draft out of his money belt, handed it to Flynn, and counted out one hundred twenty-dollar gold pieces, then started loading them into his money belt. He groaned as he finished. "Damn thing is bulky as hell. I look like I've got a belly now!"

Flynn laughed. "Go buy a couple of new shirts that are larger than you normally wear. I'm glad we only got what we did in gold. Last year, we had to carry half of it in gold to Denver and put it on deposit there."

The adjutant came out of his office and asked, "Are you gentlemen finished? Can I have my troop move the table and chairs back in?"

Rio replied, "Yes, sir. Sorry about that, I should have let—"

Smiling the adjutant interrupted, "I just need to get my sergeant back to work. That was his desk, so he's...somewhere on post now."

Flynn added, "We do appreciate it, and I'm getting pretty dry, so I think it's time to go to the sutler's store before the cowboys drink all his whisky." Flynn opened the door and motioned Rio out. "Let's get while the getting is good. And I do want a beer!"

They were walking across the fort when they saw Pronto staggering toward them, a group of decrepit characters staggering along with him as they sang something at the top of their lungs. "Oh shit. Pronto's drunk as a lord. Who—"

Smiling, Flynn said, "Looks like Pronto found some friends of his. Those are some of the old mountain men. They come down out of the mountains in the fall and take jobs working for the Army. That way, they get to sleep inside and get fed during the winter." He shook his head. "I wouldn't be surprised if Ethan doesn't know half of them, located where he is. Pronto will sober up in a day or two...maybe...until then, just stay out of their way. They're dying off in a hurry, and they all know it. I'll bet there isn't a single one of them under seventy. And don't try to drink with them, whatever you do."

"But Pronto...I've never seen him drunk. He doesn't drink in Texas, does he?" Rio asked plaintively.

"Only once in a while, but he doesn't get drunk. He...your mother would kick his ass if he did." They watched the gaggle stagger toward the gate and went on to the sutler's store.

***

As the sun peeked over the horizon, Rio was just finishing saddling a fractious Red, both of their breaths streaming in the morning cold. Flynn and Cavanaugh walked over leading their horses, and Rio asked, "You leaving now, Rene?"

Cavanaugh shrugged. "I don't have any reason to stay, and I'd like to get home. 'Sides, the money would be a help." He glanced at Flynn. "And Mr. Flynn has offered me a job as a hoss wrangler for him."

Rio nodded. "I'm not surprised. You've done a good job, Rene." He swung up on Red. "Let's make tracks. It's two days to Cheyenne from here before we can get on the train." The three of them trotted out of camp and headed south toward the ford of the North Platte river.

Ten hours later Flynn said, "That should be the breaks dropping down into Bear Creek. We can water there and either cross or camp by the creek."

Rio stood up in the saddle and arched his back. "I think...I had my druthers, I'd like to be off the plain, but at the same time, I'd like to be able to see what's coming at me."

"Well, make up our minds, Rio." Flynn was smiling when he said it, and Cavanaugh laughed.

Pursing his lips, he said, "Your call, Rene. Up or down?"

Startled, Cavanaugh looked between them as they continued riding. "Uh...down? If we can find someplace to...maybe fort up, if we need to?"

Flynn made a come on motion, and Cavanaugh added, "Umm... If we're off the plain, then we're not being sky lined."

"Okay, you pick the camp then, Rene," Rio said as they started looking for a way down the breaks to the creek itself. It was running fairly full and maybe five yards wide from what they could see. They finally found a place where the rim had collapsed into a fairly shallow ramp and rode slowly down to the creek. After the horses drank, they refilled their canteens upstream of the horses and started scouting for a place to cross. Rio had gone down stream and found what he thought was a shallow stretch, whistled, and waited for Flynn and Cavanaugh to ride back to him. He found a piece of driftwood, poked at the bottom as far out as he could reach, and it never got over two feet deep. "I think we can cross here and not get wet."

Flynn motioned to him and said, "Lead on, Rio."

Rio smiled and shook his head. "Don't trust me, John?"

"Do you really want me to answer that?"

"Never mind." He rode Red into the water and had to pull up his feet to keep them from getting wet, but it didn't get any deeper. The others followed him across, and he was pretty sure he'd heard stifled laughter behind him.

Cavanaugh found a little cove on the south side that gave them a wall of the breaks behind them, and they made a cold camp there.

Late the next afternoon, they rode slowly into Cheyenne. Rio glanced around and said, "John, any idea where to stay?"

"After last year's debacle, I'd rather go to the hotel. I think I remember where it is."

"Lead on." Cavanaugh was looking around, wide eyed at the hustle and bustle around them, and Rio added, "Fort Russell is being expanded just west of town. I *think* this is the current territorial capital, and there are cattle ranchers settling in out here."

Flynn groused, "And sheep. Remember seeing them?"

"Ain't goin' to end well, they eat the roots of the grass too." Rio said.

Flynn nodded. "There's the hotel." They reined up in front of the Eagle Hotel and tied their horses to the hitching rail, then walked into the lobby. At the desk, Rio asked, "How much for a room?"

The pale, skinny man with the green eyeshade behind the counter said, "Seventy-five cents. Only got one room left," without raising his head.

"We'll take it," Rio sighed and spun the book around, picked up the pen and dabbed it in the inkwell then scrawled his name.

The clerk looked up and said, "Ain't room for three in there."

Cavanaugh said, "Hell, I'll sleep on the floor!"

"Be an extra quarter for him, then," the clerk added.

Rio started to say something, and Flynn laid a hand on his arm, shaking his head. Rio handed over a silver dollar, then asked, "Baths?"

"Quarter apiece. Down the hall on the right. Best food is down the street at the café."

***

The next morning, they mounted and rode to the train station. There was a train sitting in the station, huffing softly as they walked up to the ticket office. Rio scanned the train schedule and looked up at the clock in the back of the office, then asked, "Tickets for the eight o'clock train to Evans and Denver?"

The ticket agent picked up on Rio's accent and look the three of the up and down. "Cowboys coming off a drive?" Rio nodded, and he asked, "You got horses with you?"

"Yep, three horses. Two going to Denver, one to Evans."

The ticket agent peered through his wire framed glasses, "Three dollars each to Denver. Dollar sixty to Evans. Includes the horses. You need to get the horses over to the tracks now if you want them loaded on this train. It leaves in thirty minutes."

Rio dug out the money as Flynn and Cavanaugh hustled back out front and brought the horses around to the box car with the ramp up to it. Once Rio had the tickets in hand, he headed for the box car, knowing that getting Red on the train was going to be a battle. He finally blindfolded Red and led him, trembling, up the ramp and into the box car. Once he got a hackamore on him, he fed him a carrot he'd brought from the stable but left him blindfolded. They led the other two horses up, one on each side, and he seemed to calm down a little bit. Rio stroked him. "I know you don't like being cooped up, boy, but it's for your own good. Don't need you kicking the side out of the boxcar or trying to jump off. The conductor wiped his brow and said, "Thanks, Gents. We'd a never got that red devil on without your help." He pulled out his pocket watch and added, "Y'all better get aboard, we're leaving in about five minutes."

Chapter 8

Late that afternoon, Rio turned onto the trail beside the river and said softly, "Don't look like the river to me, but I think Uncle Ethan brought me this way before, so I guess that is the Cache la Poudre and this is the right canyon. We're almost there, Red." He started humming softly and Red, his roan gelding, twitched his ears. "Okay, okay no singing. Maybe an hour, Red, then you'll be home, and I'll get you a nice bait of grub and a stall, then I get a real bed, not a damn bedroll on the ground!"

Buck and Jack had been taking turns watching the river trail from their vantage point on the ridgeline since early morning. Jack was snoring lightly, laying in the shade of the pines, propped on his saddle. Buck saw the lone cowboy coming up the river trail. "Too far," he mumbled to himself. After fifteen minutes or so, he eased the new Sharps 44-90 rifle with its Malcolm scope across the back of his saddle, loading one round and grumbling a bit as he finally got the rider in the scope. He slowly let out his breath, and touched off a round.

The shot echoed down the canyon as Buck watched the rider fall from the saddle and lie still in the middle of the trail. The roan scampered a few yards up the trail and stopped as Jake jerked awake grabbing for his gun until he heard Buck laugh.

Buck laughed. "Got 'em. I knew I could hit him from here!"

Jack crawled forward and peered over Buck's saddle, "Are you sure? The ol' man don't want anybody goin' up that trail."

Buck replied, "You see him layin' there. If ya don't believe me, go look for yourself!"

Jack got up, "Nah, it ain't worth the ride, and it'd take us too long to get across the river from here. Whoever it is ain't moved, he's dead." Jack looked at the sun's position and continued, "If'n we're gonna get back to the ranch, we need to mount and ride. We'll come back tomorrow and get his horse and saddle. It's too far back to the crossing to make it over there today. And that horse ain't gonna stray that far."

In answer, Buck picked up his saddle and started saddling his chestnut as Jack threw his saddle over his grey gelding.

***

As dusk was falling, the roan nudged Rio's foot again. He moaned and finally rolled over. Staggering to his feet, his head covered with blood, he stumbled toward his horse. Red shied away at the smell of the fresh blood, and Rio grumped, "Dammit, Red, stand still!" He grabbed the stirrup, grumbling to himself as he climbed into the saddle. Leaning forward he muttered, "Com'on Red, go home. Go home, fella."

The roan turned and plodded slowly up the river trail as dusk turned to night, the cowboy swaying in the saddle.

Red stood ground reined in front the old stone cabin, and Rio slumped on the steps, too dizzy to even try to make it up the steps. Going in and out of consciousness, he wondered if he's going to die before his uncle, Ethan came back. *Pretty sure I sent him a message I was coming to see him on the way back. He should have gotten the message. Too dizzy...* "I'll get you in the stable, Red. You just gotta wait."

Red pricked his ears, turned and neighed as a man riding a horse came into the clearing. Rio looked up and saw an old mountain man, late 60's, solidly built, bearded, with long gray hair, dressed in buckskins, "Unk Ethan, I'm...I've been shot."

Monte Brooks, the old mountain man, tied his horse to the rudimentary stable, and walked slowly over, his old Colt Navy conversion in his hand. "Damn, I'm getting tired of findin' bodies up here." Getting his toe under Rio, he flipped him over, and Rio moaned. Monte leveled his pistol, "Well, you ain't dead are ya?"

"Help me or shoot me, but you better not kick me again, ol' man. Pretty bad when you kick your own kin."

"Hell boy, you ain't in any shape to tell me anything, and you ain't my kin." Monte shook his head and stepped around him, going into the cabin. He found the table and felt the lamp, with the chimney raised, and pulled out a Lucifer, lit the lamp and carried it back out the door. He looked Rio over, then took the lamp back inside, leaving the door open.

Shuffling and grunting, he got Rio up and into the cabin, half carrying him to a bunk and rolling him into it. "Damn boy, you a heavy one, lessee where you been shot." He held the lamp over Rio, and asked again, "Where you shot, boy?"

Rio mumbled, "I dunno, my head hurts real bad. I member falling, nothin' else."

"Only thing I see is this scalp wound, don't look like you're hit anywhere else."

"I can't see real well, 'm seein two of ya, Unk Ethan."

"I ain't Ethan, lemme see if'n I can patch you up there, boy." Monte rummaged around, heated some water, and found an old shirt that he tore strips off of for a bandage and some left over horse liniment. He turned back and saw that Rio had passed out, "Well, this makes it easy. You ain't gonna complain are you, boy?" Dabbing a corner of the shirt in the hot water, he patiently worked the blood out of the scalp wound, slapped some horse liniment on it, and wrapped a strip of shirt around Rio's head. He tied it off, grunted and said, "Huh. Dunno if you're going to make it or not, boy. We'll see if you're alive in the morning.

Taking the lamp, he went out, grabbed Red's reins, then led him over to the stable, unsaddled his horse, put it in a stall, pitched some hay in, then repeated the evolution with Red. He set both saddles over the rail of the empty stall and hung the bridles from the saddle horns, then picked up his trapdoor Springfield and Rio's Spencer and walked slowly back to the cabin.

***

Miles away, in the bunkhouse on the Circle K ranch, Buck snorted and laughed as he said, "You shudda seen it boys, at least 300 yards weren't it, Jack?"

Jack leaned back in his chair. "Maybe, but it was downhill, so it was a pretty good un."

Callahan sipped his coffee and asked, "What did the ole man say? You gonna get a bonus for this un?"

"He ain't said yet, but I think so. He wuz real happy 'bout what we done though."

Callahan spit in the fireplace. "Taint fair, I set on that damn trail for a whole week and never saw nobody but our riders. How come you get 'em all Buck? Ain't this your third one?"

Jack plopped his chair down, interrupting, "Buck's just lucky, but with the boss wantin' to get the rest of that range, everybody'll get some of that money sooner or later."

Callahan rolled his shoulders and walked to the door, throwing the remnants of the coffee out. Dropping the cup on the battered table, he said, "Maybe I get off this damn nighthawk shift, I can get some. I'm as good a shot as you are, Buck, and you damn well know it."

Buck bristled, then saw that the thong was off Callahan's pistol. He shrugged. "Ain't my call. Talk to the *segundo*."

"Maybe I will. C'mon, Murphy. We gotta ride."

Buck grinned. "Have fun boys!"

Murphy contented himself with smacking Buck in the back of the head as he went by. As he and Callahan walked down to the corral, he asked, "How come we keep getting the nighthawking and they get all the good jobs and bonuses?"

"Probably because they have no problem killing somebody by shootin' them in the back. I ain't that cold blooded."

Murphy snorted. "Or from ambush, apparently..." They quickly caught horses, saddled them and rode out into the night.

***

Monte poured a cup of coffee and walked over to Rio, kicking his foot. "You still alive boy?"

"Yeah, old man, I'm still alive. And I'm not a boy! Name's Rio, Rio Bell."

"Okay boy, and I ain't Ethan, or whatever you called me last night."

Rio sat up with a groan, holding his head and blinking rapidly. "Oh damn, so bright! Ya kinda looked like Uncle Ethan last night. And you sure as hell act like him," he winced, "I don't feel so good, still can't see worth a damn, and my head is killing me. Where am I?"

Monte pushed the cup into Rio's hands, "Here. Drink this, and I'll try to find some herbs to put in a poultice on yer head. You're in a cabin on a bench in Poudre Canyon. I found ya on the steps last night."

Rio peered around muzzily. "This...is Uncle Ethan's place. Who are you, and where is Uncle Ethan?"

Monte sat down suddenly. "I'm Monte Henderson. Your uncle Ethan Bell?" When Rio nodded, he went on, "Sorry to tell you this, but he's dead. Bear got him a couple o' months ago up on Houndstooth."

Rio slumped, dropping his head into his hands as tears streamed down his face. "No! Not Uncle Ethan! He was too...where is his body?"

"Arapaho Joe and a couple 'o other mountain men found...what was left. They buried him up there looking out over the valley. Twern't enough to bring down, and he'd been dead a while afore they found him. For what it's worth, he got the bear, too." Monte got up, came over and laid a hand on Rio's shoulder. "I'm sorry."

Rio nodded. "I gotta get to Denver and...I don't think anyone let Pa know. I gotta get there to meet Pronto, he'll know what to do."

"This Pronto, did he have a last name?"

Rio looked up at him. "Yeah, Pronto Pike. Why?"

"Hell, I thought that ol' fart was dead. I used to know him but ain't seen him in oh, six, maybe eight years." After a pause he said, "We come in this country 'bout the same time, back 'fore the war, with Carson in forty-two."

Rio sighed. "Well, he was alive an' kickin' last week. But he is getting old, he drove the chuck wagon on the cattle drive." He realized he still had the cup in his hand and finished it with a grimace. "God, that tastes bad, what is it?"

"Good for ya, boy, you rest while I go hunt up some plants and things. You ain't goin' nowhere in the condition you be in."

Rio mumbled, "Too bright." He lay back on the bunk and passed out moments later.

Monte shook his head as he picked his legs back up and put him back in the bunk. He went out and started searching the area around the cabin, mumbling to himself as he did so about various native remedies for the scalp wound that Rio had and worrying about how serious the injury was. "Iffn he can't see real well, that ain't good. He must got hit pretty hard to have that bad a rip in his scalp. Ain't gonna sew it closed. Better he heals on his own." After he picked all the herbs he could find around the cabin, he saddled up and rode off the bench down to the river.

He found some willows on the west bank and proceeded to strip a good handful of bark off one of the bigger ones. Stuffing them in his saddlebag, he turned and rode back up to the cabin. Stabling his horse, he fed him some hay, checked on Red, and racked his saddle before carrying the saddlebags into the cabin. He found Rio holding onto the table and weaving. "Unc...Monte, I gotta go piss. I...can't make it by myself.

Monte dropped the saddlebags on the table and sighed as he came around and wrapped Rio's arm around his shoulders. "You gonna have to walk. I ain't strong enough to carry yo ass."

After getting Rio to the outhouse and back, Monte set about grinding the willow bark into a powder, then fixed a plate of food. Waking Rio up, he got him to the table. Rio moaned, "Don't want anythin' to eat."

Monte shoved a cup of willow bark tea at him. "Drink this, and eat, damn yor hide! I ain't havin' you die on me!"

Rio got most of the plate of food down, then managed to stagger back to the bunk with Monte's help. "Dizzy. Don' feel good."

***

Late in the afternoon, two days later, Rio wasn't much better, and his head wound was becoming infected. "Gotta get some help for you. You gonna have to ride. I'm going to saddle the horses as soon as I get you to the door."

Rio nodded. "Okay. Don't know what else to do."

Monte helped him out to the steps, sat him down, and quickly saddled his horse and Red. Leading them around to the front of the cabin, he helped Rio onto Red and tied his hands to the saddle horn. Mounting, he led Red off the bench. "Where we goin'?"

Monte looked back. "Gotta get you some help boy, I can't get your fever down, and yor head is gettin' infected."

Just at dusk, Monte led Red with an unconscious Rio, tied to the saddle, into the yard of a small ranch on the south side of the Cache la Poudre. "Hello the house!"

He saw the light go out and dimly saw a man, rifle in hand, step out the door. "Who's there?" the voice asked suspiciously.

"It's Monte, Mister Nevell, I got a sick man with me what needs help."

"Get down and come in, Monte. You need help?" He turned and said, "Alice, get the lamp lit, and one for the back bedroom." He set the rifle by the door and stepped off the porch.

Monte replied, "Yessir, I could. This one's kinda heavy."

"Dammit, how many times I gotta tell you to call me Hank, Monte?" He reached up and helped Monte get Rio off his horse. "Did you shoot him, Monte?"

As they carried Rio into the house, he replied, "Nope, found him this way, layin' on the steps up at the cabin. Think he's Ethan Bell's nephew. I...told him about Ethan, and he broke down."

As Monte and Nevell brought Rio in the door, Hank's daughter came out of the back room. "Lamp is lit, what happened, Dad?"

"Somebody shot him and he's burning up with fever. Get some water on, we gotta try to break this." The two of them brushed by her and carried Rio into a small bedroom on the back of the house. "Alice, you're gonna have to sleep by the fireplace. I know it ain't right, I'd rather have this cowboy where I can lock him in if necessary."

"Yes, Dad." She turned to the stove, picked up the kettle, shook it, and headed out the door for the pump.

Hank and Monte lay Rio on a single bed in the sparse but clean bedroom. "Any idea who shot him, Monte?

"Don't know for sure, but his name, he says, is Rio. He's mumbled a lot of stuff about a cattle drive, so I guess he's a cowboy, and his accent is from Texas. Hell, maybe he really is Ethan's nephew. Other than that, I don't know. I think he was probably shot by some of Kidd's hands." Monte stepped back and put his hands on his hips. "I back trailed him down to the canyon trail, and I could see where he laid on the trail after he wuz shot."

Hank grimaced. "Damn, that's not good. I wonder if Kidd is trying to take over all of the range on this side of the Mountain. He's stolen about all there is in the south valley already." He shook his head. "Don't tell Alice, I don't want to worry her."

***

It took Hank, Monte, and Alice working in shifts to finally get Rio's fever to break. A week's worth of blond beard had grown, and he was still unconscious. Alice was sitting in a chair by the bed, reading the Bible when, unbeknownst to her, Rio woke and saw Alice, haloed by the light from the window. In a rusty voice he asked softly, "Are you an angel? Have I died and gone to heaven?"

Alice jumped, startled by both the question and Rio being coherent. "I'm Alice, and this ain't heaven." She got up and ran to the door. "Dad, Monte, he's awake!" She disappeared through the door, much to Rio's disappointment.

Hank and Monte came into the bedroom, with Monte in the lead. "Where am I?" He peered up at them. "How long?"

Monte answered, "You're at the Bar N, I couldn't get your fever to break, so I brought you here for help. You been out of it for a couple of days, boy."

Rio groaned. "I gotta get up, I gotta get a message to the crew in Denver, they'll be wondering what happened to me." He tried to get up and promptly collapsed on the floor.

Hank shook his head. "You're in no shape to go anywhere, Son." The two of them lifted him back into the bed. "The closest town is ten miles across the river."

Alice came back in with a cup of coffee. "Think he can drink this?"

"Is that...coffee? Please!" She handed it to him. "Thanks, miss. I, well, uh, Mister?

"Nevell, Hank Nevell, and this is my daughter, Alice."

"Mister Nevell, I don't mean to be short, matter of fact I really appreciate what you done for me. If it weren't for y'all I'd probably be dead right now."

Monte chimed in. "You're damn right, boy, and you ain't going nowhere for a while."

"Well, tell the truth, I still can't see real well. But I got to get a message to Pronto."

Hank said, "Well, there is that stage station 'bout ten miles from here. And the train...why you got to get this message out?"

"I need to let Pronto know what happened to me...and get him to send a message to dad that...Uncle Ethan is dead." He paused. "Uh, how many days have I been here?"

Monte replied, "Two days at the cabin, five days here."

He said, "Well, I do need to ride over and pick up some supplies I had shipped to the depot, so I guess I could send one for ya." He turned to Alice, "Hon, can you bring me a piece of paper and a pencil from my desk?"

She went out and came back moments later with a piece of paper and pencil and handed them to Rio. He wrote out a short note, handed it to Hank and said, "I really appreciate that, Mister Nevell."

Hank took it and asked, "Monte, can you stay here till I get back?"

Monte grinned. "Sure thing, Hank, don't want to leave these two alone, 'specially since Rio's awake."

Rio started to get up, swinging his legs over the side of the bed, he suddenly realized he didn't have any clothes on. "I'm nekkid! Where are my pants?" He jerked the sheet over his lap as Alice blushed and rushed from the room, laughing.

Chapter 9

The sun was just peeking over the hills as the triangle clanged outside the Kidds' rambling ranch house at the head of Soldier Canyon. Other than the ranch house itself, the rest of the buildings were indicative of a rawhide outfit that had grown over time. The bunkhouse was chinked logs, with cobbled together bunks for two dozen cowboys. Two pole barns sat north of the main house, nestling against a small butte that provided relief from the north winds. A ramshackle cook shack and dining room sat between the barns and the main house, forming one side of the corral in front of the barns.

Inside the main house, a serving woman cleared away dishes of the favored few allowed to eat in the dining room. Roger Kidd, fifty years old, heavily built, and going to fat, sat at the head of the table. "Emma, go get some hot coffee from the Chink."

She mumbled, "Yes sir, Mr. Kidd," as she scuttled out of the room.

He looked at his three boys, seated around the table with Pete, the oldest next to Roger. Jud, the middle son, sat next to Pete, and Todd, the youngest sat as far away from both of them and Roger as he could. Roger glanced at his ranch foreman, Billy Purcell, sitting directly across from him and leaned forward. "Boys, it's time we took the rest of the land we need." Looking toward the kitchen he added, "Buck killed another lone rider on that ridge trail leadin' up the river. We need to close off all the access to our land."

Billy sighed. "Hell boss, we cain't stop everbody. We got everthing down to the end of Horsetooth mountain and most all the way up to the river."

"It still ain't enough. I got three boys here needin' land, Billy. I want to move on that Nevell ranch on the other side of the river. I get that place, then the back door's closed." He smiled. "And that would give us another four, five hundred acres of *protected* graze futher up north that we can keep cows on without anybody being the wiser. Nevell's got a few natural ponds up there and a creek or two, so there is plenty of water."

Jud replied, "Gimme a couple of the boys, Pa, I'll take care of that old man and that girl."

Todd laughed. "You just want to get back at her for turnin' you down at the dance. She's too young for you anyways."

Jud smirked. "Yeah, well she ain't gonna turn me down agin. I'll make sure of that!"

Roger slammed his hand down on the table. "Jud, you don't do nothin' stupid. Make it look like an accident, burn the house with them in it." Glancing at the door again, he continued, "Then I'll go to the bank and pay off old man Nevell's note and we'll have that one. Pete, you make sure you're seen around town with a couple of hands."

He paused and looked hard at Pete. "Spread the word we're being rustled and warn everbody. Tell 'em we heard shots back up the canyon agin."

Pete sighed. "Sure, Pa, but how am I gonna cover for Jud and Todd?"

"Don't you worry 'bout Jud, you take Todd with ya, but stay outta the bars. Yah hear me? I don't want any problems."

"Yeah, Pa. I got it."

Roger turned to Todd, "Todd?" The boy nodded then grinned.

"Take a couple of the cowhands with ya, too. Gives you a more settled look, like we're real upstanding citizens." Roger chuckled as he said it, and the others at the table laughed dutifully. Todd's laughter was a little wild, causing Billy to bite his lip, but he didn't say anything.

Emma came in with a coffeepot and asked softly, "Sir? More coffee?" Roger and Pete held out their cups, and she filled them silently, then walked around the table to Billy.

As she filled his cup, he said quietly, "Thank you, Emma." She gave a little nod and quietly left the room.

A few minutes later, Todd said, "Pa, I gotta go. Gotta get *ready* to go to town." Roger nodded and, as everyone got up, he motioned to Pete to wait.

After the others had left the dining room, he stepped up to Pete. "Keep Todd out of trouble. Do not let him get into the saloon by himself. We don't need another *situation* like the last time. And take two of the regular cowboys with you, not the gunnies."

Pete grimaced. "I'll try, Pa. That's...all I can do. He ain't right, and he's gettin' worse."

"Hog tie him if you have to, I got to see some people about moving some cows," Roger said briskly and walked out of the dining room.

***

Hank drove the wagon up to the Evans water stop as the station agent walked to the edge of the platform. "Morning, Mr. Bellingham," Hank said.

Nodding, Bellingham said, "Morning, Hank. Ain't figured out why you keep coming over here to get your stuff rather than pick it up at Fort Collins. That be a two day trip for you, when you could..." He waved his hand distractedly. "Anyway, your goods come in yesterday evening."

"Yep, need to get them. The reason I come all the way out here is that it's less expensive to have things shipped to here, and I don't want people in Fort Collins knowing what I'm ordering." He reached in his pocket and added, "Need to send this message." He handed it to Bellingham, along with a dollar.

Bellingham looked at it curiously. "I kin get it out right now. You want to wait for an answer?"

"Nope, it's from a cowboy laid up over at my place. I'll just load my goods while you're doing that."

Bellingham turned and yelled, "Billy! Run over and see if there are any cowboys hanging around the café willing to help load a wagon!" Billy darted out of the office and waved as he ran around the corner. Bellingham shook his head. "Kid is ate up with the whole telegraphy and communication thing. He's almost as fast as me. And don't ever play him at chess. He's a sneaky little shit."

Hank chuckled as he walked toward the storage area. "Can I borrow the cart?"

"Of course. You don't need to ask."

Bellingham walked back to the office as Billy came back at a run. "There wuz only two, and one was hung over, but the other one is coming." He ran to the office, sat at the telegraph key, and Hank heard him ask, "Kin I send this one, Mr. B? Kin I?"

Hank and the lone cowboy got the wagon loaded in a half hour, then pulled a piece of canvas over the load. He flipped him a dollar. "Thanks for the help. Tell Jim I said for the Rafter J to be careful around Fort Collins. Cowboys are getting shot over there for nothing." The cowboy nodded as he pocketed the dollar and strolled back toward the café.

He walked over to the office and stuck his head in. "Mr. Bellingham, I'm loaded and going to head back. Anna is supposed to be coming home in the next week or so. She's going to ride the rails to here, and she's bringing a horse with her, so tell her to ride careful coming home."

Bellingham nodded. "I will. Hell, I'll see if I can find somebody to escort her. Ain't safe out here anymore. I heard what you told that cowboy."

Glumly, Hank replied, "Yeah, that's why I'm carrying a rifle all the time now. I better get on the way. I can make it home afore dark if I hit it steady all day and nothing happens."

Bellingham shook his head. "Next time, rather than camp out, come on in and sleep here at the station. Whole lot safer."

"Thank you. I'll consider that." He climbed up on the wagon, clucked at the horses, popped the reins, and started down the dusty trail toward Fort Collins as he waved over his shoulder.

***

It wasn't quite dusk when Hank drove into the ranch yard. He climbed down off the wagon with a groan and stretched his back before heading for the outhouse. Alice came out and asked, "Where's daddy?"

Monte chuckled. "Takin' care of *things*," pointing to the outhouse. Monte and Rio helped unload the wagon, carrying the various small barrels and boxes wherever Hank or Alice told them it needed to go. Monte commented, "Layin' in for a siege, Hank?"

"Naw, I get better prices if I order by the barrel, especially on flour and beans. 'Sides, the store in Fort Collins charges way too much, and everybody knows your business and what you're buying. With...the issues with the Rocking K, I'd just as soon they not know how short we are." Hank carried the last barrel toward the house. "Alice, you get supper started yet?"

"Not yet, Daddy. I'll start right now."

Rio reached out and stopped Monte. "Can I ask you something, Monte?"

"Sure, boy, what is it?"

"I ain't a *boy*, dammit! Did you ever seen a man about fifty, brown hair, right handed, walks with a limp around that cabin up yonder?"

"Cain't say thet I did, but I come in this part of the country again 'bout six-eight months ago." He paused. "I found that cabin 'bout a month ago, right after the Arapaho said there wuz a dead man just up the ridge from it. 'Cordin' to Arapaho Joe, he'd been dead a while, been kilt by a bear from what he could tell. They buried what was left o' him in that meadow above the cabin, right where he fell. Said they never did find a horse or anythin else. I figgered sooner or later some kin might show up, and I'll tell 'em what happened. Guess I need to plan on movin' on, iff'n you want the place."

"That must have been my uncle Ethan. He found that place, pretty rundown and nobody around. He...bought the land from the Arapaho and fixed the place up. He was raising horses up here. That's how I got there, Ethan raised Red from a foal and gave him to me about four years ago. I just told him to go home." He rubbed his face. "Why didn't you let someone know?"

Monte scuffed a toe. "Hell, Rio, I cain't read. There's a bunch of papers in a desk, but I couldn't make head nor tail outta them." He bit his lip then looked up at Rio in the gathering darkness. "Anyway, there ain't many people what know about that cabin, and Joe said he was going to let somebody at the Fort know when he got up there. Hell, Hank didn't even know about it 'til I tole him the first time I came down this way to go to Fort Collins. It's pretty well hidden up there."

"He told me whoever built it kinda hid it up against the ridge to keep people from seeing it. Besides, it's almost seven thousand feet up, so there ain't no cowboys gonna go that high looking around."

Monte replied, "I'm sorry, Rio. Guess there ain't much I ken say."

"Thanks, Monte." He looked around. "What happened to Hank's hands? He's got a bunkhouse, but we're the only ones in it, and Alice said they were running about five hundred head."

"They been run off or kilt I guess. He didn't ever have but two or three. Kinda a low level war with...Rocking K from what Hank said."

Hank came to the door and said, "Supper's on. Y'all coming?"

Monte said quietly, "He ain't runnin many head right now, so he can get by with just him and Alice doing the work. He's got most of 'em back up the north fork of the Poudre right now. Got another daughter down in New Orleans, goin' to school." He turned toward the house. "I'm hungry. Let's go eat!"

Rio looked up as the cold wind gusted and shivered as the clouds obscured the moon. "Yeah." *Why am I suddenly cold? Did somebody just walk on my grave?*

***

Meanwhile, at the Cliff House hotel in Denver, Flynn, Pronto, Jeb Green, Juan and Jesus Rodriguez, Arthur, and Rene Cavanaugh sat around a table in the dining room, enjoying a good dinner. The manager of the hotel walked into the dining room, looked around, and saw them. He walked over and said, "Mr. Flynn?"

Flynn looked up. "Yes, I'm John Flynn." The manager gave him a telegram. "I'm sorry, apparently the telegraph office didn't know where you were staying. This was sent from...the Evans water stop this morning."

Flynn opened it and read through it, his face going white. Pronto said, "What happened, John?"

Jeb chuckled. "That from Rio? What'd he do, find him a woman?"

"He got himself shot, and Ethan ain't at the cabin. Ethan's apparently killed by a bear a couple of months ago. I gotta let the boss know."

Juan asked, "He is alright, isn't he, *Señor* John?"

Pronto threw his napkin on the table. "Where is he, John? We need to be ridin'."

"He's at the Bar N, north of Horsetooth Canyon, up on the north fork of the Cache la Poudre," he paused for a second, shook his head and added, "Says to come careful." He looked across the table at Pronto. "Pronto, he says tell you Monte is there. Who's that?"

"Damn, he and I used to ride together, back, oh hell in the forties. He's hell on wheels. Called him Monte cause he was a fool for thet three card Monte game." He laughed at a memory, then quickly sobered. Getting up, he said, "Let's go, boys, we got some miles to ride."

Jeb asked, "We leavin' tonight?" Almost to himself, he added, "Yeah, we better, 'fore Rio gets well and goes huntin'."

Juan shook his head. "What and spoil all his fun? *Amigos*, we will just get there in time if we are very lucky."

Arthur grumbled, "I'll go get the damn horses as usual. Jeb, grab my kit will ya? Rene, you want to help me?"

Cavanaugh jumped up. "Sure, Arthur."

Flynn held up a hand. "Wait a minute. There isn't any point in trying to leave tonight. We get a good night's sleep and catch the train in the morning with our horses." Or mule, in your case, Pronto."

Pronto started to argue, shook his head and said, "You're right, John. I forgot all about the train. I'm gettin' old. What, two hours on the train, 'stead of a two day ride." He got up and headed for the door. "Gonna make some arrangements with the stable to leave Mabel here 'til I get back."

Flynn stopped at the front desk, borrowed two pieces of paper and a pen. He quickly wrote out two messages and motioned to the manager. When the manager walked over, Flynn said, "We've got a problem we need to take care of. We will be leaving at first light for the train station and should be back in a week or so." He slid the two pieces of paper across the desk. "And I'd appreciate it if you could send these two telegrams for us."

The manager took them, replying, "No problem, Mister Flynn. I'll get them sent tonight. We'll also hold your rooms. And please convey my condolences to Mr. Bell on getting shot."

"I'll do that, sir, and thanks for holding the rooms."

Chapter 10

The sun cleared the hills in the east as Jud and two gunnies, Wade and Peck, crouched at the top of the rise south of the Nevell ranch house. They could dimly see movement in the house, lit by the lamplight. Jud said, "Now remember, there should only be two people there, the old man and his daughter. We'll shoot the old man from here." He laughed. "Then we'll go down there and have some fun with that little bitch before we burn 'em out. Got it?"

Wade spit to the side. "Yeah, Jud, I hear ya." Peck nodded as he stepped back, leading the horses down off the rise. Jud lay down and sighted on the window, chuckling as he waited. A red shirt appeared in the window, and Jud fired first, then Wade shot a second later.

Alice was thrown across the table by the force of the bullet. Hank, Rio and Monte dived away from the table in fear as a second round ricocheted off the stovepipe. Hank moaned, "No, no, *noooo...*" as he crawled to his daughter. Monte eased up to the window as Rio scrambled back to the bedroom, returning with his carbine, ducking low to keep from being seen through the window.

"Did you see where the shots came from?"

Monte replied, "I think it was up on that rise by the trail." He ducked back and turned to Hank. "Hank, is she alive?"

He'd pulled Alice to the wall, frantically checking her for the entry wound. "I think so, she's hit high up."

Getting her shirt open, he found the entry hole above her collarbone. "Oh God, why her and not me?"

Rio said, "Calm down, Hank, you gotta take care of her. We'll do—"

Monte cursed, "Lookit these bastids, ridin' up like they own the place. He eased over to the door, followed by Rio. "Let's get 'em close—"

Hank grabbed the rifle by the stove and aimed through the window, screaming, "Die, you bastards!" He started firing and Rio and Monte scrambled for the door, Monte threw it open and they started shooting as they stepped out on the porch.

Peck grunted and fell from his horse as Jud and Wade turned and raced away, abandoning Peck to his fate.

Hank and Monte moved Alice to the bedroom as Rio kept watch out the door. Propping her head on a pillow, Monte rolled her up on her side as she moaned, and he saw the exit wound. "It's all the way through. Don't look like it mushroomed, so maybe didn't hit anythin' major." He picked up the sheet Hank had ripped and made two pads, wrapped the rest of the sheet around her shoulder and added, "Hank, she's got to have a doctor, I can't do much to help her, other than get some liquid in her."

Hank got up. "I'll go, Rio's in no shape for that ride, and you're all that's keeping Alice alive, Monte." He hurried out of the bedroom heading for the door as he mumbled, "I still can't figure out why they shot her."

Rio said somberly, "I think that they were aiming for you, Hank. She's wearing shirt and pants, and they probably didn't even know we were here. I don't see them now, but my vision is...still not right. You keep watch, and I'll saddle your horse, Hank."

Monte came out to the main room. "Which way you goin, Hank? You're liable to get caught up with them Kidds if you cross the river at the usual place."

Hank said grimly, "I'll go through the bastards if I have to, Monte. I'll be back as soon as I can with the doc."

Rio led a saddled horse out of the barn, then whistled. Hank came out and swung up on the horse as Rio held the bridle in one hand and a rifle in the other.

Looking down, Hank said, "Keep 'em off the place if you can, Monte. I'll be back as soon as I can with the doc."

"Don't worry, Hank, we'll be here when you get back. You just worry about getting the doc." He slapped the horse on the rump, and Hank galloped out of the ranch yard.

***

Pronto, Flynn, and others rode into Fort Collins just after nine in the morning, having caught the first train out of Denver. Arthur grumped, "I need to eat sumthin'. At least in camp, Pronto had breakfast cooked afore we went out." They rode down the street and reined up in front of the saloon. "Wonder if they got grub here?"

Pronto dismounted. "One way to find out." The others got down, tied their horses to the hitching rail with Pronto's mule, and walked into the saloon. There were two groups of people in the bar, one group of older men was in a desultory game of cards, and the other group was three cowboys sitting facing the door with a bottle on the table. The bartender was polishing glasses at the end of the bar when Pronto and the others walked in.

The bartender walked to their end of the bar. "Help you gents?"

Flynn tipped his hat back. "Y'all serving any food here?"

"Lemme check in the back. Might be." He stepped through a door into the back of the saloon, coming back moments later. "Sorry, cook ain't showed up. Best bet is the café down the street. But I got beer. Can't guarantee how cold it is, but it is beer."

Pronto glanced around and said quietly, "A little information if you don't mind?"

"If I can."

"Lookin' for a place called the Bar N, it around here close?

The bartender said quietly, "'Bout five-six miles northwest of here, north side of the river, but it's a hard ride and you gotta cross the river."

The saloon door slammed open and Hank rushed in, rifle held by the fore stock. He looked around, then headed for the table where the card game was.

The bartender added, "Matter fact, that's Hank Nevell there, he's the owner."

Hank put his hand on Doc's shoulder. "I need you to come to the ranch, somebody shot Alice this morning, and she's hurt bad!"

Doc Ferrell looked up in surprise. "What? Somebody shot Alice? Where?" He started up as he added, "Let me get my bag."

One of the cowboys started laughing, and everybody turned to look as he said loudly, "Guess she got what she deserved."

Hank spun around at the comment, and the cowboy jumped up, drew his gun and shot Hank twice in the chest, stunning everybody in the saloon. He smiled as he shoved his gun back in the holster. "Well, he ain't gonna be a problem anymore. Everbody can tell he was fixin to shoot me!"

Doc bent over Hank then looked up, shaking his head. Pronto walked over and looked down at the doc. "Doc, you gonna ride out there and help her?"

Rising, he answered, "Yeah, Hank's gone, but if I get there in time, maybe I can save her."

The cowboy, still smiling, said threateningly, "Ain't no use to go, Doc. We might need you at our place. Sounds like the Bar N is done for, but the Rocking K is riding high."

Pronto turned on the cowboy and the tension ramped up in the saloon. "Shut up, punk. The doc is going, and we'll ride along to make sure nothing else happens!"

"I'm Todd Kidd," the cowboy said his hand hovering over his gun. "Don't need some old man telling me anything. If I wanna stop the doc, I will! Or I'll just stop you!"

Pronto, knowing the others had his back, walked toward him growling, "I'm right here, boy! Why don't you try me for size, at least I'll have my hand on the action of this pistol." He crowded him, coming within arm's length. "What's the matter boy, you yella? Or just afraid to stand up to somebody who's ready for ya?"

"I'm Todd Kidd, we *own* this town!" the cowboy said, his voice going up as he backed up trying to get room to get away from the crazy old man. He shot a panicked look at the two cowboys still at the table. They had their hands on top of the table and weren't moving or saying anything as they watched Arthur's shotgun swing in their direction.

Pronto stopped, spat on the floor, and said disgustedly, "Yeah, you're yella. Afraid to face somebody that's ready for ya."

He turned away with a hiss of disgust. Juan yelled "Pronto!" when he saw Todd grab for his gun."

Pronto dropped to a knee as he turned, drew and fired in one smooth move, putting two rounds into the left pocket of the cowboy's shirt. Todd's one shot went into the table next to him as he fell back, dead on his feet. Flynn, Juan, and Jeb drew and covered the rest of the room as Arthur turned his shotgun toward the door. Rene drew his gun cautiously, turned and faced the back door, nervously looking back over his shoulder.

Pronto, still holding his smoking pistol, walked over to the table where the two cowboys sat, hands on the table. "You boys want in?"

The younger one looked up in terror. "No, Sir! We ain't moved! But you played hob, that's Roger Kidd's youngest. He'll come huntin' you fer sure."

Pronto holstered his pistol and turned to the doc. "You ready to ride, Doc? Looks like we might have worn out our welcome here."

"Ah, sure, let me get my bag and saddle my horse." He started for the door, but it slammed open as Pete and two more cowboys entered the saloon at a run. The first thing they saw was the shotgun in Arthur's hand swing to cover them from a few feet away. They slid to a stop, not willing to risk moving. Pete saw the two bodies on the floor, glared around and ran over, first to Hank, then to Todd. He dropped to his knees cradling Todd. In anguish, he asked, "What happened?" When no one answered him, he yelled, "*Somebody tell me what happened!*" Tenderly laying Todd's body down, he started to get up as the young cowboy said, "Uh well, Todd shot Nevell, then the ol' man," he pointed to Pronto, "He crowded Todd inta tryin' him. And that crazy ol' man killed him."

As Pete's hand went to his gun and he started to turn, the bartender slammed a sawed off double barrel on the bar, freezing everyone. "That's enough! Pete Kidd, you stay right there, ain't gonna be no more shootin' in here today!" He pointed at Todd with the shotgun. "Todd killed Nevell and Nevell didn't even have his hand on the action. Killed him just because he turned around when Todd laughed about his daughter bein' shot." He nodded toward Pronto saying, "Then this old man crowded and challenged him to shoot him since he was facing him, and he backed down. The old man started to walk away, and Todd tried to backshoot him, but didn't make it. That's it! Now all of you cowboys clear out!" He motioned toward the door with the shotgun, and Pronto and the others with him backed toward the door, followed by Doc Ferrell.

Pronto held his hands up as he asked, "Will you make arrangements for a wagon to take Nevell home? And let the Sheriff know?"

The bartender barked, "I'll get the undertaker. Sheriff Mason's down in Denver, ain't no deputy here now, he's somewhere out on the range. Now y'all *git*!"

Arthur led the way, Pronto and the others escorting the doc out the door. Pete and the others glared at them as they walked out, but didn't do anything. As soon as they left, Pete motioned to the others, and they picked up Todd's body, carrying it toward the door.

***

Out at the ranch, Rio prowled restlessly, carrying his rifle the whole time. Looking into the back bedroom, he saw Monte hovering over Alice. "I got the dead one outside on his horse. Horse stepped on his reins and stopped. How's she doing?"

"In and out, she's lost a lot of blood, but I think it's stopped." He wiped her face with a wet rag. "I hope I can keep her from movin' too much. What did you find?"

Rio smiled grimly. "I tracked 'em back across the river 'til they turned around the butte. They were still runnin hard at that point." He said angrily, "The brand on the horse is a Rocking K, guess that's the Kidd brand?"

"Yep, stay here with Alice, hold her hand or somethin' while I go look at thet cowboy and his horse." Monte got up, and Rio sat down and tentatively grasped Alice's hand on top of the covers. She rolled her head, and he realized that Alice's eyes were open and looking at him.

Rio wasn't sure what to say or do, so he said gruffly, "You lay still. Monte got the bleeding stopped, but you can't move!"

Alice, pain etched on her face, said softly, "It hurts! Why did they shoot me? Where is Dad?"

"They must have thought you were your Dad. He's gone to Fort Collins for the doc, they should be back soon."

"Can I have some water? I feel so thirsty."

Rio picked up a cup, then lifted her head. "Don't move too much, and don't drink too much.

After she drank a couple of sips, he gently lowered her head back to the pillow. "Thank you, Rio. Who are you? Why did you come here?"

He squirmed, suddenly uncomfortable. "I'm just a cowboy, Alice, I came up here to visit my Uncle Ethan. He lives...lived up on the river."

"Where? I didn't think anyone lived up there, except maybe Monte."

"Monte is living in the cabin Uncle Ethan had. It's on a bench 'bout seven thousand feet up. He rebuilt it after the war. He pretty much kept to himself after the war, so I'm not surprised you didn't know him."

"What about you? Who are you?"

"Well, I'm from Texas, San Felipe del Rio is the closest...settlement, down on the border. I work for a ranch down there." Alice had nodded off or passed out, he didn't know which, but he could still feel a pulse, so he just sat and held her hand until Monte came back in, shaking his head. Rio got up, giving the chair to Monte. "Well, did you know him?"

"Yeah, he's one of Kidd's gunnies. Peck, I think his name was. He usually runs with that middle Kidd boy, Jud."

Rio growled, "If Alice dies, I'll get 'em all, Monte." He blew out a breath and added, "Every damn one of them."

***

Two hours later, the doc, Pronto and the others rode into the ranch yard to be met by Rio at the corner of the corral, rifle pointed at them, and Monte, standing in the door, rifle in hand. Once he recognized Pronto, he decocked the rifle and came forward. "Doc, she's in the house."

The doc looked at Rio, seeing the scalp wound and was confused. "I thought Alice was shot?"

"She is, mine's a week or so old. She's inside and needs you bad, Doc. Monte is with her now. He kept her alive somehow." He looked up at Pronto. "How the hell did y'all get here so quick, and what the hell are y'all doin' out here?"

Pronto shrugged and dismounted. "We figgered we better get up here afore you tore the country apart. 'Sides, I wanted to say hello to Monte."

Rio noticed that Hank was missing, "Where's Hank?"

Pronto spat in the dirt. "He's dead, some punk shot him down in the saloon when he came to get the doc."

"Oh hell, who's gonna tell Alice?" He blinked and focused on Pronto. "Where is the bastard that killed him?"

Jeb drawled, "He's dead, too. Pronto pushed him, and he turned yella then tried to back shoot Pronto." Jeb chuckled. "If it hadn't been for Arthur and his little pop gun, we'd a had a real shoot out when his...brother show'd up."

Monte came to the door and said, "Damn, you really are alive you old bastard."

Pronto laughed. "Same to ya, ya ol' son of a bitch!" He started walking toward the porch.

Monte replied, "I thought they kilt you ten or twelve years ago down Mexico way."

They met at the bottom of the steps, pounding each other on the back as Pronto said, "If it hadn't been for Rio's Pap, I wouldn't be here. He found me and got me back to the ranch after I got shot down in Ol' Mehico." They broke apart, and he added, "I kinda stayed around and kept an eye on the pup for 'em."

"The pup?"

"Yeah, that's what I used to call Rio, he follered me round like a puppy." Cocking his head, he asked, "What happened to Rio? I see the scab and missing hair."

"I found him layin' on the steps of the cabin I'm...was livin' in. 'Pears it actually belonged to Ethan Bell. Rio'd been head shot, and I guess he had a concussion. I had to bring 'im here, cause I couldn't get the fever down, and his head wuz gettin' infected. We wuz here when Alice wuz shot, and we got one of 'em. He paused as Flynn walked up. "Doc tole me about Hank, damn shame, too. I guess I'll have to try to hold this place 'til Alice gits better, if she lives."

Juan interrupted, "Has *Señor* Rio gone after them yet?

Monte glanced at him. "What you mean?"

"The ones who shot him, *Señor*."

"Naw, he ain't in no shape to ride. I'm surprised he wuz able to ride today and backtrack them Kidd riders."

The doc came to the door and yelled at Monte, breaking up the reunion. "We gotta get Alice to town if I'm gonna keep her alive. She's lost a lot of blood." He looked around and added, "See if you can find a wagon and get it hitched up!"

Monte nodded and turned toward the barn. "Boys, I think there's a wagon in the barn, the team should be in the corral 'bout three hundred yards up the draw."

Flynn snapped out, "Jeb, you and Juan get the horses. Arthur, see if you can get the buckboard ready to go. Maybe some blankets to ease the ride?"

Everyone scrambled to get things done, and fifteen minutes later, Rio came out gently carrying Alice in his arms, tears streaming down his face. Doc was holding her left arm steady and holding a pad over the entry wound. He'd already given her a dose of laudanum, and she'd passed out again with a moan when Rio picked her up. He gently handed her up to Pronto who was kneeling in the back of the wagon, and he gingerly laid her on the padding they'd found as the doc climbed into the wagon.

With Flynn driving, Doc in the back with Alice, and Arthur riding shotgun, Juan sat on a fresh horse, cautiously feeling him out as the doc turned to him. "Son, you got to ride to town and let my wife know I'm bringing Alice in. She'll need to prepare for me to do surgery, and I'll need water heated and everything laid out as soon as we get there. Go two blocks past the saloon, turn right, go one block east, and it's the whitewashed house on the corner."

"*Sí, Señor!* I ride like the wind!" Juan gigged the horse into a fast trot, then a gallop, dust flying from the hooves as he bolted down the trail toward Fort Collins.

"Let's go, Mr. Flynn, times a wastin'."

Monte stepped back from the wagon. "We'll hold things down here 'til you send the boys back." Flynn snapped the reins, and the wagon rolled out of the ranch yard, followed by Jeb and Pronto.

Cavanaugh looked at Rio, "Where do you want me?"

Rio bit his lip for a second. "Rene, can you get up in the hayloft? That would...give us eyes down the trail."

Chapter 11

A cavalry patrol came riding through the gates of Fort Laramie. Fat Jack Jensen, late 60's years old, six feet four but stooped, rail thin, bearded, in dirty buckskins, followed the lieutenant as they reined up at the adjutant's office. Fat Jack dismounted with a groan, rubbing his backside as the lieutenant hopped nimbly down. "Sergeant, dismiss the troops to their barracks. Weapons inspection in two hours." He glanced at Fat Jack. "Another patrol with nothing happening. I thought the Indians were on the move."

Jack shrugged. "They are. They ain't interested in fightin' us this close to winter. They're heading for their winter camps, huntin' for the winter and getting' ready to hole up 'til spring."

"So, what do I say to the major?"

"Whatever you want. Me? I'm glad it's quiet. These old bones ain't up to a bunch of shootin' and runnin' hard. I'd say we're probably good 'til spring, but that's just me."

The lieutenant sniffed, then coughed. "Well, I'm going to say my scout thinks we're done for the year." He smiled. "After all, you have *many* years of experience on me."

Jack started to lay into the lieutenant when the sergeant major walked up. "Damn, Fat Jack, I didn't know you knew anybody that could write."

"Whatta ya mean, Sarmajor? You sayin' I'm old and dumb?" he asked with a smile.

"Nah. Well, old anyway. This come for you from Cheyenne," he handed Fat Jack a telegram. "Courier brought it late last night. Guess somebody's got some problems down Fort Collins way."

He took the telegram and read it slowly, then replied, "Thankee, Sarmajor, is Smiley around?"

"Last time I saw him was at the smithy."

Jack mounted up and rode across the parade ground to the smithy as the sergeant major turned to the lieutenant. "Guess you didn't see anything?"

The lieutenant shook his head as he laughed at Fat Jack riding across the parade ground. "I swear Jack would ride to the jakes if he could. Tracks, mostly days old. Jack said they weren't worth following. He thinks all the Indians are heading for their winter camps."

The sergeant major glowered at the lieutenant. "Lieutenant, Jack walked out of the mountains three winters ago with just a pair o' moccasins on his feet. He'd lost his horse a week before. Lost a couple of toes. Iff'n I were you, I'd be listening to Jack, not laughing at him. Or, hell, any of these old men. They've been out here for years, and they know the Injuns better than damn near anybody." The adjutant stepped out on the porch, and the sergeant major added, "I think *somebody* wants their report." He waved in the direction of his temple in a casual salute and headed for the smithy.

The blacksmith was pounding on a horseshoe while Smiley Peters, another mountain man in his late 60's, stooped, skinny, no teeth, bald, and bearded, wearing fancy buckskins with scarves around the waist, lounged as close to the fire as he could get. Isom Grissom, one of the few black mountain men, wiry and lean, with a fringe of white hair, sat comfortably on a stump, reading a thick book. Two others looked on: Arapaho Joe, dark skinned and beardless, and Long Tom Oats, kibitzed and stayed as warm as they could.

Jack waved the telegram. "Smiley, Pronto's ridin' into a dust up, 'cordin to this, Monte's there, too. And thet kid, Rio, got shot by somebody." Smiley cocked his head, and Jack asked, "You comin'?"

"Hell ya, lemme git my possibles. Where we goin'?"

As he got up, Jack said, "North of Houndstooth, round the Poudre crossing."

Isom put a strip of rawhide on the page he was reading and closed the book. Getting up slowly, he asked, "What about us, you ol' Fart?"

"You want to go, git yer kit."

Chuckling, Isom replied, "I've owed him for saving my life for thirty years. Maybe now I can pay that bastard back and git him to shut up."

Long Tom didn't say anything but got up and buttoned his coat as he followed Isom and Smiley out of the smithy.

Smiley shook his head. "Miss a fight, 'specially with Pronto and Monte in it? What, are ya crazy? Don't leave without me." He walked out muttering to himself as the blacksmith smiled.

"Crazy damn mountain men."

Jack laughed. "You just now figgerin' that out?"

A half hour later, the sergeant major walked up to Jack as he finished tying his bedroll on the back of the saddle.

"What's goin on, Jack? I ain't seen that bunch move that fast since the last Injun attack."

"We got to ride down the country a little bit, Sarmajor. Make my apologies to the Lieutenant, will ya?"

"Well, y'all did sign on for the duration, you know."

"We should be back in a couple o' weeks. Ain't like there is much goin' on right now anyways..."

"Anything I can do?"

Jack shook his head. "Nah, looks like there's gonna be a little dust up down around Horsetooth and the Poudre. Pronto and Monte are in the middle of it, so we're goin' to help 'em out."

The sergeant major shook his head sadly. "Sounds like there's gonna be some shootin'." He glanced around to see who was nearby. "I'll see if I can get the Colonel to send a courier to Fort Collins and a patrol thataway in the next couple of days with a doctor."

"Thankee. Not sure we'd need it, but somebody might." He looked at the other four mountain men and added, "Let's go, boys. Time's a wastin'."

***

Late in the afternoon, Pete Kidd drove the buggy he'd borrowed from the hostler into the yard, two horses tied to the back, and surrounded by the cowboys that had been sent to town with Pete and Todd. Pete pulled to a stop in front of the house as Roger came out the front door.

"Pete, what the hell is goin' on? Who's in the buggy?"

Pete didn't know what else to say and blurted out, "It's Todd, Pa. He's dead."

Roger grabbed at a post holding up the porch and blanched, swaying on his feet. He asked querulously, "What? Dead? Did you kill the sonfabitch that did it?"

When Pete didn't answer, he screamed, "*Dammit tell me!*" He stumbled down the steps, suddenly looking every day of his age as he staggered tentatively toward the buggy.

As he got to the back of the buggy, Pete finally said, "He went to the Palace and...well he killed Nevell when he came in for the doc cause somebody," he glanced venomously at Jud as he rode up, "shot his daughter. Then some ol' man called Todd out and Todd backed down." He shook his head sadly. "Then Todd tried to backshoot 'em and wasn't able...the ol' man turned and shot Todd down right there."

Roger lifted the tarp with a trembling hand, then glared at Pete. "Where were you? Tell me you killed that bastard!"

"I was down at the general store, spreadin' the story we talked about. I didn't know Todd went to the saloon. When I got there, we walked into a bunch of drawn guns. There was nothin' I could do."

Roger reached down and smoothed Todd's hair off his face, gently replaced the tarp over him and turned to the cowboys. "What you mean nothin'! Who was with 'em?" The two cowboys hung their heads and he roared, "Why didn't you back 'em?" When they didn't answer, he drew his pistol and shot both cowboys. Waving his pistol at the rest of them he said, "I oughta shoot ever damn one of you," as tears rolled down his face.

Jud dismounted and walked up, flipped the tarp back and looked at his little brother. "Well, at least he's at peace now."

Roger, stunned, looked at Jud. "What happened? I told you to burn Nevell's house with him in it. Not shoot some damn girl!"

"Pa, we shot into the house, I thought I'd killed the ol' man, so we went ridin' up, and they opened up on us."

"They, whatta you mean they?"

"I dunno, but there wuz at least three people shootin' at us. They kilt Joey, and we had to git away. We come down the long way so nobody would see us and met Pete just before the butte."

Roger drew himself up. "So you screwed up, shot a girl, the whole town knows and the doc is out there? You dumb sonofabitch. *You* caused your brother to git kilt!" Waving the pistol around again, he added, "Two of y'all go dig a grave. We're gonna bury Todd, and then you're gonna go finish what you were supposed to do, Jud. I'm gonna send Harvey back with ya. Don't come back here 'til it's done!"

***

As dusk fell over the Nevell ranch, the small living room was crowded with cowboys. Monte and Pronto were conversing in low tones as Pronto started cooking supper. Jeb was sitting at the table as Juan prowled the room. He stopped and picked up a tintype off the mantle, turning to Monte. "*Señor* Monte, who is the other *Señorita* in the picture?"

Monte took the tintype, "I think that is Anna, Juan, I've never met her. She is Alice's sister though." He handed the tintype back. "She's down in New Orleans, going to finishing school. I *think* her aunt, Hank's sister, runs one down there."

Juan took the tintype and sighed. "She is very beautiful, no?"

Jeb laughed. "Lemme see Juan, and I'll tell you. You think anything in skirts is beautiful." Juan showed it to him, and he added, "Yep, she's...beautiful is a good word." He whistled.

Pronto looked around. "Where's Rio and Cavanaugh?"

Flynn said, "He's prowling, Pronto. You know how he gets before he goes off. And Rene is up in the hayloft.

"Jeb, Juan, go find him, and round up Arthur, too. Supper'll be ready soon. Hogtie Rio if you have to. We can't afford for him to go after these assholes 'til we find out exactly what's goin' on." The two of them grabbed their rifles and headed for the door.

Monte looked up from the stove. "Goes off? Hogtie 'em? Damn it almost sounds like you're afraid of that boy, Pronto."

"I'm not afraid of him, Monte, I'm afraid of what he will do." He shook his head. "He's gonna go after those that shot Alice and Hank, ain't no way to stop him."

"Hell, they'll chop him to pieces. He cain't see, and he's hurt."

"That won't stop him, Monte. He's got a side you ain't seen yet." Pronto idly picked up the shotgun by the door, thinking. "Monte, Rio is the Rio Kid. He gets like this, he's a stone killer, ain't got a nerve in his body, and is as fast with a pistol as anybody I've ever seen."

Monte looked up skeptically. "That was five or six years ago I heard of him. Rio ain't old enough."

"He killed his first man at fifteen, Monte. A rustler he run up on at the ranch. The rustlers tried to bluff the kid, but it didn't work. Seems the rustler had relatives, and they come huntin'."

Setting the shotgun down, he sighed. "Three of them caught up with him one day in the settlement at

Del Rio; Rio, he come walkin' out of the store suckin' on a piece o' peppermint. They braced him right there, and he dropped all three of 'em. They got lead into him, but we got him outta the settlement and back to the ranch. I saw it from down the street, but by the time I could get there it wuz all over."

"So, he got a reputation then."

Pronto laughed. "Oh, that wasn't the end of it. He went down to Old Mehico with a crew to pick up a herd from Alvarez. On the way back, some rustlers decided they wanted to take it at Lajitas crossing. They come up on Rio and the boys at the fire. There were eight of them and six of the boys. Rio dropped the loudmouth ringleader in the middle of his yappin' about how they wuz gonna take the herd. Now the ringleader, he had his gun out when Rio got 'em. It was touch an' go, but they got outta that OK, a couple of the boys got burned and Rio got shot in the leg. He killed three of the eight. One of the rustlers got away, and he spread the story.

"Damn, that is quick! That boy's gonna have it hard. They ain't never gonna let him go. Somebody will try comin' after him to prove they're faster."

"I dunno, Monte, he's been fairly quiet these last couple of years. He kilt five more on this drive, but three wuz Injuns trying to steal the herd, and the other two were herd cutters down by Denver."

***

Late that night, north of Cheyenne, Fat Jack and the others sat round a campfire, finishing off a deer Long Tom had shot earlier. Smiley burped and leaned back against a log. "What you think's happenin' down there, Jack?"

"Sounds like somebody might be doin' a land grab, and Pronto and Monte done ended up in the middle of it." Jack threw the stick he was toying with on the fire, sending up sparks. "Ain't the first time we seen this. One o' the reasons I left Ohio all those years ago."

Isom asked softly, "Are we going directly to the Nevell place?"

"Yeah, that's where we're s'posed to meet. Anything happens afore we get there, one of them will be leavin' us some sign."

"Thet's a long ways round that set o' ridges, ain't it?" Long Tom asked.

"'Bout seventy miles round them ridges. Done it a couple o' times."

Isom leaned back against another log. "There's another way down there. We kin go up Bitter Canyon and branch off at that crack with the white rock in it. Bear Molina and I did that two, no three years ago."

"Didn't know you been down in that part o' the country, Isom." Smiley said.

Isom chuckled. "Yeah, I wintered one year there with Bell, Ethan I think his name was. He had a copy of the Odyssey. Finished it 'fore spring. Smart man!" He eased his back and continued, "Besides, this'll get us in there without any noise. There's one little ranch at the bench on at the head of Deer Canyon, but we can get round it easy."

Joe smiled sadly and added, "Ethan was good man. My boys tole me that bear thet got him didn't get away. They took the horses that wuz on the bench, ran 'em up to the winter camp. We ain't goin' up there, are we?"

Jack finally said, "No, what we're goin' to do is catch the steam cars tomorrow in Cheyenne, ride them to Evans, and get off there. It's...maybe fifteen miles to that little ranch you're talkin' about Isom. That's the Nevell place."

Long Tom poked out his lantern jaw and looked at them glumly, "Ain't never rid any steam cars. Not sure Ol' Bessie will even get in one o' them fancy cars. She don't even like stalls in a barn."

Jack spat off to the side. "You cheap bastid. I'll pay for you and Bessie. Saves us two days of ridin'."

"Thankee. What we gonna do when we gets down there?"

"Whatever be needful of doin'."

Smiley grumped. "Too damn many folks around. All clustered up round the fort and...these idjits in these towns...like a bunch o' damn ants crawling over one another."

Jack sighed. "You don't have to go, Smiley. You kin go back to the mountains, like you allus threaten to do."

Throwing a stick in the fire, Smiley said, "Oh, I'll go along. Ain't gonna miss a ruckus."

Isom laughed. "Smiley, you like being warm too much to go back up in the mountains and we all know it. We aren't young men anymore. We're not as fast as we used to be, nor are we in as good a shape as we used to be. I've seen Fort Collins, and there aren't many people there...yet."

Tom nodded. "Quiet down that way. 'Cept for that bunch down south of the Poudre. I come up that way from the mines, six maybe eight months ago. They was running in gun hands and had cows with a bunch of different brands."

Jack spit again. "Damn, I didn't...well, we'll just have to go careful. If we gotta fight gun hands, we need to get them up where we live. In the mountains. They won't get off a horse and walk."

Isom laughed. "It's those...what are they calling them? Cowboy boots or some such. Y'all saw that bunch that Pronto rode in with. They ride everywhere!"

Tom muttered, "They'd never make it in the mountains." All of the others agreed, and Tom continued, "If you're done yapping, I'm gonna get some sleep." He got up and walked over to his bedroll, rolled up in it, and pulled his hat down over his face.

Jack yawned and threw one more log on the fire as the others headed for their bedrolls. *Bunch of old farts. Can't even ride all day, glad we get on the steam cars tomorrow.* He made one more check of the horses and stumped over to his bedroll, joining the others as they dropped off to sleep.

Chapter 12

The next morning, everyone had been rousted out and eaten in shifts around the small table in the kitchen. They couldn't find enough coffee cups in the house, so the cowboys had dug into their saddlebags and brought their own. As they passed another pot around, Rio said, "Well, if Alice is still alive, we better try to hold the ranch for her. Monte, you know the area the best and know the people involved. How 'bout filling us in?"

Monte found a piece of paper on Hank's desk and turned it over, and picking a piece of charcoal out of the fire, he started drawing out a rough map. "Well, lemme see; south of the river, the Kidd's are the biggest ranchers in the area. They came in about three years ago with a herd and partnered up with ol' man Brewster. He was one of the first settlers out here and had laid claim to about ten thousand acres. 'Bout two years ago, Brewster got thrown from a horse and died. Since he didn't leave any heirs, Kidd and his clan took over the ranch. They run a couple a thousand head below the river, to the end of the canyon and out on the plain."

He pointed to what the Kidds claimed as theirs. "They're real touchy 'bout anybody crossin' their range or even getting on the land they claim. They've been buyin' out or runnin' off the small ranchers for about six months or a year now." He drew the ridges and features on the north side of the river. "Nevell here, he's been here for 'bout fifteen years, here at the head of Deer Valley. He claimed 'bout five thousand acres and owned a thousand outright."

Rio asked, "What about Ethan? Where did he fit into the picture?"

Monte shrugged. "Not sure. Guess your uncle mighta owned some land up by the cabin, but I don't know. Like I said earlier, I never knew him. Biggest town is Fort Collins, over here. The Sheriff only works the town and the other side of the ridges. Out here there ain't no law, 'lessen they come up from Denver or you can find a US Marshal."

He sketched in the town and railroad. "Over here is the railroad. Got that depot out here at Evans, and that's it between Fort Collins and Cheyenne. Depot's primarily there for water and cattle and a stopover if Cheyenne is snowed in. I didn't get to town much, so I don't know what wuz happenin' down there."

Rio nodded. "Okay. Pronto, I want you and Monte to come with me to the cabin. Jeb, you and Juan go up the canyon and see how many cattle are up there. Rene, you and Arthur go down to the river and sweep back this way. If you get a shot at a deer or elk, take it. We're going to need to feed everybody. Look for the waterholes, any line cabins or anything else. John, if you would, stay here and look around. Make a list of things that need to be done." He looked around at everyone. "Everybody goes armed. One of each pair rides with a rifle out. Something happens, three shots and hunker down. We'll come a runnin'. I want everybody back here by supper."

"*Señor* Rio, what if someone, they shoot at us?" Juan asked.

Rio's smile was a rictus of hate. "Kill 'em."

Rio led them out, and everyone got their horses saddled, heading out in pairs as the three of them rode slowly toward the cabin, Monte in the lead.

Two hours later, after crossing the river at the upper ford, the bench came into view above the river, and Rio sighed as they rode up to the cabin. Monte quickly checked around. "Nobody's been here since we left." Tying the horses to the corral, Monte led the way into the cabin and Rio sank gratefully into a chair at the table as Monte got a fire started in the fireplace. "You okay, Rio?"

"Little dizzy."

Pronto came in and spun a chair around, then sat. "Five stalls, all empty. No tack, but plenty of hay. Corral hasn't been used in a while."

Monte added, "When I found this place, it was...a mess. Somebody, probably Injuns, had been through the cabin, but nothing was really tore up. All the food were gone, along with the blankets, but that was about it. There weren't any horses or tack around, just the stable."

Rio sighed. "Uncle Ethan was breeding horses up here. He...had two he'd brought from Texas. Spike and Rose, Red...is one of their foals. He was also breeding them with some mustangs, mountain horses. They..." Rio shook his head. "They were the basis of what he hoped would be a new line of horses. He...liked the horses more than people. But I think from what he said, he got along with the Arapaho pretty well. He...made some kind of deal, I don't know what else to call it, for the land this cabin was on."

Getting up, Rio went to the right side of the fireplace, counted with his fingers, and worked one stone loose. Pulling out an oilskin, he brought it back to the table. Moving the lamp, he untied it with shaking fingers. "Uncle...Uncle Ethan told me...where to find this. He said this was my...legacy." Ten gold coins rolled out, with one falling off the table. Ignoring it, he carefully unrolled a deerskin and said, "I think this is something he got from the Indians."

Pronto and Monte stepped up beside him, and he stepped back so they could see. Pronto cocked his head and asked, "Monte, is that...like a grant? It's pictures, but..." He pointed to one place then another, "Looks like that's Horsetooth mountain, and here's the river. With the markin'...northern Arapaho?"

Monte nodded. "I think so. Looks like they...maybe are givin' him 'rights' to that area." He tapped the deerskin. "This here is where we are now." He looked up at the ceiling, then sighed. "Rio, I'll move out so you kin have the place back. I'm...sorry."

Rio shook his head. "Don't...we don't have to make any moves right now. I'm...not sure I want to stay here." He turned and started for the door.

Pronto started to roll the oilskin back up and an envelope slid out. "Rio! Here's sumpin' you might want. It was under the deerskin." He handed it to Rio as he walked out of the cabin.

Walking aimlessly around the bench, Rio finally walked back to the stable and sat on a barrel by the door. Opening the envelope, he took the paper out with a shaking hand.

To whomever finds this. This is my last will and testament. I, Ethan James Bell, do give all my worldly possessions, this cabin, and the horses to my nephew, Rio Austin Bell of the Bar B ranch in Texas.

Ethan James Bell
October 10, 1868

Make sure to keep the rats out of the stable, Rio.

Rio looked at the paper as tears rolled down his face. *Rats out of the stable? There was only one rat, and I killed it out here. There weren't any...oh... That hole in the back. I'll have to wait until I'm up here by myself to get back in there.* He carefully folded the paper and put it back in the envelope, then folded that and put it in his jacket pocket. Scrubbing his face, he looked around.

Well, Uncle Ethan, the horses are gone, and I don't guess I'll ever find them. I bet the Indians got them, but at least Monte has taken care of the place and saved my life, so maybe I'll just let him stay here, cause I kinda want to go home. He got up and walked over to Red, took the envelope out of his pocket and slipped it in the saddlebags, then strode back to the house.

Stepping inside, he said, "I don't think we're going to find anything else up here." He picked up the oilcloth, walked to the fireplace and replaced it in its hiding place, then tapped the rock back into place. "Let's head back down to the ranch. By the time we get back, maybe somebody will be back, and we'll have some idea of what we're dealing with."

***

It was after noon when Roger Kidd turned away from the grave while Todd's body, in a cobbled together coffin, was lowered by Pete and three others using their lassos. He climbed on his horse, scowling as he watched them fill the grave and mound it up. Pete walked over to the wooden cross they'd fashioned with Todd's name on it and brought it to the head of the grave, then looked up at his dad, saying, "This is all I could do, Pa."

He didn't say a word, merely nodded, and Pete shoved the cross into the dirt, then held it as Billy pounded it down with the shovel. Once that was done, they stood around nervously, waiting to see what the old man was going to do. They'd buried the other two cowboys early that morning, well away from Todd's grave and hoped the old man wouldn't notice.

Roger finally glared around and said, "Everbody back to the house. I got decisions to make." He rode off, leaving everyone else scrambling to their horses as he galloped away. Roger slid the horse to a stop at the steps, dismounted, and stomped up the steps. As the rest of the riders came into the yard, he turned and bellowed, "Billy, Pete, Jud, git your asses in here." Slamming through the front door, he called out, "Emma! Dammit, woman, where are ya?"

She came timidly from the back pantry and said, "Right here, Mr. Kidd."

"Get the Chink to put some coffee on, and bring me a plate o' beans and cornpone."

"Yes, sir." She disappeared back into the house. Roger stomped toward the dining room, grabbing a bottle off the table as he went through the office. Slumping back in his chair at the head of the table, he pulled the cork and took a long pull from the bottle, then set it carefully on the table in front of him.

When the others had filed in, he took another swig of whisky and said carefully, "Billy, you take Buck and Jack. You go to town. Find out who those bastards were. Find out where they went." He paused long enough to take another drink and added, "I'll hunt 'em down and kill em myself."

"You want me to leave now, Boss?"

"Go, and don't come back 'til you got answers." Billy got up and headed for the door as Roger rounded on Jud. "I want revenge for Todd. Jud, you gonna take Harvey and...pick three others. You gonna go back over to the Nevell place and burn it. Kill whoever is there."

"I'll leave right now, Pa."

"No! You...will wait 'til Billy gets back and I know where them others are." Pausing, he took another drink and continued, "And tell Harvey he's in charge, since you ain't gettin' the job done."

"Pa, he's—"

"He's family. He's my...our cousin. He's been with me from the start." He picked up the bottle and took another drink, wiped his chin and said, "We ain't movin' agin! Ain't runnin' no more! I ain't leavin' Todd!" He said softly then looked up at them. "Both of you get outta here and leave me in peace." Pete and Jud looked at each other, and Roger roared, "Out! Damn you useless little...out!"

They scrambled out the door, and Pete closed it softly as he looked at Jud. "Pa ain't right in the head right now. We gotta keep...we can't let anybody else know." Jud gulped and nodded, then almost ran for the front door, as if the devil were chasing him. Pete saw Emma coming down the hall with a pot of coffee and whispered to her, "Be careful, Pa is...in one of his moods."

She paled and nodded as she tapped softly on the door. "Mr. Kidd, I got your coffee."

Pete and Jud walked out of the house and saw Harvey Dunn lounging against the corral. Jud started that way and Pete followed until Jud hissed, "I can do this on my own. I ain't gonna cross daddy right now."

Pete nodded sharply and continued on to the bunkhouse. Seeing Ed Cory standing there, he asked, "Where's Ivan?"

Cory looked up in surprise. "Far as I know, he's out at the line cabin. Billy sent him and Obadiah down to the south line cabin. They supposed to be pushin' the cows up toward the high meadow. Billy wanted to get it grazed while the cows could still get to the grass. Didn't Billy tell ya?"

Pete grimaced. "Billy's got other things on his mind right now. Who else is here?"

"Me and Malachi," he nodded toward the bunkhouse, "And them others. But Billy apparently can't send them out 'cause..."

Nodding, Pete said, "Well, we need to get ready for the cold. Last I counted we'd got ten or eleven wagons of hay in the barn, but I'm not sure it's gonna be enough."

"Mebbe, mebbe not. Depends on how much snow, and how cold it gets. 'Member last year? We didn't get snow 'til January, and it didn't get real cold until February."

Pete looked up at Houndstooth mountain and shivered. "Yeah, but this year, snow's already a third of the way down the mountain. And the Injuns are long gone. That tells me they know it's gonna be bad, and they're holing up wherever they go in the winter."

***

Fat Jack sighed as they crossed the last ridge, and he could see the tops of the buildings in Cheyenne. "Almost there, boys."

Joe said, "Don't like this place now. Too many folks. Liked it better when it was end o' track."

Tom spit and replied, "Ain't nothin' here for us now but trouble."

Smiley laughed. "Well, iff'n you stay outta the damn saloons, you won't have no trouble."

Tom bristled, and Isom rode between them. "Gentlemen, we have a job before us. That does not mean we can fight among ourselves, or get in fights before we get there."

There was some grumbling, but they rode the last miles in silence. Jack led them to the train station by a roundabout way, missing the town and saloons. Dismounting, he grunted and stretched, then walked up to the ticket office. He looked at the young man across the desk and asked, "When's the next train south?"

"Not 'til tomorrow morning. Last southbound left a half hour ago."

Jack grimaced. "That ain't good. We need...five tickets on the morning, and five horses, too."

"To where? Denver?"

Drawing a blank, Jack fumbled and finally said, "That...whatever the stop is for Fort Collins."

"Oh, Evans. Five people and five horses, you said?"

"Yep."

"That'll be fifteen dollars. Two dollars for each person, and a dollar for each horse."

Jack shook his head. "Fifteen? Damn, boy, we ain't wantin' the horses to ride in the coach with us!"

The young ticket agent threw up his hands, "Old timer, I don't make the rules. Y'all don't like it, don't buy a ticket. Ain't no skin off my nose, one way or t'other."

Grumbling under his breath, Jack rooted around in his sash and pulled out a twenty-dollar gold piece, then slapped it down on the counter. "You gonna write us tickets?"

Nodding, the young man pulled out five tickets and quickly wrote them out, then pulled his cashbox open and counted out five silver dollars, sliding all of it across the counter. "Train leaves at eight. Gotta load the horses, so be here by seven thirty. You ain't here in time, the horses don't get loaded."

Jack grimaced. "We'll be here." Scooping up the dollars, he slipped them in his sash and folded the tickets, sticking them in with the money. Striding back out of the ticket office, he went over to the others. "Ain't no more trains today. We're on the first train in the mornin'. Gotta be here by seven thirty. Anybody got a watch?"

Isom shook his head sadly. "Jack, you *know* I'm the only one with a watch. Let me make sure my watch matches the clock here." Quickly stepping up to the door, he looked through the glass and saw the big clock behind the agent. Pulling out his pocket watch, he glanced at it, smiled, and turned away. "We are good. My watch and the clock match. Now, what are we going to do?"

Smiley grinned. "I could allus use some food that ain't burnt. And a real bed."

Joe shivered. "Ain't goin' to Bessie's agin. Got bugs last time."

The others laughed, and Tom said, "*You* got bugs? You mean more than normal?"

"Aw shut up. I'll go sleep in the livery stable."

Tom nodded. "Me too. Eat first though."

Jack sniffed and said, "Alright. Café and then the livery. At least the hayloft will be cheaper than Bessie's and won't smell as bad." They led their horses around the corner and tied them in front of the café, then trooped inside.

The menu was chalked on a board and said beef, beans, taters- 15¢ Apple pie 5¢. An older woman with her hair up in a bun and a clean apron came over to the plank table. "You boys want supper? Coffee or water comes with it." There were nods around the table, and she added, "Be a couple of minutes. I'll get you some coffee now."

She came back shortly, carrying five cups and a beat up coffee pot. "Coffee's good. Only used the mother once this afternoon."

Jack looked up and said, "Thankee, Ma'am. I want apple pie, too."

"I'll see if there's any left. I do a pretty good pie, if I do say so myself. I do bear sign too."

Tom perked up. "You do *bear sign*? I ain't had any of them in...mebbe two years."

She shook her head. "Lemme see, maybe there's one or two in the back. Ain't makin' no promise."

As she walked off, Tom mumbled, "She makes bear sign, I'll marry her."

Isom chuckled. "Tom, that's...oh, never mind."

Joe replied, "He don't, I will."

A half hour later, stuffed with the meal and dessert, including two bear sign Tom had enjoyed with his coffee, they walked out of the café, and Joe said, "Lemme talk to the hostler. I know him."

Mounting up, they rode down the street to the livery stable, and Joe, good to his word, went in and a couple of minutes later came back out and waved them in. "Got good stalls, and feed. We can sleep in the hay loft. Fresh hay. Dime apiece for the horses and us."

As they dismounted, led their horses into the respective stalls and stripped the saddles, blankets, and bridles, Smiley shook his head. "This's gettin' to be an expensive trip. I already spent more today than I spent in the last two weeks."

Jack spit in the stall's corner and replied, "Dammit, Smiley, you're makin' fifty dollars a month scouting. I know you be squirreling it away. You do this same stuff ever couple o' years. This is for a good cause."

Smiley grinned, showing his gums. "I know. But I can only stand to be around people for so long before I gotta go back in the mountains and get away from everbody."

Taking their blanket rolls, they climbed into the hayloft and found places where they could spread their blankets. Within minutes, they were all asleep.

Chapter 13

Roger Kidd was badly hungover as Emma served breakfast to them. He slurped his coffee and moved the eggs around on the plate, finally eating a biscuit and a piece of bacon as he stared at Pete and Jud. "I want you to have everbody pair off and git out on the range. Tell 'em anybody they see, they don't know 'em, kill 'em."

Pete asked carefully, "Pa, aren't you overreacting a little bit?"

"No by God, I ain't. It's time to take over! I ain't never gonna leave here now. Not with Todd buried out there." He pointed wildly at the door with his coffee cup, slopping coffee everywhere. "Ya'll get out of here, *git!*" Pete and Jud got up quickly and headed for the door, but Roger added, "Not you Pete, I need you here. I ain't gonna run no more. You an' Billy got to keep the ranch goin'. I want at least two in ever line shack we got!"

"Ok, Pa," Pete replied softly as Jud looked back and shook his head.

Jud stumbled down the front steps and hurried to the bunkhouse, throwing the door open. "Pa's mad. Everybody needs to get up and out. Pair up, get out on the range. Shoot anybody you don't recognize."

As the cowboys hurried out, Jud looked around and saw the gunnies were still lounging around. Biting his lip, he said, "That includes y'all. Buck, you and Jack go up by the river to where you can watch that trail up on the north side. Shoot anybody you see. Harvey, dad wants us to ride up that way later today, but you might want to keep the boys out of sight."

Harvey spit out the piece of straw he was chewing on and regarded Jud curiously. "Okay. We'll saddle up and ride out. We'll be up around the far side of the butte. Buck, Jack, git up to the river, you got the good rifles."

Buck and Jack looked at each other and smiled. Buck said, "Git the horses saddled, Jack. I'll go git a bait of grub from the Chink. Meet you at the corral." He reached under his bunk and came up with the scoped Sharps 44-90. Cradling it in his arm, he strolled out, winking at Jud on the way. "We get anybody, the old man's gonna pay, right?" Jud nodded sullenly as Buck brushed by him, closely followed by a smirking Jack. A few minutes later, Buck walked out of the cook shack, a poke in his hand. He smiled at Jack. "Got biscuits, bacon, and I stole the mint outta the Arbuckles' sack. It shore is good!"

Jack grimaced. "Thanks a lot. Gimme a biscuit. I'm hungry now."

"Let's get outta sight o' the house first. I heered the old man rantin' at Pete, and I don't wanta be around if..." He shrugged. "I think Todd gettin' killed has...he's just goin' wild."

Jack reined the buckskin around and headed north, looking back over his shoulder. "Fine by me. Youse right. The old man ain't right in the head, ain't been for a while now." Buck sneaked a look back at the house as he mounted and gigged the horse to a trot, quickly catching up with Jack. They dipped into an arroyo as quickly as they could, and both relaxed once they couldn't be seen. Buck dug into the poke and handed a biscuit and a piece of bacon to Jack as they rode. Jack munched it slowly, then asked, "We goin' to the usual place?"

"Sure. I figger we can hide out up there all day."

***

Fat Jack kicked Smiley's foot. "Wakee, wakee, you old fart."

Smiley grumped, "Damn, I'm gittin' too old to sleep in a barn like this." He sneezed loudly, causing Joe and Tom to jerk awake. "Got the sneezes now. Prolly have 'em all damn day now."

Isom laughed from the floor of the barn. "Hell, Smiley, you're just getting old, period."

"You ain't no youngster yore self, Isom. I notice you ain't jumpin' for joy this mornin' either."

"Well, I've already done my ablutions, saddled up, and I'm ready to go. We have..." He glanced at his watch in the lamp light, "an hour before the train leaves."

Jack interrupted, "Y'all stop jawin', and let's mount up."

Joe shuffled over to the ladder and climbed down as Smiley said, "Damn, y'all are testy this mornin'."

Jack shook his head. "Shut up, Smiley, git your horse saddled, and lets go." He looked around asking, "Where'd Tom git off to?"

Joe replied, "His horse is gone, so I'm thinkin' he's...somewhere other than here."

Isom laughed again. "You know where he is. He's got to be at the café, looking for some bear sign. Tom is Tom, he's not going to ever change."

Jack mumbled, "Sumbitch better be at the train, otherwise I'ma cash his ticket back in. Let's *go*!" The four of them mounted and rode slowly and quietly out of the livery stable, brushing straw from their clothes in the early morning chill.

Isom said softly, "Winter isn't far off. Cold and still. It's going to be a long cold winter."

Jack replied, "A pox on you, Isom. I don't want long and cold unless I got me a bed warmer."

Joe snickered. "You couldn't get a squaw now, your life depended on it, you old fart."

They rode up to the train station, and the agent said, "You the ones going to Evans?" When Jack nodded, he added, "Get your horses loaded. Second cattle car back. Ramp's already in place. I'll get your tickets when you get ready to board."

Jack looked around and shook his head. "Tom ain't here. I ain't gonna go lookin' for him. Let's go, boys." Riding past the engine spooked the horses a little bit as the escaping steam whistled out of the engine's bypass. It took them a minute to get the horses calmed down, and Isom, as usual, was the first one to lead his horse up the ramp. The others got their horses on and started back down the ramp just as Tom rode up, bag in hand.

Dismounting quickly, he handed Jack the bag. "Hold that poke while I load Bessie." They finally got Bessie loaded after Isom took over, blindfolded her, and had Tom lead her up the loading ramp.

Once she was secured, Isom said, "Leave her blindfolded. She can smell the other horses, and as long as they stay quiet, she will, too. Otherwise, I'm afraid she'll kick the hell out of them, the cattle car, and everything else as soon as the train moves."

Tom spat on the loading ramp. "Mebbe I need to stay with her, too."

Jack shook his head. "Iff'n you want to, go ahead. Me, I'm gonna ride the cushions." He opened the bag and smiled. "And I'm gonna eat your bear sign, too!"

Jack turned and headed for the passenger car, and Tom charged down the ramp after him. "Come back here, you damn thief! Them are *my* bear sign!" The others laughed and headed for the passenger car as the railroad workers moved the loading ramp and shut the cattle car sliding door. Tom finally got his poke back as the train pulled out of the station, but it was short four donuts, and Smiley was laughing as he gummed his, licking the sugar off his moustache after every bite.

An hour and a half later, they had the horses unloaded at Evans and were headed to Fort Collins. Jack said, "We'll go to the café and git some food, nose around a bit, and ride out, quiet like."

Isom chuckled. "Jack, we're not exactly...unremarkable, if you take my meaning."

Shrugging, Jack replied, "Well, iff'n we keep our mouths shut..."

Smiley sniped, "Iff'n *you* keep your mouth shut," prompting a round of laughter.

***

At the Nevell ranch, Pronto, Rio, and Monte sat at the kitchen table, sipping coffee as the sun came over the horizon. Pronto looked at the other two and said, "Rio, Monte, I got to tell y'all somethin'," he took a sip of coffee before he continued, "I sent a telegram to some folks and tole 'em to come on down."

Rio looked sharply at him. "Why and who, Pronto?"

"Well, I jus' got a feelin'." He glanced at Monte. "Monte, when I heard you wuz here, I sent a telegram to Fat Jack. Last I heard he wuz at Fort Laramie."

Monte leaned back. "Fat Jack? Hell, I ain't thought of him in years, either. Think he'll come?"

"If he gets it, he'll be here. He was out scouting for the Army when we dropped the herd up there. I don't know who might come with him. Hell, I don't even know who's still alive outta that bunch we used to run with."

Rio said thoughtfully, "If nothing else, they'll help if we gotta hold this ranch, Monte."

Monte nodded, a faraway look in his eyes. "Yeah, thet they will. Fat Jack...ain't one to be messed with." Turning to Pronto he asked, "Who else have you heard about, or heard from?"

Before Pronto could answer, the front door banged open, and everyone grabbed for their guns as Arthur and Cavanaugh came in, shivering. Arthur raised his hands. "It's just us, Boss! Is there coffee, Boss? It's downright *cold* out there!"

Pronto slipped his pistol back in the holster and got up. "Where's your cup, Rene? Ain't enough to go 'round. You know that." Cavanaugh looked at the ceiling, mumbled something under his breath and headed for the door.

Arthur pulled a cup out of his coat pocket with a smile. "I have mine right here."

Pronto said gruffly, "Then you get coffee, as soon as you come back with another bucket of water." He handed the bucket by the stove to him and smiled as Arthur's face fell. "Arthur, you got a *long* ways to go to put one over on me." He started to say something, thought better of it, grabbed the bucket, and headed for the door. Pronto said, "Guess I better get cookin', the rest of 'em will be coming in shortly, wantin' to be fed." He picked up a knife and started slicing bacon into the skillet. "Rio, go git me some eggs."

Rio knew better than to argue and got up, slipped on his coat, and went out the door. Monte levered himself up and said, "I'll make the biscuits. You never could do 'em right, you old fart."

Arthur came back with the water, closely followed by Cavanaugh, and they got cups of coffee, standing close to the stove until Pronto threatened them with the knife. "Git outta here! Go stoke the fire in the fireplace, you're thet damn cold."

Rio finally came in, "I could only find a dozen eggs."

Pronto grimaced. "Ain't enough. Go git some taters out of the root cellar. I'll mix 'em in with the eggs."

Rio came back a couple of minutes later, four potatoes in his hands. Pronto glanced at them. "That'll work. Rene, go roust everbody out. We gotta get movin' on gettin' things done."

Rio looked around. "Has anybody seen Juan and Jeb?" A chorus of negatives answered him, and he scratched his head where the scab was. "Soon as we eat...Arthur and I'll go look for them. Maybe they found a...line cabin and stayed there last night."

Monte frowned. "Or, somebody saw 'em and potshotted 'em. Not like we coulda heard it all the way down here."

A half hour later, as Arthur and Rio looked at Red's off hind hoof, the two missing cowboys rode up. "Where the hell have you two been?" Rio asked angrily.

Juan put his hand on his chest, "*Señor*, we have been working. We found..." he pulled out his tally book, "Four hundred sixty-one cows north of the ranch house. Some of them were hidden in draws and up on the buttes to the north. By the time we got ready to start back, it was getting dark."

Jeb added, "We found a line cabin with a small corral 'bout five miles north of here. Figgered we'd be better off spending the night up there than trying to come back in the dark, as 'techy as everbody is. We left at first light, come straight here." He looked at Red. "What's wrong with Red?"

Disgusted, Arthur said, "He's tryin' to throw a shoe. I gotta try to find somethin' to fix it. I didn't search the barn yesterday like I shoulda."

Rio cocked his head. "Well, let's see what we can find. You two go on in and eat. I think Pronto saved you a bit of breakfast, just in case."

Juan took off his hat and bowed, "We thank you, *Señor*! As soon as we take care of the horses, we will enjoy *Señor* Pronto's *muy magnifico* cooking."

Arthur snorted. "Jeb, take that boy's temperature. I be thinkin' he's sick...at least in the head." The two of them laughed and led their horses toward the corral as Rio and Arthur fanned out searching the barn.

***

Down in Denver, Anna Nevell was quickly packing her valise as Elizabeth Morgan came into the bedroom. "Anna, I wish you didn't have to rush off. I know you want to get home but—"

Anna, twenty, lithe, and pretty, tucked her hair behind her ears. "Mrs. Morgan, I can't tell you how much I appreciated the bath last evening and being able to wash my underthings. But I wrote dad that I would be home before the twentieth, and that's tomorrow."

Impulsively, Mrs. Morgan hugged her. "I know, dear. But we haven't seen you in...almost two years. And Caroline has decided to stay with Bea, saying she'd rather complete her studies and come home for good next May. I truly did appreciate the letter and the tintype you brought, besides, if we hadn't welcomed you, Bea would have come up here and skinned me alive!" She smiled at Anna, who chuckled.

"So Caroline and I are carrying on the tradition you two started?"

Mrs. Morgan bit her tongue and cocked her head at Anna. "Well, we've known each other for...a lot of years. We went to school together all the way through college. And your dad sending you and then Alice down here to go to school did nothing but cement those relationships. With you and Caroline both going to Bea's finishing school in New Orleans, yes, you are continuing the tradition!"

Anna made a face. "But you don't use your...education, do you?"

Mrs. Morgan laughed softly. "Oh, I help Jack out. I just don't let him know how *much* I help him. Speaking of Jack, he should be getting the carriage ready to take you to the train station."

Anna closed the last strap on her valise and smiled. "I'm ready. I promise I'll be back to see you." She hugged Mrs. Morgan and sighed. "And I'll bring Alice with me. Now that the trains run to Cheyenne, it's only an hour or so trip, instead of two or three days!"

Jack Morgan called from the base of the stairs. "Liz? Anna? I've got the carriage out front, and your horse on a hackamore, ready to go. We need to get going if you're going to get your gelding loaded!"

Mrs. Morgan chuckled. "We'll be right down, Jack! You know us females, we're always late."

Anna smiled and picked up her valise, leading Mrs. Morgan out the door and down the stairs. "Thank you for doing this, sir. I do appreciate it."

He smiled as he took her valise and led her to the carriage. "Well, it's the least we can do. Tell Hank I said to come on down and see us. And bring some of that good elk meat when he comes."

She laughed. "I will, I surely will, sir."

The ride to the train station was short, and Mr. Morgan supervised the loading of her horse while she dealt with the two trunks that had been stored overnight in the baggage room. As soon as everything was loaded, she made her goodbyes and settled into a seat in the rail car. *Home! I'll be home this afternoon. I can't wait to see Dad and Alice! And I won't ever make another trip like this one! I'm tired, so tired.*

Chapter 14

One very tired and grumpy young lady, wearing a split skirt, boots, and blouse with a short jacket, stepped off the train at the Evans water stop. Dropping her valise on the dusty boards, she ran her fingers through her shoulder length dark brown hair, making sure it was still up in a bun. She looked around and finally saw a skinny old man, with a full head of white hair and wire rimmed glasses, coming out of the small office. "Sir? Are you the agent here now?" She asked rather shortly.

The older man stopped and peered at her. "You lost, Missy?" She smiled, lighting up her whole face, and he straightened up. "Yes, I'm the agent, for better or worse. What can I do for you?"

"I need my trunks off loaded from the train, and I also need my horse from the cattle car, too."

He scratched his head for a second then looked around and whistled. A kid stuck his head out of the office. "Leave that checkerboard alone and run get a couple o' gents from the café, Billy. Got a lady here needs some help." Billy nodded and took off at a run. He turned back to her. "I'm Ryan. What be your name, Missy?"

"Anna Nevell. My...my family, we have a little ranch over on the Cache la Poudre up north of Houndstooth Canyon."

The conductor came up and said, "Mizz Nevell, as soon as I get some help, I'll get your horse off. Ryan, can you get the baggage cart over here? She's got a couple of trunks."

Ryan nodded. "I'll go get it, Charlie. Been busy here today, bunch of mountain men on the first train south and Circle J loading beeves out. Any problems so far today?"

"Nah, smooth run so far. I was wondering why the southbound was still here. Bunch of antelope off to the east, too far away to shoot." Four younger cowboys came around the corner of the office, and Charlie said, "I think your help is here." He whispered to Anna, "I don't think they see real live girls that often."

Anna smiled. "I'll be on my best behavior. I *do* owe you an apology. I'm just tired from traveling. Five days up to St. Louis on the *Natchez*, then another four days on the trains to Denver, so two nights of decent sleep in a week and a half does not leave me at my best."

The conductor grinned. "A pretty lady like you doesn't need to apologize. You're forgiven for being tired. I have a bed in the caboose, and it's still a long trip from St. Louis to Denver. That's why I work this route now." He turned to the cowboys. "Gents, can you help me get the ramp down on the cattle car, please? Mizz Nevell needs her horse unloaded."

"We can. C'mon boys!" He nodded politely at Anna. "My name's Jake. I...we work for the Circle J up north of here."

Anna smiled prettily at them. "I do appreciate the help, Jake."

The cowboys quickly got the ramp down, and Charlie led a chestnut mountain horse out of a box car, then went back and got a side saddle and blanket. The cowboys brought the two trunks out that had been in the cattle car and put them on the baggage cart Ryan had brought over.

"Mizz Nevell, I'll be happy to store your things until somebody can get back with a wagon and pick them up."

"Thank you, it might be a couple of days." She opened one trunk and took out a canteen and saddle bags, then put her small bag in its place. She closed it and smiled at Ryan. Spotting the olla hanging in the shade next to the office, she asked, "May I get some water, please?"

He nodded as Jake led the saddled chestnut around to the hitching rail and tied him there. The conductor asked, "Missy, you sure you gonna be all right out here? There ain't much civilization once you leave here, and it's a long ride to Fort Collins."

Anna smiled. "Don't you worry, sir. Contrary to what it may look like, I grew up out here and it's only twenty maybe twenty-five miles to the ranch. I've done it a few times." She turned to Jake. "Thank you for the help. I do appreciate it."

Charlie shook his head. "Pardon me, Missy, but you sure don't look like no girl that ever sat a horse before, much less grew up out here."

Ryan added, "She shore don't. Guess the old man, Bellingham, I relieved will be sorry he missed you, but he had to go to Denver on an emergency. They sent me down from Cheyenne last night, but he'd already gone." Ryan paused for a second or two. "I wish I could ride over with you though, don't feel right 'bout no woman out here alone. Maybe one of those cowboys..."

Anna patted her handbag. "Well, I've got a little bit of equalizer in here. Please, tell Mr. Bellingham I said hello."

The train whistle blew, the conductor handed her up on the horse, and she looped the canteen around the pommel and made sure the saddle bags were secure. He shook his head. "Time for us to go. Good luck to ya, Missy."

"Thank you, Sir." She looked over at Ryan. "Someone will be here in the next day or two for the rest of my bags." With that she turned the chestnut and rode toward the mountains.

Two hours later, Anna was kicking herself for not bringing something to eat. She crouched at the side of a fast running stream, tentatively tasted the water, and refilled the canteen as she wiped her brow. *I smell the trees. It's so good to finally smell pines again, rather than the stink of the river and New Orleans, much less the funk of the people on the train.*

***

Jack and the others rode into Fort Collins and pulled up in front of the café. "Looks quiet," Isom said softly as they dismounted and tied their horse to the hitching rail. They trooped into the café and were surprised to see real tables and chairs.

Tom said, "Probably can't afford to eat here."

Joe smiled. "They got fish. I'm tired of beef and beans. Gonna try that."

Jack looked around and noted a wiry man sitting by the front window wearing a badge. He was looking curiously at them, and Jack sat down with his back to the man. "Somebody be curious," he said softly as the cook came out of the kitchen.

"What you folks want?"

They all ordered coffee and various things off the menu board. The cook disappeared and came back with cups and poured them coffee. "Gonna be a little bit for the fish. I gotta fry it up."

As they waited for their meals, the man with the badge came over. "Where y'all headed?" He asked.

Jack looked up, acting surprised. "We'uns be headin' for the mountains. Tired of people."

"Y'all goin' north or south?"

"What difference it make to you?" Jack asked testily.

The wiry man dropped a hand over his pistol butt. "Y'all might wanta go north of the river. South o' the river ain't safe."

Joe looked up at him. "Why that be? I been goin' south to Horsetooth for years"

The cook brought out their food and said, "Dammit, Talbot, go harangue somebody else. They ain't skeered o' you. And they ain't gonna tell you nothin'."

The wiry man sneered. "They'll be findin' out. Old men like that better be careful out there."

He stalked out, and the cook shook his head. "Little bit o' power, hidin' behind that tin while the sheriff is down in Denver. He...y'all be careful iff'n you're goin' south. Them Kidds be shootin' to kill down there."

Jack nodded. "Thankee. And thankee for the food."

Twenty minutes later the five of them rode out of Fort Collins, purposely crossing to the south side of the river as Talbot watched in frustration.

***

Another hour and a half of hard riding and Anna looked around and smiled to herself, the creek she just crossed marked less than a mile to the ranch. *Thankful I'm almost home. My behind hurts. What little riding I did in New Orleans didn't prepare me to do this today. What was...* She started to pull up as she looked back, then saw five men splashing across the creek, bandannas covering their faces. *I don't like this, but I don't...run, dammit girl, run!* She popped the chestnut on the rump and hung on as it took off at a fast canter up the trail between the trees.

The first rider on a fresher horse, a blue bandanna over his face, caught her within fifty yards, reached out and grabbed her arm. She tried to jerk out of his grip. "Let go of me!"

"No way. I got you now." He peered at her. "Hey, you ain't Alice, who are you?"

"Let me go, please. I don't even know who you are. All I want—"

The rider chuckled nastily. "Oh, but you will." He yanked her off her horse and jumped down. "I get you first, then everbody else that wants gets a turn."

She started fighting him for all she was worth and screamed, "Let go of me, you sonofabitch."

The rider slapped her across the face. "Stop it, you little bitch!"

A voice from further up the trail said conversationally, "Now you shouldn't oughta done that, boy." The two of them froze as an old mountain man dressed in buckskins stepped onto the trail. "Now you just let her go, and you can ride away."

The second horseman with a red bandanna, rode around the two standing in the trail and up to confront the old man. "I don't think so ol' man, you gonna die right here."

"If you think you're good enough boy, start the music."

The man laughed as he pulled a pistol from his waistband and shot as he said, "Die, you ol bast..." he coughed as the mountain man's bullet took him in the center of the chest. The man on the ground pushed Anna away and drew but didn't have a shot. The other horsemen drew their guns but couldn't see around the horse and rider.

The mountain man reeled back, blood flowering on his buckskins. "You gonna go with me boy!" He straightened up and continued to pump bullets into the red bandanna until his pistol clicked on an empty cylinder. "C'mon boy, I thought you wuz gonna kill me."

Suddenly, as the man fell from his horse, the side of the trail erupted in gunfire. The three other men died quickly, without ever getting off anything other than a random shot. Anna used the distraction to reach into her reticule and get her hand on the .32 pistol there. She turned and fired under her arm into the man's body next to her. As he doubled over and fell, his bandanna came loose.

Jud Kidd! What is he doing all the way up here? She ran to the chestnut, grabbed the reins, got a foot in the stirrup and smacked him on the rump as she got her seat, riding hard up the trail for the ranch.

As the powder smoke cleared, four more old mountain men came out of the woods and met on the trail at their friend. The oldest and skinniest mountain man got on his knees and cradled the dying man, holding him like a baby. The man's eyes opened slowly. "Fat Jack, tell me I got that bastard...didn't I?" He coughed. "Thought he could kill me? Didn't work so well for him."

Fat Jack asked sadly, "Dammit, Smiley, why couldn't ya wait?"

Smiley looked around. "Cause he hit her. Never could stand to see a woman git hit." He coughed again, and blood ran from his lips. "Did we get em all? Did she git...git away...?" His eyes rolled up, and he died in Fat Jack's arms.

Bowing his head to hide his tears, Fat Jack mumbled, "Yes, she got away, damn you. You bastard, you just couldn't wait." He gently lay Smiley on the ground and closed his eyes, then said harshly, "Git the horses, we gotta ride. Got to make sure she's safe. We'll come back an' bury Smiley later."

Isom Grissom, the spare black mountain man, clean shaven, but with a halo of white hair trotted back up the trail and said, "One of them, the one on the ground, got away. The other four are dead." The remaining mountain men, led by Fat Jack, hustled toward their horses. Arapaho Joe spit on the body lying on the trail as they rode by. As they rode off, Jud Kidd staggered out of the brush and climbed slowly on his horse, then rode the opposite direction, holding his side as blood stained his shirt and hand.

***

Dusk was touching the ridgeline as Jud rode slowly up to the line cabin. Hunched over like he was, Meacham, one of the cowboys there, almost shot him before he realized who it was. "Ferguson, come help me. Jud Kidd's out here, and it looks like he's been shot!"

Ferguson jumped out of the bunk. "Aw hell, that's just what we need. We can't let him die out here," he looked out the door and added, "And it's too damn dark to try to carry him back to the ranch." The two of them got Jud off the horse, and Ferguson asked, "What happened, Jud? Who shot ya?"

As they helped him into the cabin, he moaned, "That Bitch. She shot me. They ambushed us at the creek."

Meacham glanced at Ferguson then asked, "Who ambushed you? Where are the rest of the crew, Jud?"

Jud mumbled, "I'm all that's left. They killed us for no reason." As they lifted him gingerly into the bottom bunk, he moaned and said, "Somebody gotta tell...Pa...Harvey—"

Meacham stepped back and looked piercingly at Ferguson. "Harvey...Dunn is dead? Is that what you mean?" Jud just moaned, and Meacham bit his lip, turned, threw some wood into the stove and said, "We gotta see how bad Jud's hurt. Need to heat some water, and...you got a spare shirt? We need somethin' for a bandage."

Meacham had already pulled Jud's vest open and his shirt. There was a ragged hole through the union suit, and he used his knife to expand the hole. "Bring me the lamp. Jud mighta got lucky." Ripping the union suit wider, he shook his head in disgust. "Ain't deep. Right along the bottom rib. Don't look like it really went in him at all." Taking his bandanna off, he started to wad it up, then stopped. "Hep me cut his shirt tail off. Gotta have sumthin' to tie the 'dadder on.

The two of them managed to get Jud's shirt cut, then Meacham finished wadding the bandanna and placed it over the wound. "Gimme that shirt tail." He got it over the wound and said, "Roll him up on his side." Ferguson did, and Jud moaned. They finally got the shirt tail tied and let him roll back flat.

Ferguson asked, "Shouldn't we tie him on his hoss and take him back to the ranch? He ain't hurt that bad, and I'd rather he be off'n our hands."

Meacham scratched his scruffy beard. "Yeah, makes sense. His horse still outside?"

Ferguson went to the door and looked out. "Yep. Ground reined. Lemme tie him to the post. Horse probably don't like blood smell." He got the horse tied up, stuck his head in the door and said, "I'ma go saddle our broncs." Fifteen minutes later, he was back. Between them, they got Jud drug out and on his now fractious horse. "Tole you he wasn't gonna like the blood."

Meacham spit. "Just tie his hands to the damn saddle horn. Gonna take us a while to git back to the ranch in the dark." He stretched his back and grimaced. "But you're right, we don't wanna have him on our hands if sumthin' went wrong." They mounted and led Jud's horse as they started toward the main ranch house.

***

The darkness was broken only by the light of a lamp Anna had on the table in the Nevell's house. Rio had asked the cowboys to keep watch, expecting some kind of reaction from the Kidds, but so far, nothing had happened. The mountain men, plus Monte and Pronto, were sitting on the steps as they passed a bottle Monte had found. The bottle of whisky helped keep the cold at bay as Monte asked, "Weren't that at the Rendezvous in thirty-nine?" Anna cocked her head, listening as they talked.

Pronto replied, "I think so, we'd come in with Smith and Sublett, best I recollect."

Jack took a sip and passed the bottle. "I allus thought it was forty-two."

Isom shook his head. "Couldn't have been, I wasn't there in forty-two because I was with Beckwith up at Crow Nation. And I 'member seeing it.

Rio chuckled as he passed the bottle to Pronto. "Smiley actually talked a guy to death? That's hard to believe."

Joe sighed. "Not if you listened to him yap for thirty years."

Tom smiled. "Course that ol' boy had a mite to drink 'fore they started, and his finger did slip off'n the hammer on his pistol."

Monte laughed. "Yep, that was the last time he had that pistol in his lap playin' with it." He took an appreciative sip. "Hell, Smiley did good. Ya know, thet was the last o' the good rendezvous."

There was a round of laughter, and the bottle made another circuit as Juan said sadly, "I wish that I could have met the *Señor*. He sounds like a man of honor."

Isom smiled at Juan. "Smiley was that, not that you could see, but he never stood for any bad treatment of any woman; White, Indian, or otherwise. Hell, I remember one time he fought that one guy for those trade beads, over at the Hole, I think it was. Just because he wanted to give them to that squaw he was sweet on."

Pronto laughed. "Yeah, damn near got kilt, but he got them beads. Him and that squaw disappeared for a coupla years though."

Jack added, "Yeah, he tole me the squaw died the next winter, and he went with Bridger to see the big water."

Anna shook her head and smiled, *If only dad and Alice could hear this. This is...like a history lesson come to life. And they saved my life without a second thought. I don't understand why...people think they are dangerous. I've...well, they wouldn't try to do to me what Jud wanted to do. I hope I killed that...sumbitch.*

Chapter 15

Anna clanged the triangle and yelled, "Breakfast!" The mountain men and cowboys, most of them the worse for wear, shuffled out of the bunkhouse and barn toward the house. "There's two pots of coffee and some biscuits and beef. It's not much, but it is going to have to pass for breakfast." She stepped back in the house and waited as they straggled in.

Juan, carrying his coffee cup, was the first through the door and said, "*Señorita*, you do not have to do this."

Anna pointed at the coffee pot. "My daddy never turned anybody away, and neither will I."

Arthur nodded to her as he stepped in the door. "It's much appreciated, ma'am."

The others trickled in one by one, grabbing biscuits and beef and a cup of coffee, then heading out on the porch while the mountain men enjoyed the warmth of the cabin until Pronto looked around and asked sharply, "Where's Rio? Anybody see him?" He stuck his head out the door and asked, "Rio?"

Jeb replied, "I was the last one out, and he wasn't in the bunkhouse." Pronto mumbled something as he stepped back in.

Anna asked, "Where could he be?"

Flynn said, "Jeb, check and see if Red is in the corral." He paused then added, "Juan, see if Rio's saddle is in the barn." The two of them went off the porch in a hurry, bumping Monte on the way out.

Monte looked askance at them as he walked in and glanced at Pronto. "Who put a burr under their saddles?"

"Rio, damn him. He musta slipped out last night."

Monte shook his head and Anna asked, "What do you mean, slipped out?"

Jeb and Juan trotted back to the house, and Juan stuck his head in the door. "*Señor* Pronto, he is gone."

Arthur grimaced. "Well, I guess he's gone huntin'.

Anna said, "Well, we do need meat, especially to feed all of you."

Flynn said sadly, "No, ma'am, you don't understand." He glanced around at the mountain men. "He's gone people hunting. He's after those that did this to you all."

"What? Oh my God, you've got to stop him. He'll be–" The laughter from the cowboys stopped her in mid word.

Pronto smiled grimly. "Ain't that easy, Ma'am. Rio gits started, he's kinda hard to stop, leastways stop 'fore he kills everbody." He took a sip of coffee. "He don't kill that easy either. So we might as well finish eating, cause he's long gone by now." He took another appreciative sip of the coffee. "Gotta admit, you make some good coffee, ma'am."

Jeb and Juan sat on their horses as Pronto, Monte, Flynn, and Arthur stood on the porch. Anna stomped her foot. "I *am* going to see my sister. I *have* to!"

Monte put his hands up. "Will you wait, please? Let me ride in and see what's goin' on with yore sister and in town. I can get some supplies, too. Ain't no point in you goin' in and gettin' in the middle of...anything."

Pronto added, "We jus' want to protect you, 'specially now. You...and Alice are all that's left. Let

Monte do this. Also, we don't know what's coming at us from them Kidds. Ain't like them to give up.

Anna said disgustedly, "*Fine*! But tomorrow, I *am* going to see my sister." She turned toward the door, grumbling, "Even if I have to go by myself."

Isom shook his head. "Spirit. She's definitely got some spirit." He stepped off the porch. "I'm going to ride up in the hills a ways and see if I can bag a deer or elk. We're getting low on food with this many people here."

Pronto nodded. "Jeb, you and Juan see if you can track down Rio. Stop 'im any way you can, short o' killin' him." He looked over at Fat Jack. "Jack, y'all want to stay here while we go get the cows rounded up?

Jack nodded. "Can Arthur stay and look at our horses? Mine's kinda limpin'. We'll stay here and hold the ranch."

Monte took off for the corral. "I'll get supplies." Before Pronto could interrupt him, he added, "And I'll get some canned peaches or apples, iff'n I can find 'em."

Arthur looked at Flynn, then nodded. "I'll look at the horses and also check the ones in the corral."

Anna said softly, "I do appreciate what all of you are doing for me and my family. But I *want* to see my sister!" She turned and walked back in the house, before the tears came.

***

Roger Kidd looked blearily up from the table as Billy walked in and sank into a chair. "Didn't get back 'til late last night. Sorry. Seems a bunch of mountain men came through Fort Collins yesterday mornin'.

Talbot said they wouldn't tell him where they were goin', even after he flashed his badge at them."

"No idee which direction they wuz goin'?"

Billy shrugged. "Talbot said they rode out headin' west."

Emma came in with a bowl of eggs, another of biscuits, and set them quietly on the table. "Be right back with the bacon, sir."

Roger nodded abruptly at her, then added, "Go have somebody wake up Jud. He shoulda been here already."

"Yessir," she mumbled and scurried out of the dining room.

Shaking his head, he continued, "Pete's out rounding up stock, pushing it to the south range. Dunno where Jud is, that boy hadn't come back when I went to bed last night." He pointed to the bowls. "Help yourself." Billy nodded but waited until Kidd had served himself before he took a small portion of the eggs and a couple of biscuits.

Emma came back with slices of bacon on a plate and said, "Cookie went to wake Jud up. He don't like me going in his room." Kidd nodded as he took a handful of bacon and transferred it to his plate, then started eating.

They had both finished when Jud limped into the dining room holding his side.

"What's the matter with you, boy?"

Jud slumped in a seat as far from his father as possible. "I got shot yesterday afternoon. We...we were ambushed by a bunch o' mountain men."

Roger slammed the table. "What?" He stood, almost upsetting the table. "Why the hell didn't you tell me?"

Jud edged back, saying softly, "I...was...I don't remember getting back here."

"Where's Harvey? Why didn't he come tell me?"

Jud shook his head. "They...Harvey's dead, Pa. They all dead. They...ambushed us up by the creek. We...didn't do nothin'."

Roger's face reddened, and he started to yell when somebody started ringing the triangle outside. Billy jumped up and ran for the door. "I'll find out—"

They heard somebody yell, "Somebody git the boss!"

Roger charged out the door, yelling over his shoulder, "C'mon Jud. This..." the rest was lost in the growing clamor of voices. He got out the front door and onto the porch and stopped dead. There were three horses with bodies over the saddle being led toward the house by one of the gunmen. "Who?" He yelled.

"Dunn, Glazer, and Hill," the gunman yelled. "Couple of boys went north to see if they could find any more hosses."

Roger Kidd slumped against the post momentarily, then walked stiffly down the steps as the horses were led up to the porch. "Git 'em off the horses." A few of the cowboys helped lower the three bodies to the ground and respectfully stepped back as Roger looked at them. Harvey Dunn had five bullets in him, all in the front. The other two had been shot in the sides and front. Spinning around he looked up at Jud and said, "Why are all the shots in Harvey's body in the front? Who..."

Jud stood holding to the post on the porch. "Some crazy ol' mountain man. He...just stepped out on the trail and started shootin'. Harvey killed him, but my hoss was jumpin' and threw me just as they shot me.

Musta knocked me out, cause when I came to, they were...ridin' off north."

"North?" Kidd stomped over to the porch. "North? Toward Neville's place? What were you doin' north of the river? I tole you to stay *south* of the river."

"I...Harvey...he thought...he saw somebody and went after 'em."

"Where were you? Why didn't you tell him to stop?"

"I was right behind him. You know he don't listen to me."

Roger Kidd threw up his hands in frustration and turned to the assembling cowboys. "Go dig some more graves. Bury 'em with the others." He stomped back up on the porch and glared at Jud. "You better not be lyin' to me, boy."

***

Rio rode slowly across the rolling terrain, pausing occasionally to look for tracks of the horse he was following. Seeing a line cabin in the distance, he stopped and checked his pistol was loose in the holster. Riding in a wide circle, he approached the cabin from the blind side and rode to the corner of the cabin. "Hullo, the cabin."

Ferguson opened the door a crack and looked out blearily. "What you want, cowboy?"

"I'm trackin' a man that tried to rape a woman yesterday."

He opened door fully and goggled at Rio. "You what?"

"I said, I'm trackin' a man that tried to rape a woman yesterday, over at the creek north of the river. Tracks lead straight to this cabin."

Ferguson stepped out, showing his hands. "Jud ain't here. We took him down the ranch house yesterday evenin'. You welcome to come in an look iff'n you want." He stepped to the side as Meacham came to the door.

Meacham stuck his head out and said, "Jud said they wuz ambushed, didn't say nothin' 'bout no rape."

Rio dismounted carefully, keeping his eye on the two cowboys and walked to the door. "Him and four others grabbed Anna Nevell and were going to rape her until a bunch of old mountain men stopped them. 'Pears this Jud played possum then ran."

Ferguson spat, wiped his mouth and replied, "I ain't standing for that. I may not be the best person, but by God, I don't believe in messin' with no woman."

"Then you better ride. I'm gonna take him and all his kind down."

"Yessir, I'll ride. I'll ride right now, lemme get my poke together." He started to go back in the cabin, stopped and looked meditatively at Rio. "You can't take on ol' man Kidd and all his rannies. There must be twenty of em."

"I don't care. One or twenty don't make no difference to me."

Meacham laughed coarsely. "Who are you? You crazy or jus' plain stupid?"

Rio's smile was not pretty. "Well, sometimes they call me the Rio Kid."

Meacham looked sharply at Rio, taking in the Texas garb and saddle, and stepped back. "You just might be him. But I ain't stickin' around to find out. I'm ridin', too. Jus' let us clean out our pokes."

A half hour later, the two cowboys rode northeast, toward the railroad. Rio sat on Red as he decided whether to burn the line cabin or not. He heard horses coming from the northwest and eased Red behind the cabin as he waited.

Juan, in the lead, said, "Jeb, I don't know if that bodes good or evil that those two are riding away."

Jeb cantered up beside Juan. "Mebbe, mebbe not. Rio coulda told 'em to clear out or die, and they cleared out. So mebbe he ain't too far ahead of us."

Rio recognized their voices and rode around the front of the cabin. "What the hell are you two doing down here?"

Juan, visibly relieved to see him, said, "*Señor*, the *Señorita*, wishes you to come back to the ranch house."

"Wha...why?"

"She wants to go see her sister. *Señor* Monte has gone into town for supplies and to see if anyone is watching. The other...mountain men, they are helping around the ranch."

Rio grimaced. "Helping? More like eating her out of house and home. I'll bet not a damn one of them has worked on a ranch in...God knows how many years, if ever." He gestured toward the direction the two Kidd riders had ridden. "Those two said Jud was here and taken back to the main house last night. Apparently Kidd has twenty gunnies down there."

Juan sighed. "*Señor*, as good as you are, you can't take all of them on!"

Rio shook his head. "Maybe not. Or at least not with the three of us. I...dammit." He turned Red north. "Alright, let's get back before she does something stupid, like riding off without us."

***

Isom walked into the barn and heard Flynn and Arthur talking about one of the horses. He cocked his head, grinned, and walked closer. "Mister Flynn, is that by chance Old Virginny I hear in your voice?"

Flynn sniffed and said, "Yes, 'fraid so, Isom. How did you pick up on it?"

Laughing, Isom said, "Grew up listening to that. You would not by chance be a Flynn of the Flynn Flyers, would you?"

Flynn's jaw dropped. "How...what do you know about..." He shook his head sadly, "What *did* you know about our horses."

Arthur stood quietly, not completely understanding what was playing out, but he'd never seen Flynn look so troubled. Isom said softly, "I used to ride for old man Bennett. Con...Conway Bennett. I rode Silver Streak."

Flynn sagged back on a bale of hay. "You...my grandfather...hated you!" He shook his head again, as if shaking a memory away. "Supposedly my grandfather threatened to buy you just so he could whip you. Did you know my father? Egan?"

"I remember him as a young man. He was just starting to spark the ladies when I left."

Arthur asked, "You left?"

"Yes, Con's younger boy, Clayton, made lieutenant and he was being sent with Colonel Grissom on a mapping expedition out here. The old man sent me along to care for him and the horses."

Flynn nodded. "Makes sense. How did you...become so well read?"

Isom laughed. "I was a house boy, and a little one at that, so I was taught my letters and ciphers so I could help in the house. The love of horses turned out to be a bonus, when Con found out I could ride and had a way with the horses, it...got a lot better for me and my momma. Right before we left out, the old man manumitted me."

"So you've been out here a long time."

Isom grimaced. "Yeah, not all of it good. Back in '44 or '45, I got lost from Fairmont's Party. I was tracking a damn mule down and got completely lost. They left me, guess they thought Injuns had got me. Three days later I come up on a camp of some boys, and they strung me up like that, till I convinced them I'd just got lost, not run away. Then they felt bad and let me stay. Damn, that was almost thirty years ago! Spent one winter holed up with the Arapaho, had a Bible and a copy of the Iliad. Had them both memorized by spring."

Arthur goggled. "I never heard 'bout any of our kind bein' out here thet early. I'm proud ta meet ya. And I guess that 'splains how you talk so good."

Isom solemnly shook hands with Arthur and Flynn. "Yep, funny how helping with the horses and mules after one of the skinners got killed in an Indian raid kept me in food and shelter for a long time." He glanced at Flynn then asked Arthur, "How'd you get out here?"

Arthur replied, "My pappy come to Texas with Rio's granpappy back in the late '30's. We were manumitted by the ol' man 'fore they left for Texas, but Pappy, he come anyway. I was born in Texas, was in Natchez during the war, came back in sixty-three, and I got a wife and a little one down at the ranch. I kinda handle the remuda and shoe horses for 'em."

"Never had any problems?"

Arthur spit on the dirt floor. "Hell, I never had any problems till after the War, when them carpetbaggers come in. They tried to say we were runaways, but Rio's pappy stood up fer us and had the papers from his pappy.

Isom shook his head, saying, "Well, we here now, an" in a fight where neither one of us has a stake."

Flynn started at that, but Arthur put a hand on his arm. "Maybe for you, but I ride fer the brand. They stood by me, an' I'm a gonna stand by them. Rio done got hurt by 'em, now the brand's gonna take care of it."

Laughing, Isom replied, "Oh hell, I didn't mean it that way, I'm standing by my friends the same way. Besides, I was getting bored riding with the damn Cavalry. Damn young officers think they know everything, and they don't know bear scat from moose scat." The three of them laughed, the tension broken, and went back to examining the horses.

***

Monte rode slowly into Fort Collins, enjoying the relative warmth and sunshine as the skies cleared. He'd purposely come in from the north, the pack horse plodding along behind as he headed for the mercantile. Reining up in front of the store, he tied both horses to the hitching rail and looked casually around. A few people were moving around town, but not many. The café looked fairly busy, and a cavalry patrol was riding east as he watched. Stepping up on the porch, he opened the door and stopped, holding it for an older woman. He touched his hat and said, "Mornin', Ma'am."

She looked him up and down and finally nodded as she swept by, her arms full of packages. Shaking his head, he slipped into the store, reveling in the smells of leather, tobacco, and could it be? Sweet cookies? He made for the counter in back and watched a middle aged man with round glasses ringing up a purchase for a cowboy.

His mouth watering, he started down the aisles, getting a handful of items each time, and bringing them back to the counter. After the fourth trip, the cowboy was gone, and the storekeeper walked down to where he was piling items up. "Can I help you, old timer?"

Monte nodded. "Flour, a bag, iff'n you got it, sugar, salt, bakin' powders, side o' bacon, and...can I ask what is that that I smell?"

The storekeeper chuckled. "The wife is baking for the church social on Sunday. Cookies. I can probably sneak one, if you are spending a lot of money, which it looks like you are."

"Gotta get supplies for the winter. I ain't comin' back down 'til spring." He gnawed his jaw. "Say, is there a doc or a...whatyoucallem, dentist in town?"

"Ain't got a dentist. There might be one at the fort. All we got is Doc Farrell. Don't know that he does teeth."

"Mebbe he can take a look. Tooth's hurtin' terrible bad." He looked at the ammunition behind the storekeeper. "Need four...no, make it five boxes of thet forty-four and five boxes of thet fifty-seventy carbine ammo." Once everything was piled on the counter, the storekeeper disappeared into the back, then came back moments later with two cookies. He handed them to Monte and started totaling up the goods while Monte enjoyed the cookies. "Mighty fine cookin', my compliments to your wife."

The storekeeper patted his stomach and replied, "I know, thank you, but I don't think I'll tell her right now. Might get me in trouble." He chuckled then said, "Your total is...ten dollars."

Monte reached in his belt and counted out ten silver dollars then asked, "Where be that doctor?"

"Go south a block and west a block. He's got a...he doctors out of a building next to his house. He usually eats lunch at the café." Pulling out a pocket watch, the storekeeper looked at it, "But it's early, so he's probably at his building."

Monte continued packing the goods into sacks and said, "Thankee."

The storekeeper asked curiously, "You meet any other mountain men? A few of them came through here a day or so ago."

Monte shook his head. "Nope. Ain't seen nobody." Taking up his sacks, he nodded politely and eased out of the store. Packing the sacks on the pack horse, he mounted and ambled down to the doctor's place.

Tying his horses, he walked up to the building and knocked. Hearing a distant voice say, "Come in!" He opened the door and stepped in the room, sliding to the side as he smelled an astringent odor. "Be right with you," came the voice again. A few moments later, the doc came through a door in the back, sleeves rolled up. "What can I do for you?"

Monte looked around and asked quietly, "Wanted to check on Alice Nevell. You 'member me from the ranch?"

The doctor looked sharply at him then smiled. "Yes, sir, I do. She's...better. She's over at the house in the spare bedroom. You want to see her?"

Monte shook his head quickly. "No, sir. Her sister, Anna, come home, and wants to come see her. Did you get Hank buried? And how much do we owe you?"

Nonplussed for a few seconds, the doctor said, "We took care of Hank. He's buried next to his wife in the cemetery. His horse and rifle are in my possession.

The undertaker took five dollars from us to bury Hank, since he didn't have any money on him when Kidd killed him." Biting his lip, the doc thought for a minute. "I don't see a problem with Anna coming to..." He grimaced. "Well, if anybody from the Kidd place is in town, it might be a problem."

Monte nodded. "We kin figger somthin' out. Probably tomorrow mornin', iff'n I have to guess. We'll ride in with her. She'll want to know iff'n she can take Alice home."

"Not yet. I got the infection down, but she's still hurting pretty bad. I'm giving her just enough laudanum to take the edge off the pain, but I don't want to get her addicted to it. She...didn't take the news of her daddy's death easy, but having Anna home might help her. Let me think on it, and we'll make a decision tomorrow."

"Thanks, Doc. Oh, and iff'n anybody asks what I wanted, say I talked to you 'bout a toothache. I'm going to ease out of here and head back to the ranch. We needed supplies, and I don't think the storekeeper knows I'm staying there."

He headed for the door, and the doctor said, "I won't say anything. Watch out for the deputy, he's on Kidd's payroll, along with the sheriff, although we can't prove it." Monte nodded sourly as he stepped out of the building.

Mounting up, he led the pack horse north, planning to be back at the ranch before sunset.

Chapter 16

Pete Kidd walked into the old bunkhouse where the cowboys slept. "Anybody seen Meacham and Ferguson?"

Tate, one of the oldest cowboys replied, "Naw. They went up to the north line cabin, far's I know, they are still up there."

Pete rubbed his face and sighed. "How about you and Perry go up and relieve them. Take enough supplies for a couple of days."

Perry sat up. "Hey, boss. What happened to Dunn and the other gunnies? Somebody shot the hell outta them and put them on their hosses. We brought Anselm and that French dandy, Alfon's bodies in yesterday afternoon after we found their hosses up on the north flat. By my count, whatever happened took out five of the old man's gunnies."

Pete sat heavily in one of the chairs at the table. "Jud...says they got ambushed by...mountain men. Dunno why, he said they just shot them down for no reason."

Tate mumbled skeptically, "Everbody 'ceptin' Jud?"

"He...said his horse bucked him off. That's what he says saved him."

Tate snorted, but didn't say anything more. Pete got up wearily. "Just get Meacham and Ferguson and... don't stay up there. Just push any cows you see south. Pa wants all the cattle down on the plain before the snow hits."

The two cowboys shrugged into their coats and stumped out as Pete walked slowly back to the main house. He'd no sooner gotten inside than Roger yelled for him. "Pete, I need you in the office!"

He looked up at the ceiling and turned toward the office at the back of the house. "Yes, Pa?"

Roger Kidd, harried and unshaven, looked up at him. "I want the gather completed by tomorrow. Day after, we're gonna take care of that bunch north o' the river for once and for all. I mean to have the Nevell place by new year."

Pete nodded. "Pa, you know the cowboys ain't getting fighting wages."

Roger snorted. "If they be willing, I'll pay 'em fighting wages. They can't be any worse than that bunch that got kilt."

"We got enough money to pay them? We haven't sold many cows this year, have we?"

"Don't you be worryin' about money! There's enough. Now git! And take that no good brother of yours with ya."

Pete walked upstairs mumbling to himself, "Take your brother, and do what? Punch cows, go kill people? Damned if I know." He got to Jud's room and knocked, but didn't hear any response. Pushing the door open, he saw a lump under the covers and kicked the end of the bed. "Get up! Pa wants us to go move cows."

Jud moaned and rolled over. "I ain't goin'. I been shot, fer God's sake! Go 'way." He pulled the covers over his head, and Pete noted the half empty bottle of whisky on the floor and turned away in disgust.

At the door he said, "Better not let Pa find out you're sneakin' his whisky." He went quietly down the back stairs and out the back door toward the corral shaking his head.

***

After breakfast, Rio turned to Monte. "Is there a way to get down to the Kidd's place through the mountains?"

Monte thought for a minute, then said, "I'm pretty sure there is. I ain't followed it all the way out, but Redstone Crick comes down pretty much dead straight at the butte behind their place, iff'n I 'member right."

"I want to take a look at it. Maybe ride up that way today."

Anna interrupted, "I want to go see Alice! You *said* you'd take me to see her!"

Rio looked down at his coffee cup as everyone else backed away. "Anna, Monte told you your sister is in and out. Why not wait a couple of more days? If you go see her now, all you're gonna see is her layin' in bed. And if she's that bad, we sure can't bring her back here."

Anna stood rigid for a second. "I...oh...you *damn* men." She stomped out of the house, and Rio shook his head.

Monte took a deep breath and said, "That...didn't go real well, did it, boy?"

An hour later, after putting various cowboys to work and setting up a guard rotation, Rio and Monte rode up toward the cabin, intent on scouting out a route to the Kidd ranch that Monte thought would be possible. Rio was still ticked off at Anna and was mumbling about her.

Monte was chuckling to himself, but Rio heard him and snapped, "What's so damn funny?"

"You and Anna are about like two damn porcupines tryin' to mate. Y'all are all bristly with each other, cause you're too damn scared of the other one."

Rio glared at him. "I'm not scared of her. She's just...mad all the time. And blaming me for everything that has happened."

"No, she ain't. Damn, Rio, pull yore head outta yore ass. Thet girl done lost her pappy, and her sister been shot. You expectin' her to be all sweetness and light?"

"I'm worried about her or one of us getting killed. Hell, somebody shot me from...somewhere that first day up here. If they can do that to me, and Alice, they can damn sure do it to Anna. And she's too damn stubborn to stay in the house!" He threw up his hands, startling Red, who almost bucked him off. "Dammit, settle down, Red!"

Monte laughed. "You are lettin' yore upset git to yore horse. You need to calm down. This country, not payin' attention will get you kilt!"

Grumbling, Rio calmed down, and they continued to the cabin in silence. After they'd checked the cabin, Monte led off to the southwest. "Gotta find Redstone Crick. We can foller that right down to the butte behind Kidd's place. It's gonna take a while, but we should be back afore dark."

***

Unbeknownst to Rio and Monte, Anna had gone out and saddled her horse and started to ride out before she was stopped by John Flynn. "Where you going, Missy?"

"*I* am going to see my sister. And *nobody* is going to stop me!" Her hand rested in her bag on the saddle, and Flynn knew there was a pistol there.

"Now you just wait a minute. We'll get some people to go with you. If you're going to be that stubborn, you are *not* riding off by yourself." Fat Jack walked out of the barn, stretching in the bright sunlight, and Flynn said, "Jack, can you round up the rest of your friends and accompany Ms. Nevell to see her sister?"

Jack nodded. "Gimme a few minutes, and we'll be ready to ride." He let out a piercing whistle, and Long Tom and Arapaho Joe came running out. "Git the horses, we'z gonna escort Ms. Nevell to town!"

Tom smiled, "Good! Mebbe I can find me some bear sign. I been hankerin' for some more of them."

Anna couldn't help but smile, and decided she would get the fixings from the store and bake some for him. *It's the least I can do for these men. They...saved me and maybe will save the ranch. And those cowboys...Damn Rio's hide. Why does he hate me? I've never done anything to him.*

Three hours later, Anna and the Mountain Men rode quietly down the street to the Doc's house. Anna and Isom dismounted and walked toward the door as the others drifted slowly away. Doc opened the door and was surprised to see Anna standing there. "Anna? What are..." He glanced over at Isom as he casually leaned against the roof post. "Who are these men?"

"They escorted me in from the ranch. I'm sorry I didn't get here sooner. I guess you knew I've been in New Orleans at school, living with my Aunt who runs it. Alice wrote me and told me what was happening with daddy and the ranch, so I decided to come home." After that rush of words, she paused, then asked, "How's Alice, Doc? Can I see her?"

"She's alive, Anna, but she's in and out of consciousness." He opened the door and added, "Come in. Did you know that Monte and that kid Rio kept her alive till I could get there?" She nodded, and he said, "And I guess you know about your dad?"

"Yes. Monte told me. I want to see dad's grave. We buried Smiley up at the ranch day before yesterday."

Doc Farrell looked curiously at her. "Smiley?" Then his face darkened. "What else has happened?"

Anna shook her head as she slumped into a char. "Oh God, I was riding home from the depot, and a bunch of cowboys led by Jud Kidd grabbed me. Smiley was one of the mountain men that stepped out in the trail and told them to let me go. They didn't, and he shot it out with somebody named Harvey. Smiley killed him, and Isom, Jack, Joe, and the rest of the mountain men killed the others, except for Jud, who apparently got away."

Doc shook his head sadly. "Those damned Kidds, they've been nothing but trouble since they showed up here. You know Todd Kidd was the one that killed your dad?"

Anna nodded. "Yes, and Pronto told me how he shot him down." She looked up at the doc. "May I please see Alice now?"

"I'm sorry, Anna, of course you can." He led her back to the spare bedroom. "She may not know you, you realize that?"

He opened the door to a sunlit bedroom, gauzy curtains covering the window for privacy as Alice lay in bed with her hair nicely arranged and covers up to her neck. Anna could see a large lump under the covers on the left side of her chest. Mrs. Tillman, the nurse sitting with her, got up and hugged Anna. "I'm so sorry, dearie. She's been awake a couple of times this morning. But..."

Anna slipped into the chair. "Alice? Oh, Alice." She took her sister's hand and said in anguish, "What have they done to you?" She bowed her head and let the tears come.

Doc Ferrell said softly, "She was shot once high up in the shoulder. I've got her bandaged and put in drains to help the infection as much as I can. I get a little laudanum into her by drippin' it in her mouth when I can. She occasionally will drink a little, and eat, but she's still in and out a lot."

Anna gripped her sister's hand hard. "She *is* going to make it, isn't she, Doc?"

"I think she will. I'd just like to watch her a few more days."

"Can I stay with her for a while?"

"Of course, just let us know if you need anything."

Doc came onto the porch with two cups of coffee. "Thought you might could use this, it's a bit chilly out here." He handed one of the cups to Isom and leaned against the porch rail. "She's sitting with her sister right now."

Isom took the coffee gratefully. "Thanks, Doc. The girl is gonna make it, isn't she?"

"I think so, but it's been touch and go. She...got an infection that...took a while to get cleaned up."

Isom mused, "I think you going to get real busy here, Doc."

"What do you mean?"

"That boy, Rio, has started man hunting those who hurt this family."

"He's going to take on the Kidds? That's beyond stupidity!" Doc Ferrell started pacing the porch, agitated. "The Sheriff will be back next week. He should handle it!"

Isom said gently, "I hear tell that the Sheriff only handles the town and is being paid by the Kidds."

Doc continued almost as if he didn't hear Isom. "Well, he can get help from Denver if he needs it." He turned back toward Isom. "That boy won't make it. They'll kill him."

"Maybe not, Doc, we are going to pitch in and help him a little."

Doc bit his lip, then said, "If you are, you better get Anna to some place safe. If they shot one woman, they won't hesitate to shoot another." He made a sweeping gesture. "I can protect Alice, cause she's my patient; but I don't know if I can protect Anna."

"We'll get her back out to the ranch in an hour or so. Then we'll just hunker down until things pop. One of us will come in to check on Alice every couple of days." He met Doc Farrell's eyes. "Once she's able to be moved, we're going to take her back to the ranch, too."

"I guess that will work," the doc sighed and continued, "I guess I better telegraph Denver for more supplies."

***

Tate and Perry rode up to the line shack and stopped in front of it. Tate looked around and said, "Don't look right. Ain't no smoke outta the chimney. Check the stable." He slipped the thong off his pistol as he eased down off the horse. Perry did the same and rode slowly toward the little stable off to the side of the cabin.

Tate eased up to the door and said, "Meacham? Ferguson? Anybody awake in there?" He didn't hear a response and pulled the lanyard to open the door. Drawing his pistol, he eased in as the door swung open, covering more of the cabin as the door swung further. When it hit the stop, he stepped in and blew out a breath he hadn't realize he was holding. *Tain't nobody here. Their blankets are gone, it's...empty.* He stepped over and touched the stove. *Cold. So a day, mebbe two days. Where?* He snapped around when Perry stepped through the door.

"Don't shoot me, Tate!" Perry exclaimed, hands high.

Tate slumped on the bench. "Sorry. Kinda on edge. Tain't right they be gone. Stove's cold. They...ain't been here in at least a day. Wonder where they went?"

Perry nodded. "Stable's empty too. Wherever they went, they wuz ridin'. No horses, no tack, nothin'. Kinda scary. Ain't like either of 'em to just pick up and leave."

"Unless they ain't left on their own. Mebbe somebody..." Tate got up and rushed out of the cabin. Walking quickly around the cabin, he pointed to the ground on the side of the cabin. "Somebody ridin' a big horse snuck up on 'em. He sat his horse right here, and then got down and stepped up on the porch."

Walking further out in front of the cabin, he saw where two more sets of tracks intercepted the set he was following. He shook his head and walked back to Perry. "Whoever it was, met up with two more riders out front." He stared at Perry. "Don't know 'bout you, but I ain't stayin' here. I'm thinkin' I'm gonna ride down south and stay there."

"What we gonna tell Pete?"

Tate mounted up and rode over to the stable. Picking out two more sets of tracks, he followed them east for a hundred yards. "The truth. We didn't find 'em." He blew out a breath, took his hat off and pushed his hair back before putting his hat back on. He reached down and put the thong back on his pistol as he turned his horse. "I think...we won't see Meacham and Ferguson agin. I think they...somebody let them go." He took one more look at the line cabin and cantered back toward the main ranch.

Perry trailed behind him and said to himself, "I ain't gettin' paid to fight."

***

Late that evening, two horses plodded slowly into the ranch yard at the Nevell's ranch. Arthur, just inside the barn, shotgun at the ready, asked, "Thet you, Rio?"

Rio replied, "Yeah, we're back. For a while anyway." He and Monte dismounted, and both stretched and groaned, almost in unison. Monte headed for the outhouse handing his reins to Arthur.

Arthur smiled and said, "I'll git your horses, y'all go on in the house and eat. I think there's some food left."

Rio asked, "Where's Anna?"

"She went to town to see her sister, but she's back safe."

Angrily, Rio asked, "Who let her go? Dammit man, they'll kill her too!"

"Twern't no stoppin' her. Fat Jack an' them rode in wit her."

Flynn walked up. "I really don' think too many folks were going to mess with them. I got her to at least let the mountain men go with her.

Rio sighed. "Yeah, you're right, ain't no stoppin' a woman. They're worse than any damn mustang I ever saw."

Rio walked in, closely followed by Monte. Anna jumped up when she saw them and said, "Alice is going to make it! She...I got to talk to her for a few minutes! And I want to bring her home in the next few days." She bustled into the kitchen adding, "There's some beef, biscuits, and beans left. I...made some bear sign, but..." she shrugged, "They're all gone." She continued prattling brightly as she dished up two plates and put them on the table. Rio didn't say a word, glaring at her until Monte chuckled. Anna looked between them, got quiet, and quickly left the kitchen.

Monte dug into the food, then said softly, "Temper, temper."

Rio glared at him, but didn't say a word. After they'd eaten, they went into the living room, and Monte pulled out his maps. Rio did remember to thank Anna for the food, but otherwise kept silent.

Monte said, "They done started a range war up here. We figgered out a way to take it to 'em."

Rio traced the route they'd followed earlier in the day. "We can't get right up to the ranch house, but we can get...maybe within a hundred yards."

"No closer'n 'bout 200 yards. Not without bein' seen anyway." Monte corrected.

Pronto asked, "What you thinkin', Rio?"

"Well, I saw some of that new dynamite in the barn. I was thinkin'..."

Pronto interrupted, "Well, ya cain't throw it that far—"

"No, but if we could injun down..."

Monte laughed. "Hell yeah, injun down there put the stuff where you could see it and then shoot it.

Jeb smiled. "That would stir things up."

"That's the idea, I want to take the fight to them." He looked up at Jeb and Juan. "I scared a couple of hands off yesterday, and this might scare a few more off. 'Specially if they're not getting fighting wages."

The planning continued, with the mountain men chiming in with ideas and approaches. Anna sat quietly in the corner, watching Rio, but never saying a word. *He's like a...general. But he listens to everybody. I...wish he'd say something about me going to town. I know, I just know he's mad about it.*

An hour later, she slipped quietly out of the living room, her passage only noted by Rio. When she didn't reappear, he figured she'd gone to bed.

Chapter 17

Rio, Monte, Fat Jack, Long Tom, Arapaho Joe, Isom Grissom, and Pronto, dressed in buckskins or worn clothes had worked over their horses making sure nothing rattled on their tack. Rio had six four-stick charges of dynamite in a sack behind his saddle, while Monte carried a sack with blasting caps on his horse. Anna, Flynn, Jeb, Juan, Arthur, and Rene stood on the porch as Rio looked around then at Anna. "We're gonna take the fight to 'em tonight. Anna, I want you to go up to the cabin with the boys. It's easier to defend than this place is."

Anna's chin came up, and she bristled. "No, damn you. I'm not leaving my home. I'll stay here by myself if I have to," she yelled, "*but I am not leaving my home!*"

Flynn said, "We'll protect her Rio, don't worry about it."

Juan stepped up beside Flynn, "*Si Señor.*" He grinned. "Besides, nobody will argue with Arthur and his shotgun."

Rio threw up his hands, spooking Red. Once he had him back under control, he said, "I give up! Let's go boys, let's go get in a fight where we can win." The mountain men followed him out of the yard and up the trail toward the cabin.

As they rode out, Anna said, almost to herself, "Be careful!" She hugged herself and turned back toward the front door.

Juan cheerfully said, "Not to be sorry, *Señorita*, he is the Rio Kid now. If he dies he will take many hombres with him."

Anna stopped and turned back to Juan. "Rio Kid? I thought his name was Rio?"

Flynn stepped up angrily. "Shut up, Juan!"

Anna rounded on him. "No! I want to know what's going on. *Who* is Rio, or maybe I should say *what* is Rio?"

Arthur sniffed and said sorrowfully, "Somebody better tell her."

Anna shivered and led them into the house, busying herself in the kitchen with another pot of coffee. When everyone had been served, she turned to Flynn. "Tell me the truth, please, John."

Flynn sighed. "Well, ma'am, Rio, well, he's kinda got a bad side, ma'am."

"Tell me, dammit!"

"Jeb, you tell her, you seen most of it."

Jeb set his coffee cup down and said quietly, "Well ma'am, Rio, he's also known as the Rio Kid."

Rene Cavanaugh and Anna both started, and she blurted, "He's not old enough! The stories—"

Jeb went on relentlessly, "Old enough or not, he is. Rio grew up with the Texas cowboys on the ranch, and they taught him their code. You ride for the brand, he watched what happened when his daddy and others rode off to war. And he's seen what happened when them damn Reconstructors comin' in."

Anna put her hand over her mouth. "No! He can't be, he's not old enough. He's...not any older than I am!"

"He's...twenty-two. He never shot anybody that didn't deserve it." Jeb grinned. "Fact is, if he weren't as fast with that pistol as he is, he'd already be dead."

Flynn shook his head as Anna sat sharply. "Oh no! I..."

Jeb squatted and looked Anna in the face. "You didn't start it, ma'am. They did, but Rio or the Rio Kid *is* gonna end it or die tryin'. When he gits like this there's no bloody backup in him at'all."

Anna looked around at the men. "I don't want him to die because of me!"

"He won't die because of you, ma'am; for you maybe, but not because of you. We'll all fight for the brand. We sat at the table and broke bread. We ain't gonna leave you in the lurch, 'specially not now."

Arthur interjected softly, "Ma'am, we all Texans now, wherever we mighta came from. We ride for the brand, and we'll fight for it. We may be accidental like, but we here now. 'Til Rio tells us different, you are our brand."

Anna got up. "I...I don't know what to say." She ran to the bedroom and shut the door before collapsing on the bed in tears. *What have I done. What is this? I...I...do I love him?*

***

Monte held up a barely seen hand in the cold stark moonlight. Rio rode up beside him and asked softly, "Are we there?"

Monte replied, "No. Smelled smoke and got to lookin', see that flicker down there?" When Rio nodded, he said, "Guards. I guess ol' man Kidd ain't takin' any chances. We...can prolly get round them, but I'd rather wait. We can ease down another hunnert yards and stop at that little bench with the cave. Build a fire there and warm up for a while. I figger we got three hours to sunrise. Give 'em an hour to git real sleepy, then take 'em out."

"Let's do that. It's *cold* up here. Guess my nose is stuffed up, that's why I didn't smell anything"

With a snort, Monte led off again, the others following closely behind until they reached the bench. Monte said, "Y'all get some o' that driftwood. Don't break any limbs, just bring 'em back here." A few minutes later, a small fire burned in the mouth of the cave, men and horses crowding around it.

When Rio complained again about the cold, the others laughed, and Joe said, "Yore blood ain't thick enough for here. You ain't seen cold yet. Wait a couple of months, when there's six, mebbe eight feet of snow up here, and yore spit freezes afore it hits the ground."

Pronto disappeared for a few minutes, then returned and looked at Isom. "We need to take out the guards, you and Joe want to take them we spotted. They're 'bout two hundred yards down the ridge, jus' past a lightnin' struck rock. I seen one moving and looked like one sleepin'. Do what you think best. Kill em if you have to.

Isom turned to Arapaho Joe. "Shall we, my friend?"

Joe's smile was feral. "Let's go." The two of them left without a sound.

***

One of the guards was stooped over fire, dropping bacon in a pan on the fire, and the other appeared to be asleep in his bedroll as Isom and Joe stopped at the edge of the firelight.

Joe asked jocularly, "Isom, you want to kill this's or thet'un?"

The guard froze in position, only raising his head and looking around at Isom.

Isom grinned. "Hell, guess I'll take this one. That way when I shoot him, he won't land in the fire and spoil breakfast.

Joe walked quietly over to the guard asleep in his bedroll and put his old long rifle between the guard's eyes, jerking him awake. "Yeah, thet'll work, it is your turn to cook anyways." He glanced at Isom. "Least ways when I kill this'un I don't got to worry 'bout where he falls."

The first guard protested, "I ain't done nothin'! We jus' sittin' up here as guards. I ain't kilt nobody. I promise!"

Isom nudged him to sit down. "You boys have stepped in it. Somebody down there shot a friend of ours. And somebody from down there shot that girl, Alice, and killed her daddy, and somebody named Jud tried to have his way with Miss Anna." He poked the guard in the chest. "As far as we're concerned, all of you deserve to die for that."

Joe chimed in, "Lessen you got somethin' you think you can tell us thet might make us spare ya."

The other guard looked up at Joe past the rifle barrel still resting between his eyes. "I'll tell ya anythin' you want to know. Iff'n I do, will ya let me ride? I promise I'll never come back!"

Isom asked, "How many men down there? And how many are cowboys and how many gunnies?"

The guard on the ground said, "It wuz thirty-five, 'til Dunn and the others got kilt. There's fifteen of us drawin' gun pay, and ten reglar cowboys. We took the old bunkhouse, it's got more room and easier to sneak in and out of."

Joe spat at the fire. "How much they payin' for gunnies?"

'Fitty a month. 'Ceptin the two that been killin' anyone usin' the north route up the river. They get extry."

Isom chewed his lip for a second. "So, there are two who just kill people for just being in the wrong place?"

The guard sitting in front of him said, "Stiles and Henry. They...come in with a couple o' fancy rifles, one with one of them...long tubes on top of it. They kilt five or six men that wuz goin' up the Poudre. Kidd...wants all of the range, and losin' his boy just made him crazy!"

After a few more questions, including where their horses were, Joe retrieved their lariats from the saddles. Gagged and tied up, they hung the two guards upside down from a pine tree on the edge of the fire. Isom smiled at them, "You boys stay nice and quiet, and when we're done, we'll cut you loose."

Back at the cave, they told the others what they'd found as Tom fitted blasting caps into one stick in each of the six charges. Tom said, "Now these should go off when you hit 'em with yore rifles. But for God's sake, don't throw 'em or drop 'em. I ain't sayin' they'll go off on their own, but tain't worth takin' a chance."

Rio asked curiously, "Where'd you learn about dynamite?"

Tom chuckled. "Worked with this here giant powder a while down around Georgetown. Can't do it no more, it gives me too much of a headache."

Pronto looked around, counting noses. "Looks like we got six charges. Everbody remember the map Monte drew of the ranch yard?" They all nodded, and he started handing out charges and locations where he wanted them placed.

When Rio didn't get one, he asked, "What about me?"

Pronto smiled. "You ain't worth a damn when it comes to sneakin' around. Leave that to us. You can bring the hosses down to that last rise before the flats where we gonna shoot from. Put 'em on the backside o' that rise. By the time you get there, we should be up there too." He kicked the fire out and smiled at Rio. "And don't ferget my mule don't like to be tail end o' the line."

The six old mountain men disappeared into the darkness leaving Rio cussing as he strung the horses together behind Pronto's mule. He finally got them in motion and led them carefully down the creek to the agreed location, thankfully without any problems. Tying them to separate saplings gave each horse enough room to graze a little on the dry grass that remained. He realized he could make out trees, and the sky to the east was lightening, so he grabbed his carbine out of the sheath and hurried to the top of the rise.

He heard the click of a hammer being drawn back and stopped suddenly. "Pronto?" he said softly.

"Dammit, boy, you're noisy as a herd of squirrels. Everbody is back 'ceptin Isom. He was gonna try to stick one on the front porch."

Isom said, "I'm back got, within about ten feet of the porch, and somebody opened the front door. Got the charge behind a little pile of rock."

Joe added, "I got mine on the outhouse."

"Water trough in front of the bunk house," Tom said.

Monte chimed in, "Edge of the corral."

"Barn door," Jack said with a grin.

Pronto smiled. "Put mine on that big tree in front of the house. *Think* it might just knock that tree down." He motioned Rio in. "You gonna have to be the watch, since there's only six charges and six of us know where we put 'em."

Rio sighed. "I guess I'll dust any of them gunnies that come outta that old bunkhouse."

Pronto chuckled. "We'll fire on my owl hoot." Rio shook his head and smiled, and Pronto laughed. "Never did learn that did ya?"

Rio glared at him. "All the rest of the sounds I'm as good as you, but that damn owl, I just never could...."

Monte asked, "Am I missing something here?" He looked up at the sky. "We better git movin', we'll have enough light afore long.

***

Pronto hooted like an owl, and shots rang out. The outhouse exploded first, followed by the water trough in front of the bunkhouse. The first of the gunnies came boiling out of the old bunkhouse, and Rio fired into them just as Pronto hit the charge on the tree. It toppled majestically, the top branches hitting the old bunkhouse, and a couple of screams sounded.

Jack was cussing as he tried again for the charge on the barn door, but it had swung so that only one stick of the charge was visible. Monte hit the charge on the corral, which blew the barn door back open. Jack hit it then, and Isom took his time and nailed the charge in front of the steps. It blew the people coming onto the porch back into the house. Rio took two more shots at two gunnies that were turning toward them and firing at random toward the top of the hill. Pronto said, "Let's go."

Roger, Pete, and Jud were sprawled on the floor when Buck and Jack came through the back door and down the hallway. They helped the three Kidds groggily to their feet. Roger yelled, "Dammit, what is goin' on? Where is this comin' from?"

Buck peered out a broken window. "Looks like up on the ridge, boss, but I think it's stopped." Hearing the screams of pain, he continued, "Looks like we got a few boys down."

Roger staggered to the door and yanked it open. "Let's go! I want them bastards! Nobody shoots up my house! *Nobody!*"

Pete leaned on the wall and watched Roger disappear through the door. *You brought this on yourself, Pa, only you. If you had just left well enough alone, and Todd hadn't been stupid...* He pushed off the wall and resignedly followed Roger out the door. Buck and Jack followed quickly. Jud, holding his side and trembling from fear, slowly followed the others, making sure he was behind someone before he stepped out on the porch.

Smoke and flames blanketed the ranch yard. Some of the cowboys were trying to put out the fires with a bucket brigade, while others tended the wounded gunnies.

Roger grabbed Buck. "You and Jack get some boys and git up there, find them thet did this an' kill 'em!"

Buck nodded. "We'll go see what we can find, boss. C'mon Jack, let's get saddled up and git a couple of the others."

Roger yelled, "Five hunnert dollars to the man what kills one o' those bastards!"

Fifteen minutes later, Buck, Jack and several others rode out of the yard as Roger ran from place to place directing people, while Pete and the cowboys collected the dead gunnies and laid them out beside the old bunkhouse. Pete noted that none of the regular cowboys had been injured and wondered about that.

***

Rio and the others sat in their saddles at the cave, waiting for Monte and Fat Jack. They finally came around a corner of the trail trailing pine boughs on ropes behind the horses. Jack smiled. "Thet oughta do it. Lessen they got a real good tracker, or lookin' close, they ain't gonna find our back trail."

Monte chuckled. "Well, there ain't a lot o' ways up this here ridge, but we shore will confuse the hell outta them, with thet false trail we laid goin' north over the butte!"

Rio turned up the trail. "Let's ride." He glanced at Isom as he went by him. "I still can't believe what you two did. I'd have never thought of that."

Isom's smile was ugly. "Well, I had it done to me before. I always wanted to do it to somebody else. Worked pretty good, too!" He laughed. "That it did, yes sir, that it did, very fulfilling it was!"

***

Buck, Jack and the others came upon the two guards, tied up and hung upside down in a tree. One of them had managed to work his gag loose. "Cut us down, dammit. This ain't funny. My head's killin' me." Buck spit and drew his pistol shooting him in the chest.

"If you'd done yo job, we wouldn't a lost eight guys." Buck cut the rope holding them in the tree, and they fell to the ground. One rolled over, but the one Buck shot didn't move.

Jack got down and cut the bindings, and the surviving gunnie ripped the gag out of his mouth, gulping air as he did so. Looking up he said, "Thank you. I thought we wuz done for."

Jack rolled the other one over. "Thisun's dead, Buck."

Buck, still holding his pistol, pointed it at the surviving guard. "You sonsabitches were s'posed to be guardin' this ridge line, you don't deserve to live."

"Wait a minnit, they come on us, an' there was nothin' I could do." Buck motioned with his pistol and the gunnie said, "There wuz two of em, I wuz just stokin the fire and he," pointing to the body, "wuz still asleep. Next thing I know, I got a Sharps stuck in my gut; with the meanest lookin ol' Black man I ever seen on the other end of it. His partner had his rifle rammed into his

head, right 'tween the eyes. Go look! I bet the marks are still there! I swear!"

Buck replied angrily, "So, you let two ol' men sneak up on ya, and they done kilt 'bout eight of our folk and durn near blowed up the whole place."

The guard on the ground held up both hands. "Listen, they wuz mountain men, dressed in furs and buckskins. There wuz more than two, cause it seemed like they wuz jest tyin' us up when the shooting and explodin' started." He pointed up the ridge. "Last I heerd 'em, they wuz goin' that way. Jus' walkin' the horses like they wuz out fer a Sunday stroll."

Buck gestured with his pistol. "Git your horse or walk and git down to the ranch. Tell Roger what you tole us. If you're lucky, he'll let you live." He looked at the rest of the gunnies. "Let's go see if we kin find thet damn trail. If they be lolligaggin' along, we might pick 'em off. Mount up, Jack! Let's go!"

Once they'd ridden out of sight, the remaining guard found his horse and the other guard's still tied to the tree. Looking carefully around, he collected his former partner's guns, money, and saddlebags. He untied both horses, put them on lead ropes, mounted, and rode quickly north on the bluff, the opposite direction to the ranch.

An hour or so later, Buck, Jack, and the other gunnies, frustrated in their search for tracks, stumbled on the false trail heading north. Buck looked at the trail and spat on the ground. "Dammit, we wasted a couple o' hours chasin' our tails up that crick." He looked up at the sun's position and added. "Almost noon. They're long gone by now. Guess we might as well go on back to the ranch. The old man can't say we didn't try." They turned their horses down toward the main ranch and rode morosely back to face Roger Kidd.

***

Rio and the mountain men rode quickly back up the creek, then followed the river back down toward the Neville place. Turning up the trail to the ranch, Rio finally relaxed for the first time. He grinned and glanced over at Pronto. "Looks like we made it!"

Pronto spat off to the side. "Mebbe. Now we gotta see what Kidd is gonna do. That means puttin' guards out down here and prolly up at the cabin too."

Rio's head dropped, then he looked up at the bright sunlight. "You don't make this easy, do you?"

"Tain't supposed to be easy. 'Specially when you in charge. Allus somethin' else to worry 'bout."

"Can we do it? Can we pull this off, Pronto?"

Pronto shrugged and spat again. "Dunno. Gonna be up to you and how well you figger out what to do."

Just how the hell am I supposed to do that, Pronto? Y'all are...no, y'all are mountain men. Your experiences are entirely different. If...maybe a melding of the two? I know how we defended the ranch at home, and y'all know the mountains. I gotta talk to Monte.

Chapter 18

Anna sat in a chair on the porch, as Rio and others gathered in the yard. Monte stood on the steps looking around. When everyone was there, Monte said, "Been two days. Kinda surprised there ain't been any reaction outta Kidd. But we can't drop our guard." He pointed to Fat Jack and Cavanaugh. "Awright, it's y'alls turn down at the creek bottom. Ride careful and if there's any problems, fire three shots and come a foggin' back up here."

Jack smiled. "C'mon kid, time for s'more lessons." Rene shook his head but smiled as he headed for the corral.

Rio said, "Pronto and I'll take the mountain tonight."

Monte asked, "You gonna stay at the cabin all night?"

Pronto rubbed his back ruefully. "Yeah, these ol bones ain't handlin' sleepin' on this hard ground in the cold."

Jack asked, "Who be our relief?"

Monte looked around. "Tom and Joe at midnight." Jack nodded and walked toward the corral.

As the group began to break up, Anna stood and motioned to Rio come over. Rather than dismount, he rode close to the step, setting Anna's teeth on edge once again. She snapped, "What's the matter, afraid I'll bite?"

"I ain't gonna take any chances. We need to get going."

"It's been almost two days, and other than that first day, nothing has happened. Monte just got back from town and says my sister is doing better." She watched Jack and Cavanaugh ride out then said, "I want to get Alice out here as soon as I can. Doc told Monte that she should be able to be moved any time.

Rio grimaced. "We'll see. I'm kinda worried that Kidd hasn't fought back any more. I don't know what he's waiting on."

"I don't know either, but I don't want my sister to be a target again or a hostage against me." She looked pleadingly at Rio. "Will you help me get her home? *Please?*"

Rio replied gruffly, "In a couple of days. We'll have to figure out who to have where to make sure both the ranch and her are covered when we make the move."

Anna smiled. "Thank you, Rio." She started to turn away, then looked back. "Why are you scared of me, Rio?"

Startled, Rio blurted, "Well, I ain't, I mean, I'm not!"

"Then why do you avoid me at all costs?" She pressed.

"Cause it ain't right. You know what I am, and you don't want somebody like me," he replied angrily.

Anna's temper rose, and she put her hands on her hips. "How do *you* know what I want?"

Pronto rode up interrupting them. "Y'all sound like two spoiled brats arguin' over a toy." He glared at Rio. "We need to git up the hill to the cabin. I want one good look at that trail afore dark. I gotta get the range to that boulder agin'. If they come back we can stand 'em off there."

"Let's go! I'm ready." Rio turned Red and trotted toward the river, Pronto following as Anna walked to edge of porch, watching them ride away. *How do you know what I want Rio? You never stay around long enough to find out.* When they disappeared around the trees, she turned and walked sadly into the house.

***

Roger Kidd was pacing the floor. Pete, Jud, Billy, Buck and Jack sat around the dining table, and two gunnies leaned against the door. "Awright, Talbot found out thet girl is getting better, an' they want ta git her outta the Doc's place." He looked around at the men. "He says thet they come in 'bout ever two days, so I'm a guessin' they gonna try to move her in the next day or so".

He stopped pacing in front of Buck, who turned and looked up at him. "Buck, you an' Jack git the three best shots we got with the rifles. I want you to take 'em to town tomorrow. I'ma take the rest and we gonna go burn that damn Nevell place to the ground and kill everone there."

Pete interrupted, "Pa! Let it go! We need to work the ranch. We've got to fix the damage, and we've got cows that need to be moved.

Roger stormed around the table to Pete. He yelled, "No, dammit! I ain't never gonna let it go! They kilt Todd, and they gonna pay!" His face red, he turned away muttering, "I'm not gonna quit 'til they're dead. I ain't runnin' no more."

Roger started pacing around the table again. Angrily he continued, "Buck, I want you an' Jack, you gonna be in the stable, up in the hayloft." He thought for a second. "That'll give you a look down the main street. We gonna take 'em when they move thet girl. I guess they gonna do it day after tomorrow, since that'll be two days. Probably early mornin', probably try to git her out o' town afore most folks wake up and start movin' around. You two'll be the last ditch." He stopped at the head of the table, gripping the back of the chair. "We'll go up early and burn thet infernal place, then ride inta town and hit 'em when they all together, either at the Doc's or in the main street.

He jerked the chair out and sat heavily, then turned to Buck. "I want you to scatter them rifles around, make sure we got good cover, cause I wanta kill 'em all!" A wild look came into his eyes as he raised his voice. "I'll challenge 'em to get 'em when they start loadin' the girl, then you shoot 'em. You hear me?"

Buck nodded. "I hear you, Boss. I'll git it done. You want me to wait 'til you draw?"

Roger shook his head. "Hell no! As soon as you see me crouch, you shoot!"

Pete interrupted again, "Pa, if you do that, they'll arrest you for murder!"

"Shut up boy, what are you? Turnin' yella on me? They kilt your brother. They gonna *pay*!" Marginally calmer he said, "I pay thet damn sheriff and Talbot enough they won't touch me. 'Sides, we can allus find a witness thet they drew first, and iff'n they all dead, who's gonna say thet ain't the way it happened?" His grin broadened until Pete got up and walked out as Roger screamed incoherently at him.

Jud huddled in his chair, looking wide-eyed as his daddy as Billy winced, wondering what was going to happen if this went wrong.

***

Late next morning, Anna gathered everyone in front of the house again. Rio stood with the men in the ranch yard. She stepped to the edge of the porch. "Tomorrow we're going to get Alice. It's time she was here and safe with us. Rio, will you come up and tell everyone what has been decided?"

Rio looked around and walked slowly up steps to stand next to Anna. Monte and Pronto, standing at the back of the crowd, a little apart, glanced at each other. Monte punched Pronto in the ribs, "They make a hell of a couple, don't they?"

Pronto leaned over, rubbing his ribs. "Yeah, but I'm afraid it ain't gonna work."

"Why in hell not?"

Chuckling, Pronto replied, "Cause I'm pretty sure once this is done, Rio's gonna high tail it, in the middle of the night if he has to."

Rio glanced quickly at Anna and said nervously, "Pronto, Monte, you ol' farts shut up for a minute, will ya?" Both of them glared at him, but he went on, "Here's what we come up with. This afternoon Fat Jack, you and your boys will—"

Jack interrupted, "Boys? *Boys*? Damn *boy*, you blind?" Everyone, including Anna, laughed as Rio turned red from the neck up.

Shaking his head, Rio cleared his throat. "Lemme try that again, will ya?" There were smiles, so he continued, "Fat Jack and those going with him, how's that?" There was another round of laughter, and he continued, "They'll ride into town this afternoon. They'll check out the town tonight and be ready in the morning with the wagon hitched up when we come in. The rest of us'll leave before sunrise, bringing Anna with us. We'll plan to be at the Doc's place around eight, just about the time it's good and light, and safe enough to drive the wagon fast if we need to." He looked around. "Won't be anybody left here, but we think it's important enough to have everybody to get Alice back here safe."

He looked out over everyone and added, "Pronto, you, Monte and the other mountain men are gonna be our safe passage. The rest of us cowboys will form a wall of bodies as we leave the doc's place. Anna is going to drive the wagon, with Alice in the back. Once we clear town, I'd like to have the mountain men watching our back trail. The rest of us will ride ahead of the wagon.

Jeb tipped his hat back and asked, "And if we git hit before then?"

Rio said grimly, "Kill 'em. We need to get Alice outta there. That's what this is all about. Just remember, Pronto and the others are probably the best rifle shots there are. They ain't gonna miss, if push comes to shove. John, you and Arthur will be in the wagon. If it comes to shooting, get Alice out of town anyway you can, and we'll cover you.

Anna laid a hand on Rio's arm. "I just want to thank all of you men for what you are doing. Without you, I'd probably be dead right now and my family wiped out. Regardless of what happens, please keep Alice alive."

Three hours later, Monte and the other mountain men rode quietly out of the ranch yard. Anna stood on the porch watching them leave and wondered what tomorrow would bring. She walked back in the house and shivered as a cold chill ran down her spine. Rubbing her arms, she busied herself with fixing supper for the remaining cowboys.

***

Everyone had eaten supper and helped clean up. Pronto had Rene cleaning the cast iron pan and was joking with Juan about the weather when Anna realized Rio wasn't in the house. Shrugging into her coat, she walked out on the porch and saw him walking away from the house toward the sunset. Curious, she stepped off the porch and followed him. Rio stopped at the head of the trail into the mountains and watched the sun dipping toward the horizon, lighting the clouds with multiple colors.

Anna stepped up beside him, and he glanced at her. "It's beautiful. Not something we ever see in Texas. And it's cold up here."

She put her hand on Rio's arm. "I grew up with this. It's...normal to me." She turned to face him. "I meant what I said earlier. If anything happens, keep Alice alive."

"Do you care so little for yourself?"

"It's not that, it's just that I'm responsible for her now. She *has* to live!" She paused for a second, then said softly, "I want to thank you, too."

Rio faced her. "For what?"

Angrily, Anna stepped back. "God! Men are so dumb sometimes!"

"Whatta you mean by that?"

"Let me see if I can get it through that thick head of yours. If it weren't for you and your friends, *none* of my family, including me, would be here."

"But you know what I am."

"Yeah, a real dummy!" Impulsively, she grabbed him and kissed him square on the lips. "Oh, damn you, Rio!" Pushing him away, she ran back to the house.

***

Up at the Kidd ranch, the dead had been buried and the cowboys were in the final throes of cleaning up the remnants of the old bunkhouse and fixing the barn door and corral. Buck looked around at the gunnies he'd selected. "Alright, boys. We done all we can here. Time to git us some revenge. Bring plenty o' ammo with you. Git yore best hoss, cause we gonna have to do some ridin' today and tomorrer." An hour later, the five of them cantered out of the ranch yard.

Jack asked, "Where we gonna stay, Buck?"

"We'll git a few rooms at Gerties. It's right between the stable and saloon, so we won't have far to go in the morning."

Burns, always taciturn, almost to the point of never speaking, cantered up beside Buck. "Why we doin' this?"

Buck shrugged. "Cause we git paid."

"Don't like shootin' no woman."

Glaring at him, Buck said, "So'right. Don't shoot the damn woman. Just shoot the men."

"We gonna get paid like you and Jack do?"

"What is with you, Burns? You ain't said this many words in...a year."

"Don't feel right. I jus' wanna get paid for my kills."

Burns' intensity worried Buck, since he'd heard stories about Burns going off the deep end when he felt he'd been insulted. "I'll make sure you git paid. Jus' don't say nothin' to anybody else."

Burns nodded. "Good 'nuff." He dropped back to his usual place on the trail, at the back of the group.

Jack rode up. "What'd Burns want?"

Buck spat off to the side. "Money, what else?"

Two hours later, they rode up to the stable in Fort Collins, and Buck told the hostler, "Want 'em watered, and fed good grain on the Circle K. We'll be ridin' out in the morning, so make sure they're ready to go."

The holster gulped and said, "Yessir. Water and grain. Ain't no room in the stalls, I'll put 'em in the corral for the night."

Buck scowled. "Feed and water 'em first." They dismounted, taking their rifles and saddlebags. They headed next door to Gertie's, and Buck arranged for three rooms. Taking one room for himself, he dropped his gear and walked next door to the saloon. Taking a back table, he sat down facing the door and waited for the others to come in. Once they were all there, he sent Jack for a bottle and to get the barkeep to get them some food.

Once everyone had a drink, Buck toasted, "Here's to us killin' them damn mountain men." They all threw back their drinks, and the bottle went around the table again. Buck leaned in. "Here's how we gonna do it in the mornin'. Me and Jack gonna be in the hayloft over the stable." He looked at Burns. "I want you on top o' the hotel. That gives you the best shot up the side street where Doc's office is. Garcia, I want you in the alley by the mercantile. Gascon, I want you on t'other side o' the street, at the corner o' the hotel. Us high shooters will hit 'em first, y'all take anybody that gits on the ground."

A couple of minutes later, the cook delivered plates of beef and beans, and Buck switched to drinking beer. "Don't y'all git too drunk. We gotta be able to see to shoot. And mornin's gonna come early.

Garcia asked, "Do we need to scout the doc's place?"

"Nah. They gotta come back to the main street and turn to go back toward their ranch. Better place to shoot here, don't wanta git back amongst them houses. Who knows who's liable to pop you out a winder." He took another drink and belched. "Sides, where I got you, ain't nobody sneakin' up behind you, and we ain't gotta worry about shootin' anybody else. The ol' man's bought the sheriff and deputy, so we can do what is needful then git on our hosses and ride outta here."

**

Monte, Pronto, and Isom were quietly planning how to best position the others the morning, when there was a soft tapping on the door. Jack and Joe slipped silently into the room. Pronto asked, "What did you find out?"

Jack replied, "Some of them gunnies are in town. Saw some Circle K brands down at the stable."

Joe added, "There's at least four or five gunnies in the saloon. They gittin' pretty liquored up. Don't think we can chance takin 'em now. Not without one hell of a fight."

Jack said, "I ain't seen Pete or the boy Jud, but I sent Tom to check out the restaurant. He wuz wantin' some bear sign. Unless we kilt a bunch, I dunno where the rest of 'em are. But I think we gotta get 'em in the mornin' for sure."

Pronto looked at Monte. "What do ya think, Monte?"

"I think Jack's right, and Tom, too. We gotta git em in the mornin'. We gonna have it to do, boys."

Isom said, "Yes, if we want keep Alice alive, we are going to have to open the ball. If we wait for them to act, it could be too late."

Tom asked, "What about we just try to git 'em at the corral? Bet they all gonna go there and check their hosses before they git ready to fight. They gonna want to make a quick getaway."

Pronto nodded. "Yep, we can do thet. Fat Jack, who's the best shot?"

"Tom."

"Why don't you git him up on the roof of the hotel in the mornin'?"

Jack smiled. "I kin do thet. I'll tell him not to shoot less'n sombody else opens the ball."

"The rest of us'll meet at the stable at dawn."

Joe said, "I'll go get Tom and drag him back here. T'otherwise, we'll never get him outta that café if they have bear sign. T'ain't never seed anyone so hung on sweets." A round of laughter followed that comment as Joe slipped out of the room.

Ten minutes later, Tom appeared, a hang dog expression on his face. "No bear sign. Didn't see none o' them. I'm goin' to sleep." With that, they dispersed to their respective rooms to get some sleep.

Chapter 19

Anna paced nervously in the darkness, *I hope we can do this without any problems or anyone getting hurt. I don't...hell, I'm not going to get back to sleep. Might as well fix breakfast.* She went into the kitchen, lit the lamp, put on an apron, stoked the stove, and started a pot of coffee. Slicing bacon, she looked at the pile, then shrugged and sliced the rest of the bacon. *Eggs, I wonder...* Throwing on a coat, she went out to the chicken coop, opened the door and winced as it squeaked. She was reaching under a chicken when she heard voices. She froze until she realized it was Flynn and Arthur. She decided to be on the safe side and said, "Gents, it's me. I'm in the chicken coop getting eggs."

She heard Flynn just outside. "Miss Anna, you need to warn folks before you do something like that."

She came out, apron full of eggs and replied, "Sorry. I...didn't think anyone else was up."

Arthur chuckled. "We all awake now, Mizz Anna."

She blew out a breath. "Well, the coffee is on."

A half hour later, with everyone fed, Flynn pulled out his pocket watch. "Five o'clock. We might as well go on in. It is going to take us an hour to get there. The earlier the better, as far as I'm concerned."

Anna sipped her coffee. "Well, there's about enough for a half cup each, so let's finish the coffee." She poured as people shoved their cups over.

Juan smiled as he said, "*Muchas gracias, Señorita!*

"*Da Nada.*"

Cavanaugh nodded and asked, "Where did you learn Spanish, Ma'am?"

Anna laughed. "I know a few words, but not many. I was learning from Aunt Bea's maid at school."

Rio got up suddenly. "Let's get going. We'll get the horses ready. You want your fancy saddle?"

"No, I can ride astride. I have a split skirt. I...think a regular saddle would be better today." The men left, and she quickly changed, put on her heavy coat, and made sure the fire was banked. Slipping her pistol in the jacket pocket, she started out the door then stopped and went back, picking up the Spencer carbine. She quickly made sure it was topped up with seven rounds and one was loaded in the chamber. She took a handful of spare cartridges from the box on the mantle and shoved them in her other jacket pocket. Slipping on her gloves, she looked around then blew out the lamp and walked out the door.

As she walked to the barn, she heard Rio cussing loud and long. She smiled, *He is human after all.* As she walked into the barn, she realized his horse had a problem. "What's wrong?"

Arthur said, "Looks like Red's goin' lame, or needs a new shoe. I ain't got time to do that."

She replied, "Well, you can ride the grey. He's a good horse. Daddy bought him...three years ago now, and he is an easy ride." She reached in the feed bin and grabbed a couple of carrots. "If I can find a hackamore, I'll go get him." Setting her rifle down, she saw one hanging with the tack and pulled it down, then walked up to the corral and lured the grey to the gate. She got the hackamore on with no problem and led him back to the barn. "Here you are."

Rio looked at him and said, "He's damn near white! I...thank you."

Arthur smiled and Flynn turned away, coughing to cover a laugh as Rio quickly pulled the saddle off Red. Arthur put Red back in a stall and finished getting Anna's horse ready. "I found a small saddle, I'm guessin' that was yours?"

She waggled her hand. "Either mine or Alice's. The stirrups should be the right length either way."

A few minutes later, the six of them rode into the early morning moonlight, Anna leading, as she knew the trail by heart.

***

Jud shivered in his thick coat as he rode beside Roger Kidd. "Pa, why'd you leave Pete at the ranch?"

Roger glared at him. "Pete ain't...somebody's gotta keep the cowboys in line. You ain't capable o' that. And I want the doc to take a look at you. Sumthin's wrong with you, you ain't been right since you got shot."

"I hurt, Pa! I think I done got infected."

Snorting, Roger snapped, "As much o' my whisky you drunk, I don't see how." He looked around, then spoke up, "'Bout another mile, mebbe two, to the river. We'll cross and burn the Nevell place, then come back to town and take care o' the rest of 'em."

Arnulf, the German gunnie, asked, "We burn it all, or just the ranch house?"

"Just the house. We kin use thet barn and them corrals. I seen 'em two years ago." He thought for a minute and added, "But iff'n they fort up in the barn, burn it too. Matter o' fact, I want you, Gonzales, and...is Morty back there?"

Morty mumbled, "Right here, Boss?"

"You go with them two. Search the barn, then hit the house."

Jud whined, "Pa, I gotta take a piss."

"Oh fer Gawd sakes. Alright, everbody stop. Do what you gotta. As soon as Judson here is done, we gonna go kill usn's the assholes that kilt Todd!"

***

All of the mountain men assembled in the lobby of the hotel as the first rays of light poked over the horizon. Pronto said, "Alright, everbody knows what they supposed to do. Tom, go head and get on the roof. We'll mosey down to the stable and see who shows up"

The group went down the back hall, out the back door, and down the alley as Tom started up the ladder nailed to the back wall. Five minutes later, they were concealed in the shadows around the stable and corral, rifles in hand.

A couple of minutes later they heard voices grumbling as a group of men came out of the front door of Gertie's. They crouched and spread out as the men came closer and they heard Buck say, "Burns should be on the roof by now. Somebody check his hoss for him. Pronto and Monte stepped around the corner and confronted them, his rifle raised. "Where you boys think you're goin'?"

Buck tried to bluster through it, "Just checkin' our hosses, ol' man. What bidness is it of your'n?"

"Is that all of 'em, Isom?"

Isom, Fat Jack, and Arapaho Joe stepped out behind the gunnies. "Yep, don't see anybody else comin'."

Pronto nodded. "Awright boys, drop 'em nice and easy. We got ya. And yore buddy on the roof is bein' taken care of, too."

One of the gunnies at the back asked, "What iff'n I don't want to?"

Pronto stepped out. "I killed that Todd kid. You wanna try me? Even up?"

Joe stepped silently up and hit the gunnie with the rifle butt. He dropped, unconscious and Joe said, "That be what happens." He spat and grinned evilly at the other gunnies, as Isom grinned behind him.

Monte chuckled. "Any more questions?" He shifted his rifle, not quite pointing at Buck, but very close. "How many more of ya are there?"

Buck started sweating, realizing these old men weren't playing any games. "Five. Countin' Burns, he's...on the hotel roof."

They relived the gunnies of their pistols, rifles, and knives then tied and gagged them. Isom pondered, "I don't know if he told the truth, but we got some of them."

Fat Jack said, "Think you're right Isom, but I'm not sure I trust 'em. Looks like we better spread out. Jus' watch out who ya shoot."

Pronto said, "I'll sit here and guard 'em." The others started fanning out, and he glanced worriedly at the roof. *I hope you got that guy, Tom. But we ain't been shot, so mebbe you did.*

The sun was peeking over the horizon as Long Tom eased onto the hotel roof. As he started toward the front of the hotel, he saw the outline of a man, crouched behind the top of the false front. Tom set his Sharps quietly on the roof and started to pull his pistol, then thought better of it, holstered the pistol and drew his knife. Thinking for a moment, he moved quietly across the roof on cat feet.

As he approached, some sixth sense made the man turn, rifle in hand. Surprised, he didn't react quickly enough and Tom was on him, knife in hand. They struggled silently, with only the sounds of blows, the scuff of feet on the roof, and heavy breathing heard.

Tom ended up on the bottom, struggling to keep the man from stabbing him, until he suddenly arched his back and blood flowed from Tom's mouth. The gunnie looked down in wonder and relaxed his grip momentarily. When he did, Tom arched one more time and stabbed him in the heart with his Bowie knife. The man collapsed on top of Tom, who struggled to lift him off. Exhausted, Tom stopped struggling and smiled as the sun shown on him. He died with his eyes open and a smile on his face, still gripping the knife in Burns' chest.

***

Anna stopped at the trees above the river just as it started to get light. Rio rode up beside her and asked, "Why'd you stop?"

"I...I thought I heard something. Maybe somebody saying something."

"That..." Rio cocked his head. Turning, he hissed, "Horses coming." He quickly pulled his gloves off and started unbuttoning his coat. "Let's get across the river!" Leading them down to the river, he pushed the grey into the water and felt him shiver, but he kept going.

Almost across, he heard a shout and Anna screamed, "It's the Kidds! Watch out, Rio!"

Jud rode up beside Roger, who had stopped short of the river. "It's that bitch!" He scrabbled under his coat and pulled his pistol, "I'm gonna kill you, you bitch! He started firing as Rio dropped the reins and drew, snapping a shot at the man. There was a maelstrom of pistol and shotgun fire, and Rio vaguely heard a carbine fire from behind him. Spurring the grey, he jumped him into the horses in front of him, firing first at the big unkempt man in front of him as he saw flame blossom from his pistol and felt a blow low down on his left side. The man disappeared, from in front of Rio and he switched guns, shooting at the man on his right who was trying to shoot and control his horse at the same time. He fell away and Rio triggered another shot at the one that had yelled at Anna, who toppled out of his saddle. He continued pulling the trigger, but his pistols were empty.

He looked frantically around and sighed when Anna rode up next to him. "Are you alright?"
Biting her lip, she nodded. He suddenly felt weak and looked down to see his shirt covered in blood. He tried to holster his pistols, but they fell to the ground as he turned to her. "I...love you, Anna. I..." He tumbled from the saddle, her scream ringing in his ears as the world turned black.

Anna jumped down, tears streaming from her eyes. "Rio...Rio!" She put her hand on his chest and felt the slow rise and fall of his breathing. Looking up, she saw Cavanaugh and Jeb ride over. "Rene, Jeb, help me get him back on his horse. He's...alive."

Juan was riding through the downed men, cussing vehemently in Spanish as he made sure they were all dead. Arthur jumped off his horse and helped the others lift Rio back into the grey's saddle, then used piggin strings to tie his hands to the saddle horn.

Flynn, pistol in hand, slumped in his saddle as he watched, blood seeping through his coat near his shoulder.

Anna turned to him, "Are you...can you make it to town?" She ran to him. "Can you? It's only a mile, but we have to cross the river again."

"I can. Were you hit? There's blood on your sleeve and your coat."

She felt the pain for the first time and staggered a bit. "I'll...let's go! Rio...we have to save Rio!" She scrambled back into the saddle and pulled the grey's reins over its head as Cavanaugh and Arthur quickly remounted. She led off at a trot and vaguely heard Flynn tell Juan to leave the bodies.

***

Pronto jerked up when he heard the rattle of gunfire in the distance. Jumping to his feet, he stepped to the corner of the stable before he realized it wasn't in town. He saw the gunnies all looking around and said, "Welp, looks like somebody started somethin'."

He saw Monte step out and wave, and he looked down at the gunnies. Making up his mind quickly, he said, "We got 'nuther one of us on top of the hotel. He can see y'all plain as day. Gonna tell him to shoot you if you move." He trotted down the street toward Monte as Fat Jack came around the corner a block further up.

When he got to Monte, he asked, "Any idea where that came from?"

"It was off to the west. I'm thinkin' the river crossin'."

"Rio 'n them?"

Monte shrugged. "No idee. But somebody was doin' a passel o' shootin'."

Jack trotted up and said, "Off to the west. Pistol, rifle, and a coupla shotgun blasts."

"Shit. That's...Arthur. But who were they shootin' at?" He looked around. "Where's Isom?"

Joe walked out from between two buildings, head hanging. He crossed the street, almost in a daze. When he got to them, tears were rolling down his face. "Tom bought it. But he took one o' the bastards with him." He pointed to the roof, where Isom waved. "I was halfway up thet damn ladder when Isom stuck his head over and said Tom was dead with the dead bastard layin' on top of him. Where'd the shootin' come from?"

Joe answered, "Off to the west. Pronto thinks it our folks."

Joe shuddered. "I'ma get my horse and go find out. I jus' might shoot them bastards while I'm at it."

Pronto shook his head. "No, leave 'em. We'll turn 'em over to the law." He started back to the stable, stopped, and looked over his shoulder. "I think we all better go, in case...just in case." The four of them headed for the stable at a trot, and Pronto said, "Need to saddle Isom's horse, too."

They were in the process of getting all the horses saddled when they heard a rifle shot. Monte ran to the door and saw Isom waving and pointing up the street. He looked and saw five horses coming in at a gallop with one man on a grey swaying in the saddle. Then he picked out Arthur and yelled back into the stable, "Looks like our folks are comin' in quick like. Somebody's been shot, barely stayin' in the saddle." He saw them turn down the side street toward the doc's place. "They goin' to the doc. We better get up there."

***

Anna slid her horse to a stop, almost losing control of the grey Rio was on. She dropped the reins and ran up the steps as the door opened. "Doc! Rio's been shot bad. He...I think he's still alive. Where?"

Doc Ferrell pushed past her as Arthur and Jeb lowered Rio to the ground. He reached down and felt his chest move. "Bring him in the office. I've got...a table to put him on." He looked at the group and saw that Flynn was bleeding and Juan was grey with pain. "Both of you shot, too?"

Flynn slid off his horse and staggered. "Hit in the arm. Juan...I think he's hit in the leg. Take care of Rio and Anna, we'll get there."

Doc turned to Cavanaugh. "Go in the house and tell my wife I need boiling water, as quick as possible, in the office." He took Anna by the arm and led her into his office, taking her coat off as soon as she was through the door. Her sleeve was ripped at the top of the shoulder, and there was blood at her waist. He pulled her shirt up and blew out a breath. "You...got grazed twice. Get my wife to clean you up while I work on Rio."

Rene took off at a run as Pronto and the other mountain men rode up, weapons at the ready. Monte jumped off his horse and helped the others as they carried Rio into the doc's office and laid him on the metal table. Doc immediately started cutting Rio's shirt open, and Monte reached down and took his gunbelt off, noting the empty holsters.

Isom and Jack came in carrying Juan, with Joe supporting Flynn. "Where's Pronto?"

"He's lookin' for Anna. She...disappeared."

Pronto found Anna hugging Alice, tears in her eyes, and Cavanaugh standing in the door saying, "Mizz Anna, you need to get the doc to look at your arm. You're still bleeding."

Pronto turned him around. "Rene, go get everbody's horses and get 'em tied off." When he left, Pronto gently asked, "What happened?"

Anna looked up, swiped at her tears and said, "I killed Jud Kidd!" Alice looked up at her in horror as she continued, "We were...at the river crossing. Halfway across, the...Kidds came down the other bank. Jud cursed at me and...drew his pistol. I...was behind Rio and...he...guns were firing and I bent over to get the carbine. I...got it out and Jud was...grinning at me. I... shot him off his horse, then shot him again. We...couldn't turn around, everybody rode toward them. When...I mean everybody was shooting. It all happened so fast." She looked up at Pronto. "And...Rio told me he loves me. He can't die! He just *can't*!" She collapsed on top of Alice, who gently patted her back and tried to soothe her.

Pronto headed for the office and met Mrs. Ferrell on the way out. "Ma'am, Anna, I think she's been shot in the left arm and down by her waist. There's blood. If you could—"

"I'll take care of her. *Do not* let anybody hurt my husband," she said emphatically.

"We won't, ma'am." He hurried out of the house and over to the office. Stumping into the office, he heard the doctor in the back and went back there. Doc Farrell was cussing and working on Rio as Isom helped by holding various instruments for him. Flynn sat slumped in a chair as Arthur wrapped a bandage around his upper arm. Juan sat in another chair arguing with Jack and Monte about cutting his pants off, saying these were his best pants. A bloody bandanna was tied around his upper thigh with blood soaking through it. Juan saw him and straightened as much as he could.

"We killed them all, *Señor* Pronto, and the *Señorita,* she killed the one that cursed her. *Señor* Rio, he led us through them." Juan slumped back and moaned. "Getting shot is *not* a fun thing. I do not like it."

Pronto stepped around the table and looked down at Rio, watched his chest moving fitfully, but moving, as the doc worked over at least three holes in his torso. He looked down at his pants and notice blood on his calf. "Um, Doc, I think he's hit in the leg, too."

Doc looked up distractedly, "Well, if I don't get these holes up here plugged, that leg wound ain't going to make any difference. Where's my hot water?"

"I'll go get it, Doc."

***

Four hours later, Rio was still alive, Juan and Flynn had been patched up, and Anna had been treated for an inch-deep through and through wound above her hip and a graze to her arm. She was knocked out in the bed with her sister as the mountain men prowled restlessly around the property. Talbot had been there and been run off without answers. When Jack went to get Tom's horse, he'd come back almost frothing at the mouth. "Somebody let thet damn bunch o' gunnies go! They rattled hocks outta here not long after we come over here, according to the hostler."

Tom's and Burns' bodies had been recovered from the roof of the hotel, and Tom lay in the shed behind the doc's house in the shed, wrapped in a tarp. Burns had been turned over to the undertaker.

Pronto, Monte, and Arthur had ridden out to the site of the attack, recovered Rio's pistols and counted bodies. Seven people had been killed. Two by Arthur with Old Betsy, and from where Rio's gun were lying, he'd taken out Roger Kidd and at least one other. Three others had also been downed by pistols, and Jud Kidd had been shot twice in the chest by Anna's Spencer carbine. Monte confirmed that Pete Kidd was not among the dead, and the others with Roger and Jud were part of the group of gunnies Roger had hired. They'd gathered up the guns and rode back to town, telling the undertaker where the bodies and horses were.

Chapter 20

Two weeks passed, Anna and Alice had been taken home by the mountain men, who guarded the ranch day and night. They buried Long Tom next to Smiley at the ranch, and Anna said a prayer over him as Alice stood next to her, tears on both their faces.

Ed Bell had shown up two days after the shooting, having gotten word through the Indians that Ethan had been killed. He'd come up the trail, changing horses at every herd he came across, and didn't know that Rio had been shot either time. He was shocked to see him lying in the back of the doctor's office, delirious and clinging to life. Glancing up at the doctor, he asked, "What are his chances?"

Doc Ferrell replied, "Well, he was shot four times. I got the bullets out, but...he was weak from being sick from the graze he got on the head. I honestly don't know if he'll make it or not. I'm giving him laudanum when I can get it down him, and a little soup when he's...able to swallow on his own. If he doesn't get enough to eat, he isn't going to make it."

He nodded. "I understand, Doc, and I appreciate everything you're doing. I'll be back."

A couple of hours later, a tense meeting had occurred in the sheriff's office between Pete Kidd, John Flynn, Arthur, and Ed Bell over the shootings and the killing spree. Pete Kidd said, "Jud was infatuated with both Anna and Alice ever since they had moved into the area. When Anna left, he went after Alice, but she wouldn't have anything to do with him." He put his head in his hands and continued, "Pa hired more gunnies and...well, he went crazy after Todd was killed. There are no gunnies left at the ranch, just a few cowboys left, and I'm not sure we can get through the winter." He looked up at the others with tears in his eyes. "This...was all so stupid. If Pa had reined in Todd, none of this would have happened. I can't believe Jud tried to kill Anna!"

Flynn replied, "Well, he first tried to kidnap her, when that didn't work, I guess killing her was his logical next step to keep her from talking."

Ed hadn't said a word, just listened to all of the conversation that swirled around him, biding his time. After the meeting he walked back to the hotel with Flynn, Arthur, and Cavanaugh. "Y'all ready to go back to Texas?"

Flynn and Arthur looked at each other, and Arthur said, "I am. Them ol' mountain men gonna keep things quiet round here. And Pronto ain't leavin' Rio."

Flynn tipped his head. "I'm ready Ed, I don't think I'm needed here, and I'd like to get back, too. Did Eli make it back yet?"

Bell nodded. "Yep, Eli got home...last month. His first trip up the Chisholm trail was apparently rather interesting to hear him tell it." He gave Flynn enough money to pay for their tickets leaving the next morning via train to St. Louis, steamer to New Orleans, and a packet boat to Matamoros. "John, I expect you to get them home. Tell Hattie I'll be home as soon as I...see what happens with Rio.

Ed saw Jeb and Juan at the ranch when he rode out to talk to Monte, and Juan professed to be hurting too badly to ride the train and wanted to stay at the ranch, hobbling around on a crutch. He didn't miss the fact that Juan made moon eyes at Alice, who blushed every time she saw him, but didn't tell him to go away.

Anna had been coming to town every other day to check on Rio, sitting with him for hours on end, reading to him, holding his hand, and, when she could, getting him to take a little water or soup. Doc Ferrell vacillated between pride that he'd saved Rio and worry that he would collapse and die without ever recovering. Ed had overheard Rio raving about Anna, once overhearing him in his delirium begging her to marry him as she held his hand. She'd wept and said yes, but that he had to survive. He never told anyone what he'd seen and heard, tiptoeing away before Anna knew he was there.

Doc was also scared of what would happen if Rio died and its impact on Anna. He's heard Rio's ravings about loving Anna and all the other things he'd been saying. Mrs. Ferrell had also seen Anna come out of the room where Rio lay, in tears more than once. She'd tried to comfort her, only to have her cry even harder. The Ferrells didn't know what to do with the two of them, and Doc had finally limited Anna to only coming in once every three days, concerned she was losing weight, not taking care of herself, and she would end up sick from worry. He'd finally convinced her to care for Juan and Alice, giving her a list of things to cook for them and prescribed Monte's willowbark tea for all three of them.

Ed Bell had taken a room at the hotel with Pronto and the two of them visited daily. Neither of them pushed Doc Ferrell, but he felt nervous around both of them as time dragged on. He'd finally gotten Rio's fever to break by using willowbark tea that Monte had concocted after all the other things failed. Twelve days after he'd been shot, Rio had finally slept peacefully for the first time. When Ed and Pronto had come in, the doc had just finished getting some soup down Rio, along with some laudanum, and he'd promptly gone back to sleep. They sat in Doc's office while Ed pumped the doc about the area. Pronto sat by the door, not saying a word the entire time, but occasionally smiling.

Ed and Pronto rode out to the Nevell ranch and he looked the place over, talked to Juan, who proclaimed he was *slowly* getting better, but not ready to leave. The mountain men had laughed at that, and Juan had blushed but stuck to his story.

***

Rio was lying in bed with shaving cream on half his face as Anna shaved him. Rio woke suddenly, clear headed and felt a 'knife' at his throat. He reached out blindly and grabbed the hand as his eyes popped open, to see Anna looking at him with a stunned expression.

She asked softly, "Rio?"

"What are you doing? I thought you were dead? I saw blood?" Letting go of her hand, he reached up and stroked her hair lovingly. "I thought I saw you fall..."

Flustered, Anna carefully put the razor down. "Well, I was trying to shave you, but since you're awake," she reached up and touched his hand tenderly, "I was just grazed." She pointed to her upper arm.

"But I saw blood on your coat?"

"I was hit down here," she pointed to her side, "But you're going to have to wait till we're married to see that part of me." She smiled at Rio's expression, then chuckled throatily.

Rio started to sit up. "Married?" He looked at her in confusion and said, "I gotta go to the outhouse. I..." He started to get up and the sheet slipped causing him to look down at his nakedness. Blushing furiously, he snatched the sheet back up and sat down. "Whatta you mean married?"

Anna's laughter rang through the office. "Rio, who do you think has been taking care of you the last two weeks?" She got up and started out of the room. "Oh, and you might want to finish shaving."

Doc and Edward Bell had come to the door when they heard Anna's laughter, and Doc came in to examine Rio. "Finally decided to join us again, huh?" he said with a smile.

He poked at Rio's sides and shoulder as Rio looked at the door. "Pa? What are you doing here? I thought I was going nuts just now when I saw you."

Ed Bell chuckled, "No such luck, Son. I got word about Ethan's death and hit the trail up here. I didn't know you'd been shot until I got here. Your ma heard you were shot, and she's on her way. Should be here in the next day or so, if she caught the packet alright.

Rio looked between Doc Farrell and his dad, "Is...everybody else okay?

"Other than you and Juan, everybody else is up and around. John Flynn got shot in the top of the shoulder, Juan got shot in the thigh, and Anna was grazed twice. Nobody else got a scratch." He lifted Rio's leg up and looked at the calf as he continued, "Long Tom died on the roof, fighting a gunnie. Best I can tell, something let go inside him. He didn't have a mark on him. But he killed the sumbitch that he was fighting.

Anna had come back and stood in the door as she said, "We buried him next to Smiley at our place."

Rio shook his head. "Um...I need to go to the..."

Doc slid a bedpan out from underneath the bed and handed it to him. "Go in this."

"What's this thing?" He looked at it curiously.

Huffing out a breath, Doc Ferrell said, "It's what you've been using for almost two weeks."

He looked up in horror. "Did Anna? I mean...did she..." Seeing the smile on the doc's face, he blushed almost beet red as he mumbled to himself, then said, "Here? Now? I mean don't I get any...privacy?"

The doc laughed. "Alright, give the boy his privacy."

A half hour later, Rio had been dressed and was sitting at the supper table, wolfing down a steak as Mrs. Ferrell tut-tutted. "You're going to make yourself sick, young man. You're eating too fast, and your stomach has shrunk."

Rio mumbled around a mouthful of steak. "Doan care. Hungry." He glanced at his dad, sitting across the table from him. "Where are the hands?"

Ed took a sip of his coffee, then replied, "Well, I sent John, Arthur, and Cavanaugh back to Texas. Jeb wouldn't leave since Juan is his partner, and Juan is *recovering* from his wounds at the ranch. Pronto has stayed too, saying he wanted to spend some time with his old friends."

Rio smacked his head. "Oh my God! I...how is Alice? I...can't believe I didn't even think..."

"Alice?" The Ferrells laughed. "Yep, she's doing fine and so is Juan." Winking at his wife, he said, "Matter of fact, I'd say both are doing outstanding."

"What about the Kidds, Childs or whoever they were that attacked us?"

"They're all dead except Pete."

He looked up, worried. "Why isn't somebody guarding Alice and Anna?"

Ed laughed, "I don't think anybody wants to try those old mountain men. They're...crazy quiet in the woods, and you don't even see them. Scared the hell out of me when I rode out to see Anna."

"What about...what's his name? Pete?"

Ed and Doc exchanged glances. "It's been handled. Guess he was the only honest one of the bunch."

Rio finished off the steak and looked around.

"You feel like getting up?" Doc asked.

Grimacing, Rio stood. "Yeah, I guess I better do this while I can. Where did Anna go?"

"She rode out, said something about getting some sleep."

***

Two days passed as Rio improved and got his appetite back. He'd taken to sitting on the Farrell's front porch in the swing, glad to be out in the air, even if it was cold. He was sitting on the porch in the swing idly pushing back and forth with the injured leg when Anna, dressed very warmly, rode up and hopped nimbly down. Smiling, she walked up and joined him in the swing.

Rio looked at her with a worried expression. "Where have you been?"

She laughed. "I went back and got some sleep. I've been sitting with you every two or three days for almost two weeks.

"You did?"

They were interrupted by Doc, Ed Bell, Pronto and Monte coming up the walk.

"How are you feeling, Rio?"

Glancing up, he said tentatively, "'Bout as weak as a kitten, Doc."

"You were hit pretty hard, Rio, I had my hands full. What do you remember?"

"I...not much. Somebody calling Anna a... drawing and shooting, and not much else. I...thought I saw Anna fall, but..."

She put her hand on his arm. "I didn't fall, you did. And I thought you'd be dead before we could get you here."

Pronto said, "Well, fresh air be good for ya. But me, I'm for warm."

They all laughed, and Doc said, "C'mon in, coffee's on." The four of them trooped in the house and Ed laid a hand on Rio's shoulder, giving it a squeeze as he walked past.

Rio turned to face Anna. "You said something about marriage?" he asked tentatively.

Laughing gaily, she replied, "Well you did ask me, oh, at least four or five times, and I said yes every time."

Pronto had stuck his head back out the door. "Yep, your dad and I even heard it a couple o' times, Rio. Oh, and your ma got here this morning. She come by, but you were sleepin' so she didn't want to bother you."

Incredulous, Rio asked, "Momma? Why is Momma here?"

Ed walked out, a cup of coffee in his hand. "For the wedding, Son."

"Whose wedding?"

Anna smiled. "Ours. Remember? You asked, and I said yes."

Rio looked around in amazement. "I...we...what? But...but..."

"You better get used to it, son. You can't dishonor this lady now. Besides, your Momma would never let me live it down. She's out at the ranch supervising right now."

"The ranch?"

Ed laughed. "Pete wanted out. I bought the ranch to give him enough to start again elsewhere. He...asked that a half-acre be set aside as a cemetery, since his pa, two brothers, and others that got killed are buried there. I did that and told him he was always welcome to visit their graves."

Anna's hand had somehow found its way into Rio's. She squeezed it. "Our ranch. We're going to live at the old Kidd place."

"Momma is driving the hands nuts with the cleaning and fixing. Says that it wasn't fit to live in. She'll be back in town tonight and wants to have dinner with you. She's already met Anna."

Stunned, Rio asked, "But what about your place?"

Anna laughed. "I think there is going to be another wedding sometime soon."

"What?"

"Well, Alice wants to go back to our home, and Juan says you're going to need somebody to manage the northern ranch. And since it doesn't have enough bedrooms," she colored slightly, "Well, it just makes sense."

Doc Ferrell came out juggling three coffee cups and passed them around. "Besides, now that you're up and around; I need the bed space."

Rio blushed as everyone laughed. Pronto said, "I'll be your Segundo for now, an' Isom, Jeb, and Juan're gonna work for ya."

Monte chimed in, "I'll gonna do the same thing for Alice. Jack and Joe are gonna stay, too. And a couple of the old hands have come back, asking for work. Alice is gonna take 'em on."

Ed added, "There are going to be enough hands straggling back to Texas that you can probably pick up enough to get through the winter. Next spring, I'll push two herds up. Story has already said he wants another herd, and from what I've seen, your new ranch can support a thousand head. And there are plenty of mines that need beef. I think we can make money the first year on it."

Rio realized his fate had been decided, and he said, "Anna, uh I, uh don' know what to say."

She pecked him on the cheek. "Try 'Thank you'."

***

Hattie Bell swept into the doctor's office like a whirlwind. "Where is that lazy boy of mine? Is he still sleeping?" Rio came out of the back room and wordlessly hugged her tightly. She pushed him back after a few seconds, looking at him critically. "Well, you're alive. Skinny, but alive. I brought your Sunday go to meetin' suit, but we might have to get it altered." Turning to Doc Ferrell, she asked, "Is there anyone in town that does alterations?"

Doc thought for a second then said, "Ah, you'll have to ask my wife, Gretchen. I...don't know."

She turned back to Rio, hugged him, and said softly in his ear, "Don't you *ever* scare me like that again, young man." She hooked her arm through his and said, "Is Gretchen in the house?"

"I believe so, Mrs. Bell."

"Come with me, Rio. It's time to get on with this."

Panicked, Rio looked at the doc, who shrugged and smiled. Mrs. Bell led him out, talking to him like he was still twelve years old.

At dinner that night, she described the 'horror' of the ranch house he was going to be living in, and how much work they still had to do. She'd put the cowboys to work, cleaned, washed linens, and noted that there was only one positive thing about the whole place. It had a real bathtub. Rio and his father barely got a word in edgewise, and later, when the two of them walked back to Doc's place, Ed said, "Your momma is...relieved to know you're alive. I...she was not happy to find out you'd been shot again, much less that you'd almost died. And...that trip wasn't to her liking. Apparently the train was not pleasant. So just bear with her. That's all I ask, Rio."

Nodding, Rio replied, "I will, Pa. It's...I guess I came real close to cashing in my chips. But, I never planned..." he shook his head. "I mean, getting married...I—"

Laughing, Ed said, "Mine was a little better, but when they get their head around something, you just go with it. And Anna is a truly lovely and smart young lady. You could have done a lot worse." Rio nodded again as they walked up to the door. "Enjoy your last night of freedom, son."

***

The next day, snow was falling lightly as Rio walked into the small, whitewashed church in Fort Collins. The preacher, a thin, bald man wearing spectacles, asked acerbically, "Are you the groom?"

"Yes, sir."

He took Rio by the arm and led him to the front of the church. "You will stand here." He looked at Ed, "Are you...the best man?"

Ed shrugged. "I guess. I'm his daddy."

Pointing, he said, "You will stand here. Are there rings?"

"No, sir," Rio mumbled. "I'm working on that."

The front door opened, and Alice walked in with Juan limping beside her, followed by the mountain men, Jeb, the doctor and his wife. There was some laughter, and the preacher said, "There will be *no* laughing in my church. Sit and be quiet. Where is the bride?"

Alice smiled at him, "She will be a moment, Reverend Clinton."

Mollified, he stepped up to the pulpit and waited. A minute or two later, the door opened again, and Rio glanced up to see a vision in white standing in the aisle as his mother walked around the outside of the pews to come sit with Jeb and Pronto. Monte escorted Anna to the altar as Alice stood and walked up to the side matching Ed's position. Reverend Clinton cleared his throat and conducted a simple wedding ceremony, of which Rio had absolutely no memory. The only thing he remembered was the preacher pronouncing them man and wife and telling him to kiss the bride. As he did so, it hit him that this was the first time he'd ever kissed her. "I love you," he whispered and kissed her again as she melted into his arms.

"I love you, too. I've seen the sickness, now I want to see you healthy, Rio!" She chuckled softly. "Healthy. You hear me?"

They turned and faced the crowd, who cheered, stomped, and whistled, much to Reverend Clinton's displeasure. Rio noted his dad slipping something to the Reverend, who smiled, and Rio thought he'd seen a flash of a gold coin. *That's one more thing I owe you, Dad, I don't know how I'll ever repay you. And I need to go back up to the cabin and see what Uncle Ethan was talking about in the barn.* He looked up and saw the slim bespectacled man sitting in the last pew of the church and smiling. He immediately wondered who he was, as he'd never seen him before.

Putting his hand on Anna's arm as people came up to congratulate them, he said, "Wait here, I'll be right back." Walking quickly to the back of the church, he saw the man stand up and asked, "Do I know you?"

Still smiling, the man said, "No, I don't think so. I'm Robert Langham, a photographer. I heard there was a wedding, and I am capturing the West as it exists today. I'd like to take your picture if I might."

He looked around and realized Anna was standing next to him. "A picture of us on our wedding day? I'd love it!" Rio was smart enough not to argue, simply nodding.

Langham said, "I'll be right back with my camera."

Reverend Clinton came back and asked, "What is that all about?"

Anna said, "He wants to take our picture. He's a photographer!"

"Photographs are an abomination, I won't..."

Clinton stopped suddenly, appearing to rise on his toes, as Pronto said softly, "You won't mind at all, will you?"

Sweat broke out across Clinton's hairline and he said gritting his teeth. "No...not...at all. But I...will not be here." He took a step, almost as if pushed, and walked head high to the front door and out into the snow, leaving it open.

Moments later, Langham came in, carrying a bulky tripod and camera, sitting them down near the pulpit. He looked at the light and mumbled something, then said, "One more minute." He went out the door and came back shortly carrying a tin and a funny looking wooden thing with a handle. After setting up the camera, he said, "If I could get the bride and groom and," pointing to Alice and Ed, "The two of you to stand where you were?"

The four of them arranged themselves in front of the pulpit, and he ducked under the black cloth, reaching around and fiddling with something on the front of the camera. He came out from under the cloth, looked around and filled the wooden thing with powder. "There will be a flash. Everybody hold real still in three, two, smile!" With a foof, there was flash of light and smoke drifted toward the ceiling causing everybody to start coughing.

Anna said, "Can we get one more, please?" Langham nodded. She asked, "Mrs. Bell? Monte, Pronto?"

They all stepped up by the pulpit, and Langham had to back the camera up. As he was doing so, Fat Jack asked, "Whut about usn's?"

Anna sighed. "Y'all too, come on."

Rio swayed on his feet, and Jeb grabbed a chair. "You better sit afore you fall over, Rio." Shoving a chair behind him. Rio sank into the chair as the others crowded behind them. Anna put her hand on his shoulder as Langham said, "Ready in three, two, smile!" Another foof, and light and smoke set everyone to coughing again. "I...can have you photographs tomorrow if that is acceptable. Would you like tintypes or paper?"

Anna asked, "Can we get..." she looked around, "Three of each?"

"Yes, Ma'am. I can do that."

She smiled. "We'll be at the hotel through tomorrow. Please deliver them there." Rio got up, and she leaned into him. "Let's go *rest*. I know you're tired." She winked at him, and he blushed as everyone laughed.

As they walked out the front door, they could hear the babble of mountain men asking for photographs of themselves and Pronto saying, "He's gonna break his camera on your ugly mugs."

Anna tucked her arm into Rio's and said, "Are you going to make it to the hotel?"

He smiled down at her. "I'll make it, one way or the other. What are we going to do now?"

She laughed, "Well, there *are* things we're supposed to do," she said archly. He blushed to the roots of his hair, and she took pity on him. "Well, your mother says our ranch will be ready to live in, probably in two days. And we have eight hands that are willing to work for us, including Juan and Jeb. There are six who are staying on at the ranch from the hands the Kidds had, plus your dad talked to their ranch foreman, Billy Purcell, and he said to keep him on to run the ranch until you get things sorted out."

Rio smiled. "So, Pa has things well in hand, and Ma is running things as usual. I guess that means we can...have a day or two to ourselves."

The End

About the author-

JL Curtis was born in Louisiana in 1951 and was raised in the Ark-La-Tex area. He began his education with guns at age eight with a SAA and a Grandfather that had carried one for 'work'. He began competitive shooting in the 1970s, an interest he still pursues time permitting. He is a retired Naval Flight Officer, retired engineer in the defense industry, an NRA instructor, and now lives in north Texas writing full time. This is the first novel in The Bell Chronicles series.

Sadly, due to changes in the printing process with Amazon, I can no longer put up links and pictures of friend's books at the end of my novels. Please check my blog http://oldnfo.org for my book promos. Thank you in advance.

Made in the USA
Columbia, SC
03 December 2024

48346171R00137